ENTER *SANCTUAR*
for once you have rea
want to leave again!

YOU CAN FIND *A PLACE TO STAY FOR A
LITTLE WHILE—*
if you have a Talent unlike any other. But watch
out, lest your Talent—or someone else's—leads
you down the seductive path to power. . . .

WHO CAN FIND A JOB FOR *THE BOY
WHO PLAITED MANES*?
it began with the horses, but when he started
weaving beauty for humankind, the pattern
became dangerously tangled with love and
fear. . . .

MAKING *PHONE REPAIRS* CAN TAKE
YOU INTO A WHOLE DIFFERENT
DIMENSION—
a realm where identities shift and blend till one
man's life can become that of another. . . .

Here are just a few glimpses of the incredible
worlds you'll discover in this latest treasure-
filled volume of both the light and dark fantastic—

THE YEAR'S
BEST FANTASY
STORIES: 13

DAW

MAGIC TALES FROM THE MASTERS OF FANTASY

THE YEAR'S BEST FANTASY STORIES 13

EDITED BY ARTHUR W. SAHA

DAW BOOKS, INC.
DONALD A. WOLLHEIM, PUBLISHER

1633 Broadway, New York, NY 10019

First Printing, November 1987

1 2 3 4 5 6 7 8 9

PRINTED IN THE U.S.A.

ACKNOWLEDGMENTS

"Beauty is the Beast" by Tanith Lee originally appeared in AMERICAN FANTASY, Fall 1986. Copyright © 1986 by Robert T. Garcia. Reprinted by permission of the author.

"Something in the Blood" by Richard L. Purtill originally appeared in THE MAGAZINE OF FANTASY & SCIENCE FICTION, Aug. 1986. Copyright © 1986 by Mercury Press, Inc. Reprinted by permission of the author.

"Pièce de Résistance" by Judith Tarr originally appeared in ISAAC ASIMOV'S SCIENCE FICTION MAGAZINE, April 1986. Copyright © 1986 by Davis Publications, Inc. Reprinted by permission of the author and the author's agent, Jane Butler.

"Long, Long Ago" by R. Chetwynd-Hayes originally appeared in the collection TALES FROM THE SHADOWS. Copyright © 1986 by R. Chetwynd-Hayes. Reprinted by permission of the author's agent, Cherry Weiner Literary Agency.

"The Old Man and the Cherry Tree" by Kevin J. Anderson originally appeared in GRUE MAGAZINE, No. 3. Copyright © 1986 by GRUE MAGAZINE. Reprinted by permission of the author.

"Phone Repairs" by Nancy Kress originally appeared in ISAAC ASIMOV'S SCIENCE FICTION MAGAZINE, Dec. 1986. Copyright © 1986 by Davis Publications, Inc. Reprinted by permission of the author.

THE TALE AND ITS MASTER by Michael Rutherford was originally published by Spring Harbor Press. Copyright © 1986 by Michael Rutherford. Reprinted by permission of the author and Spring Harbor Press.

"Sanctuary" by Kim Antieau originally appeared in SHADOWS 9. Copyright © 1986 by Kim Antieau. Reprinted by permission of the author.

"The Uncorking of Uncle Finn" by Jane Yolen originally appeared in THE MAGAZINE OF FANTASY & SCIENCE FICTION, Nov. 1986. Copyright © 1986 by Jane Yolen. Reprinted by permission of Curtis Brown, Ltd.

DEDICATION

For All THE LUNARIANS—Past, Present, and Future.

CONTENTS

INTRODUCTION

As a longtime devotee of fantasy fiction I am constantly amazed and gratified at the originality today's practitioners bring to their art. The current volume of THE YEAR'S BEST FANTASY STORIES strongly underscores this point. Here you will find stories that take place in times long past, mythical lands and in the world of today. They all have in common, however, the fact that they are sheer fantasy and could only happen in realms of the imagination.

As usual, the stories in this collection have been selected by reading through the many sources of short fantasy fiction published during the year, a year that was particularly rich in fantasy stories of all lengths.

Important collections, all of which are wholly or partly fantasy, published during the year include DREAMS OF DARK AND LIGHT by Tanith Lee, MERLIN'S BOOKE by Jane Yolen, TALES OF THE QUINTANA ROO by the late James Tiptree, Jr., VISIBLE LIGHT by C. J. Cherryh and THE CURIOUS QUESTS OF BRIGADIER FFELLOWES by Sterling Lanier.

Anthologies include SWORD AND SORCERESS III, edited by Marion Zimmer Bradley; HEROIC

VISIONS 2, edited by Jessica Amanda Salmonson; and DRAGONS AND DREAMS, edited by Jane Yolen, Martin H. Greenberg and Charles G. Waugh. The shared world anthologies continue to proliferate with increasing frequency. Two additional volumes of the first of them all, THE THIEVES' WORLD series, #8: SOUL OF THE CITY and #9: BLOOD TIES, both edited by Robert Lynn Asprin and Lynn Abbey appeared. In addition, LIAVEK: THE PLAYERS OF LUCK, edited by Will Shetterly and Emma Bull, the second in that series; and the third volume of MAGIC IN ITHKAR, edited by Andre Norton and Robert Adams also appeared. 1986 also saw the publication of two new series with REBELS IN HELL and HEROES IN HELL, edited by Janet Morris and BORDERLAND and BORDERTOWN, edited by Terri Windling and Mark Arnold. More shared world series have been announced.

Novels published during the year include Gene Wolfe's tale of the ancient Aegean, SOLDIER OF THE MIST; the posthumously published GODBODY by Theodore Sturgeon; the fourth volume of Tanith Lee's Flat Earth series, DELIRIUM'S MISTRESS; Jo Clayton's quest tale, DRINKER OF SOULS; THE TALKING MAN by Terry Bisson, a tale about the man, now retired, who dreamed our world; the final volume of Raymond Feist's Riftwar saga, A DARKNESS AT SETHANON; the second and third volumes of Guy Gavriel Kay's high fantasy trilogy, THE WANDERING FIRE and THE DARKEST ROAD; THE HOUNDS OF GOD, the final volume of Judith Tarr's medieval trilogy; Esther Friesner's tale of a knight and a dragon in modern New York, NEW YORK BY KNIGHT; the first volume of a new duology by Stephen R. Donaldson, THE MIRROR OF HER DREAMS; Jennifer Roberson's tale of swords and sorcery, SWORD DANCER; Greg Bear's THE SERPENT MAGE, a sequel to his THE INFINITY CON-

CERTO; Pat Murphy's story of archaeology in the land of the Mayas, THE FALLING WOMAN; Megan Lindholm's urban fantasy, WIZARD OF THE PIGEONS; M. Coleman Easton's Arabian fantasy, ISKIIR; the "dream" fantasy, YARROW by Charles de Lint; and THE ARCHITECT OF SLEEP, a tale about intelligent raccoons, by Stephen Boyett.

As usual several nonfiction books devoted to imaginative literature were published. Of special interest to fans of the fantastic are THE PENGUIN ENCYCLOPEDIA OF HORROR AND THE SUPERNATURAL edited by Jack Sullivan and SCIENCE FICTION, FANTASY AND WEIRD FICTION MAGAZINES by Marshall B. Tymn and Mike Ashley.

The World Fantasy Convention was once again held over the Halloween Weekend in Providence, Rhode Island, the city that was its birthplace. Among the awards presented were the Lifetime Achievement Award to Avram Davidson and a special convention award to Donald A. Wollheim.

Now for the sake of completeness it is unfortunately necessary to report the deaths of several prominent members of the fantasy community. Among them were Judy-Lynn del Rey, editor and publisher of Del Rey Books and unquestionably one of the preeminent editors of our time; two former World Fantasy Award recipients, the Argentine writer, Jorge Luis Borges, and longtime fantasy writer, Manly Wade Wellman; and L. Ron Hubbard, remembered by fantasy fans for the many fine stories he wrote for the long gone UNKNOWN WORLDS in the early '40's, all of whom died in 1986; and veteran editor, anthologist and writer, Terry Carr, who died in early April of 1987.

The world of film did not offer the viewing public much in the way of fantasy during the year, but THE GOLDEN CHILD (popular because of its star, Eddie Murphy), LEGEND and LABYRINTH should be noted.

What 1987 will bring to aficionados of the fantastic remains to be seen and eagerly anticipated. In the meantime, please enjoy the best of 1986.

Arthur W. Saha

BEAUTY IS THE BEAST

by Tanith Lee

What is truth? The beautiful Maristarre of Northfree was convinced she knew when she set out to slay a "beast" only to discover that what she perceived as truth may not have been so at all.

The land was in turmoil, and from the City of The Thousand Domes, the outlaws fled to the town of the Free North.

"How shall we be received?" they said to each other, as they rode wearily at sunset through a province of vines, and sighted such a town of fine old houses and leaning walls. In the yellow light, the world seemed peaceful. But they knew otherwise. "We bring them unrest and trouble. War—if they listen and come to our help." But Northfree, by her very name, knew the state of the land, and how terror ruled southward, from the Capital. The town opened her gates and welcomed the outlaws, gave them food and wine, and lamps; let them shine and speak out from their broken hearts and blazing rage.

It was a fact, the City of The Thousand Domes had become in these years, *altered*. In the North they had heard of the riotous insanity. The citizens had thrown down the law and the religion. They lived now by vice and cruelty, and made a fetish of dirt, rags, ugliness, for they said all things were made equal, must therefore *be* equal, nothing better than another thing, but only as nature intended—though, in the way of the fetish, they occasionally drew attention to a deformity by ornamenting it in some curious manner. Ravens perched on the towers by day and rats ran like rivers in the streets by night, exalting in the carnage. For the new deity of the metropolis, whom they called The Reasonable, was a goddess of blood and demanded frequent sacrifice. All this, the outlaws reviewed for the town of Northfree, standing in the lamplit square. A vast crowd had gathered, the windows and balconies, the very roofs were filled by silent watches, listening. Even the stars looked down.

"For a year we struggled," said the spokesman of the outlaws. "By such legal means as are still recognized there, and also by schemes and plots, to bring back some sense, some justice to our heaven-cursed City. But we failed, and in fear of our lives at last, we fled." Then he covered his face with his hands and wept, and the crowd murmured. Another spoke. He told how the City was now ruled by strange petty kings, who abused their power but refused power's name—being, of course, equal to everyone else. Evil madmen, magicians, who could ensorcel the creatures of the city, human and otherwise, bending men and women to their will, enlisting the terrifying rats as their minions, the ravens as their spies.

"To the unmerciful mercy of these monsters we were forced to leave our comrades, those imprisoned in the black dungeons on the river. They warned us to escape, and will give their lives for ours." And then the outlaws talked of raising armies here in the North, to march against the vicious rabble of the City, cast it and its masters down, and bring the reign of terror to an end. "Though they are magicians there, they are mortal. They can be killed."

The speakers enlarged upon particular tyrants, and though Northfree had heard of many of them, their names and deeds, the news had now a dreadful emphasis. Especially there was one, Chaquoh he was called, who was already well-known and infamous. It was said he wrote and uttered poison. Even to read a sentence he had penned could blind you. The malignity of his words slew, or sent mad. He stank of a terrible disease which would long since have eaten him up, but that the disease of his *spite* was stronger. Or else it was the spite itself which furnished the disease, a parasite that thrived on him, but dared not finish him entirely.

A little before midnight, exhausted, the orators concluded. The crowd shouted instead. Hands were raised and vows sworn of loyalty and protection. The young men of the town sprang forward. "We will be your army, and go with you, to blast this obscenity of a City from our country's earth. How shall we take it? Only tell us what to do."

Then there were fresh lamps lit, and bottles opened. The campaign began to be discussed.

It was only as faint color started again to come in the sky that one of the outlaws—he who had wept—said to the townsman at his elbow, "Tell me, do you know the young woman who was standing, until a moment ago, up on that balcony there? At one point there was a tall man in white beside her, but he went away. She had only one old servant for company. But she was very remarkable."

"By your description, that is Maristarre," said the townsman.

"She will have grown tired and gone home to find rest, no doubt," said the outlaw, his thoughts straying somewhat from the honorable war, for she had been exceptionally beautiful, this Maristarre of Northfree.

But then anger and pain and hope laid hold of him again, and he forgot her quite.

Maristarre of Northfree. It was true she was beautiful, with her whiteness like clear marble through which the light shines, her darkly polished hair, and darkly polished eyes that seemed always to see far off. There had been many offers, but she had not wished to leave her father, it would appear. Now she went home to one of the old houses of the town, and seating herself as the dawn bloomed, she wrote to him. "Forgive me," wrote Maristarre, "it has come to me what I must do. The young men will fight. They will form an army discernible from miles off, and all the power of the City will be turned against them. But I am one woman, and may pass unnoticed." (She was modest. At home, people turned always to look at her on the street. This very sunrise as she returned, a tall man in white had looked long after her, from the porch of a neighboring church.)

It was also true that she was a visionary, this Maristarre. She did see far off. As the orators had poured forth their flaming passion, her spirit seemed to speak softly within her. She thought, *They would fight sorcerers. What if the sorcerers lie dead?* And she beheld Chaquoh the evil one, the Beast, perhaps mightiest of the great tyrant-masters of the City of The Thousand Domes. She saw his vileness conjured by the outcry of the outlaws. And herself also she saw. She, so purely fair, and he so hideous and steeped in venom. Opposites direly attracting. As if to a magnet she was drawn to this. All her years, where another might have looked into her mirror and grown proud, visionary Maristarre had simply been puzzled at herself. But now at once she understood. She was a clean bright sword, fashioned for one incredible stroke.

So in the earliest morning she left her father's house, and the town where she had lived all her life, and the province of vines. She found transport to a town far-

ther south, and there transport to another more south-
erly. Until at length she boarded one of the rattling
black chariots that hurled itself along the rutted roads
to the City of The Thousand Domes.

She had dressed in plain slovenly garments, and her
hair hung down to her waist, for so the women wore
their hair in the Capital now, sometimes with a bloody
flower tangled in it pinned through by a stiletto.

As the coach came near the City, Maristarre saw
such things as these on the hills: Burned fields, where
corpses lay; trees with skulls tied in them by ribbons;
tall garlanded gallows of ornate wrought-iron, with the
hanged hanging. Once or twice a shepherdess drove
her sheep across the road and the carriage halted.
These girls carried pistols in their belts, and one a tall
pike with a grinning painted mask fixed to the top.
Their own faces were grinning and maleficent, and the
sheep too were changed, scarlet or ocher in color, with
sharply pointed teeth. They did not bleat, but made a
guttural sound, as if they were in the process of learn-
ing human speech, and half choked on it.

The sun had just gone down when they reached the
City. Against a dying sky, Maristarre saw its thousand
black domes, and all the points of light and rays of
smoke that rose from its hell fires.

What a place was this, worse than any telling. But
Maristarre was not dismayed. She knew her task, her
destiny, her punishment even. She had accepted all,
and had no need to be afraid.

At the gate of the City, men with broken teeth
glared in, and bade her get out of the carriage. (One
lacked an eye, but wore a patch which read *Look! I
have lost my eye!* the words picked out in gems.)

"Your business, sister?" ("Sister, brother," these were
the formal and only lawful modes of address in the
Capital, where everyone-and-thing was equal.) These
men were part of the city's Guard of Brotherhood,

and they wore the blood-red insignia of The Reasonable One.

"I am here," said Maristarre, calmly, "to join the glorious free women of the City."

The Guard approved of this. They were fascinated by beauty, too, provided it was natural; though generally they regarded it with suspicion.

"Your hands are smooth," one said her, "there's no mark on you."

"I shall gain scars of honor, in the service of Chaquoh," said Maristarre. "I have come to offer him my whole self, for even in the nothing-town where I was born, his words ring like an alarm-bell. I am his slave. I will lie at his feet."

At this, the men toasted her in a deadly inky brandy they were prone to drink, and she was allowed to go on into the City. The name "Chaquoh" would be a safe conduct. No one would touch her, if they thought her due to be his.

So she passed through the streets. In the narrower alleys, which she avoided, she heard the gutters chuckling and guessed what moved along them and how like a ruby it shone under the lamps. On the wide roads carriages whirled by, loud with drunken voices. The buildings, high-roofed and impressive always, were now much blemished from the fighting that had gone on in the City at the beginning of its alteration. Whole sections had been blasted from walls, and windows shattered, and all left gaping, so one could see in as if to a lighted picture. Quarreling, debauche, and even manslaughter, these were the normal subject of every one. Harlots went by, slender or bloated, feathers and knives in their nests of hair; and gangs of men, some of whom would have seized Maristarre, but she spoke the name of Chaquoh with such authority, they let her continue. Once, a hunchback questioned her. His humped shoulder was sprinkled with faceted jewels, though he wore foul rags. When she said she would serve Chaquoh, the hunchback laughed. He had served mighty brother Chaquoh too, he said.

On one street she came to a waxworks lit by torches, and doing fine business. The waxworks' specialty was to show life-like images of many persons who had been killed in the City, their faces having been modeled from death-masks obtained immediately after murder or execution. Several were victims of the goddess, The Reasonable One. Maristarre did not falter.

She reached a square where a forge was smoking up thick overcast and sparks. She told the blacksmith she wanted to buy from him a knife.

"See," he said, "look what I am melting down—a church bell and a holy cup to be cannon balls and swords. But here is a knife could disembowel a spider. This will do for you. Do you mean to slit the throat of some rival?"

"No," said Maristarre. "I intend to put the knife to the service of Chaquoh."

Then the blacksmith fawned on her and gave her the knife without taking any money for it.

Maristarre crossed the stone bridge over the City's river. All the statues on the bridge had been smashed and lay in piles of rubble, over which each traveler picked his way with difficulty. On days of festival, the bridges were almost impassable, due to the corpses heaped there. Down in the black river fish sometimes leapt to the surface; corpse-fed and swollen, they had grown as large as dogs, and had luminous pale eyes. From the river, too, the prisons of the City rose up out of the water, and with narrow pale eyes, not unlike those of the unnatural fish, they scanned the dark as if searching for prey. But still Maristarre did not falter. Nor when, leaving the bridge, a tall man in white seemed to bar her way—but then he moved aside and was gone.

Having gained the other bank, she walked up a long and unlit lane, where the rats might be heard rustling

and cheeping, and sometimes there came the flash of
eager rat-eyes. But Maristarre had only to whisper
the name: *Chaquoh*. She knew the rats would let her
alone.

She had had no need to ask the way. The dwellings
of all the magician-masters had been described in de-
tail. She found the house of Chaquoh with no trouble.

It was tall, and leaned heavily on both its neighbors,
which were ruined and empty, but for the scurrying,
glittering rats. From colossal chimneys, grown by over-
use seemingly too big for the building, vapors glided
into the starless night. One window dully glowed, high
up. There he would be, at his work. But even now
Maristarre did not falter.

She knocked on the door; its knocker was a severed
human hand, or so it looked—but made of white stone.

At the knock a hundred voices seemed to moan and
cry. A rat, itself big as a spaniel, slid to her ankle, and
the rat spoke to Maristarre, though its speech was
awkward and impeded.

"Whatseek?" said the rat.

"Chaquoh, my brother."

"Whyseek?"

"To be Chaquoh's slave."

"Allusissame. Noslave."

"True, brother. But let Chaquoh correct me."

"Thenshall."

And the rat licked the door, which grated and drew
open.

Beyond the doors, an empty vestibule, its corners
filled by stacks of yellowing paper, and hung throughout by curtains of dust and webs. All these, and the
paper stacks too, had been carefully spangled with
gold-leaf, so no iota of the muck should be over-
looked. On the long crooked stairway, the broken tiles
were rimmed by gold.

Maristarre went up the steps. On each landing there
were doors, fast shut, though in some cases the wood

was cracked, it was possible to see through—but only
to darkness. Finally it seemed she had reached the attic
of the house. Instead of a door, the stair opened
directly on a cramped anteroom. Nothing was in it but
a hard wooden chair, and a lamp. A statue held this
lamp, a statue of rusty iron in the shape of a snake
with a woman's head and hands. "What do you require, sister?" asked the snake-statue.

"To see my brother Chaquoh."

"Chaquoh is bathing. You must wait."

"Thank you, sister," said Maristarre. She sat on the
hard chair and folded her hands. The knife nestled at
her breast.

An hour passed. Out in the City of The Thousand
Domes, a bell struck for midnight, but the bell had a
human voice, and everyone of the twelve chimes was
some ominous word. Maristarre caught such sounds
as seemed to be *Pestilence, Despair, Hatred, Lies,
Strangling*—and several others that do not look well
written down. From the streets, too, came shrieks and
growls, stupid laughter and wicked laughter, and now
and then the noise of clashing swords, or shots.

Eventually Maristarre rose.

"What do you require, sister?" asked the statue-
snake again.

"May I now go in to my brother Chaquoh?"

The statue waited, then it said, "Yes, go in."

At this, a hole appeared in the wall, a jagged rent as
if cannon-blast had passed through there, but every
fissure was set with a pearl or a topaz. Beyond the
fissure, a disheartening stair leading down and down,
as the first stair had led up and up. But Maristarre
took the stair, and went down it, into a vague luminous dark.

Far down at the stair's foot, she found herself above
a great sewer full of murky fluid, which led away
through channels on every side, apparently out into

the City. A slight greenish slime on the water gleamed and illuminated the area.

There was a platform at the stair-bottom, jutting out on the water. Even as Maristarre stepped down on it, a creature appeared, swimming in from one of the outlets. It moved swiftly toward her, and suddenly, grasping the platform, its upper half emerged from the slime. Here was Chaquoh, it could be no other.

He was a man still, but barely. Now you could perceive the nature of his disease, his body scaled and plated—he was turning gradually, and maybe less gradually with every hour, into a sort of alligator. Yet his hands and pale face, and his bright red eyes—these were like a rat's.

"You must pardon me, sister," he murmured to Maristarre, "but it is only here I can find comfort for my body."

His red-cold eyes stared at her, all over. He put one of his little rat paws on her foot. Maristarre did not falter. "Why," he hissed, "why, pretty sister, are you here?"

"I bring you the names of the traitors who recently escaped you," said Maristarre.

"Ah," said Chaquoh with a smile or grimace, "good news. Wait. My pen—" and he drew from behind one pointed ear a dagger-bladed quill whose long, long feather seemed to touch the very ceiling far overhead under the attic. "And ink—" at which he stabbed the pen into his arm, and as the swarthy blood spurted, he dipped the pen and wrote on the air—which sizzled— *The Names of Traitors*. "I promise you," he said, "they shall die in agony."

Then Maristarre leaned close and with her knife she struck Chaquoh through the throat, where he was not yet scaled, down into the heart. He gave a thin scream, more like a whistle. And then he dragged himself upward on the platform and dropped on his side. The blood from his death-wound was not of the shade of the other blood; it was black, and where it fell the platform smoked. "You have killed me," said Chaquoh.

"Yes," said Maristarre.

"Now," said Chaquoh, "you are indeed my slave." And then he died.

But Maristarre spurned his body and his words alike. She turned from him and stood composed to wait her punishment.

Very soon there began to be a screaming and shouting and roaring on all sides. The City felt his death. Things plunged in the sewer. The great black rats spilled round, and stared at her. She thought she would be torn in pieces, and prepared herself to suffer it. But then men came, and women, rushing down the stair with torches in their hands, weeping and screeching. They took her by the arms. They called her terrible things. "To the goddess!" they cried. "The goddess shall have you."

"I am the sacrifice," said Maristarre. "I have done what I came to do. The beast is dead."

But she was dragged away into streaming fire and darkness. Battered and bruised, spat on, beaten and enchained, cast into a dungeon blacker than moonless night, in the depths of the prison in the river.

Before dawn, a voice cried her sentence out of the black. As they had told her, she must meet the goddess.

But Maristarre's eyes looked far away. Her whiteness shone in the blackness. She said nothing. She had done what she had come to do.

They took her, the next sunset, to the temple where their goddess was worshipped. It was an open amphitheater, seating many thousands, and every seat filled. At its center was a platform, and here rose two uprights of wood. They bound Maristarre between them so tightly she could not move. Then the Guard of Brotherhood, who had escorted her to the place, and bound her in it, hurried away to the edges of the arena. Drums began to beat and bugles to wail, and the multitude clapped and cawed, invoking The Reasonable One, entreating her to manifest and claim her due, this assassin of one of the City's holiest sons. The sky bled down and soon the night would come.

"How shall she know the goddess is near?" the guards had said, in grim banter, as they rode beside her chariot on the way.

"A shadow and a sound of wings," another answered.

"And then the sharp beak!"

All along the route, the people of the City had howled at Maristarre and cursed her, and made gestures of rending her. But as she was to be given to the goddess, she escaped maiming. Others danced and sang about the vehicle, describing how it would be for her, to die, when the beak of the goddess slashed her apart. Children at the wayside ate sugar skulls. In some places hawkers sold pigs' blood in which to dip various flowers so they turned the proper tint.

But then, and now in the amphitheater under the prescient sky, Maristarre showed no fear—and felt none? Between the upright stakes she stood in silence. Her eyes looked far away. *I am the clean sword, stained now by filthiness. Break me. I consent. Purity triumphs. The beast is dead. I am not their* sacrifice. *I die for the hope and beauty of the earth.*

Nevertheless, the far-seeing, far-off visionary eyes of Maristarre now glimpsed a man in the crowd, a tall man all in white, and she realized she had seen him twice, or maybe three times, before. Who could it be? Had he followed her all this way from the North? Some rescuer? No, such a rescue could not be possible.

And the last embers were crushed from the sun. The sky turned sable, a wind blew fiercely over the amphitheater, shaking garments and hair, and rattling the chains that bound Maristarre.

"The goddess! The goddess arrives! The Reasonable!"

The crowd moaned and thundered. A shadow fell abysmal on Maristarre and she heard a sound of wings—

Cold pain passed through her—but she recognized it was only the dash of the air, her chains falling away—she was in the sky, held firmly in the arms of a man, taller than any man she had ever seen, almost a giant, with a mane of pale hair flaming behind him, and vast white wings spread out, beating like the wings of a swan, as he bore her upward.

"Rescue, then?" questioned Maristarre.

"You may say so," he gently said to her.

"Where now?" said Maristarre. She did not speak of Northfree. He was the angel of death, and this she knew.

"You have seen a city of Hell-on-Earth," said the angel, as they spun higher and higher on his swan's wings, so high the sun was again visible far beneath, like a guttering lamp under their feet. "Now you must see another earthly city."

They made one enormous circle. The night revolved and was flung away like a stone; the sun, having fallen, blossomed once more.

There below, among the green lands of summer, lay a City of shining roofs and cupolas, with a silver river dividing it.

The angel spoke some sacred charm, and became a snow-white pigeon, and Maristarre a pearl-gray dove. They flew down into the shining City together, and in her visionary heart, her dove's heart, Beauty thought, *This is my doing. Good is victorious. This is how it will be.*

In the meadows girls picked flowers, and the sheep played, their wool ambered and pinkened by sunlight, their square little teeth harmlessly full of grass. Trees had paper rosettes tied on them; even the scarecrows were garlanded. The City gates stood wide, and the brave young men in their uniforms, with many honors pinned to them, saluted courteously whoever went in or out. All the women were lovely, and the men fine. Their faces were full of patience and optimism, and as they went about their work or walked to and fro, they sang sweet or gallant songs. A woman passed with a load. A man hastened after her and aided her with it. A child fell down and a score of persons ran to console it. To a shop selling bread the hungry came, and received the hot loaves without a coin asked of them. A girl with a silver ring gave it gladly in barter for a daisy.

There had been some damage done to the buildings, it must have been in a fighting past unlike this harmonious present. Now the busy workmen patched the bricks, and where the workmen had not yet come, they had hung out wreaths and plants in pots and birds in cages and hand-switched banners, to soften any ugliness.

An image-maker's shop stood on a thoroughfare, where might be seen living celebrities and deceased. It was a popular place, each figure having been modeled from the life, even in some instances after death, that no falsehood might be told or injustice done the subject.

On the glistening river, the tranquil barges floated up and down. Lions of gold had been set on the bridges, from which the statues of oppressors had long since been removed. The golden lions reflected in the silver water. Each bore an inscription which said: *Let us all be lions!* But somewhere a bell had begun to dole with a melodious sadness.

Flying with the angel, Maristarre paused in the air, and looked down to see a massive procession winding along the river bank. Girls in white and solemn musicians, incense uncurling to the sky, and green branches strewn. And a lament was rising, and on every side men and women standing to watch and weep.

Is it a funeral procession? Who has died?

One who loved us and cared for us—

Then flying lower, Maristarre the dove beheld a chair borne high in the middle of the procession, and seated in it, seeming only to sleep, a man whose handsome face was darkened by nobility, sorrow and death.

In awe conceivably, certainly with attention, Maristarre followed the bier, and all its thousands of mourners.

As the procession flowed on, she saw one on whose humped shoulder the tears of another's compassion sparkled like jewels, and a one-eyed man, on whose bandage was written: *Gladly given for my country.* The roofs about were clustered with white pigeons; white hyacinths fell, dipped in wine. Children pressed white handkerchiefs to their lips, kissing the embroidered picture of the dead lamented one. Even the alley-rats, the knaves and thieves, stared after the cortege and wept. He forgave us. He knew poverty drove us on. He was our brother, and our master.

Chaquoh! They cried, and their tears ran like rivers to a sea of loss.

"He?" said Maristarre to the angel. "Have I misheard?"

"Even he," the angel said. "Remember, he wrote in his life's blood, without a qualm."

And presently, as the funeral wound away, Maristarre found herself standing again in the sky, above a scaffold. Her own body was being removed from it, taken away for burial.

"Their goddess, that they worship," said Maristarre.

"Again, you mistook the words you listened to," said the angel. "They called it, not Reason, but Razor. It is only a common axe, or very nearly."

Maristarre looked down and observed her body, and that it was no longer beautiful, or pristine, or whole, but ugly, crippled, the carcass of a frightful beast.

"Is this, then," said Maristarre, "the truth?"

"Each sees the truth is his own way. The City strives for one truth, which it believes to be as you have now had revealed to you. Those who oppose the City's values, or fear them, see everything as monstrous, and the architectural creation of monsters—as you have had it revealed to you formerly, and on which sight you have acted."

Maristarre looked behind her, and she saw a man approaching them over the sky. It was Chaquoh. He was neither handsome and noble, nor a scaled rat-alligator with red eyes. He was merely a man, worn out with labor and fury, with his own demons, and the world's. He glanced at Maristarre and passed her, walking on into the distance which was not simply sky.

"It seems to me I must, in fact, follow and serve him. Is it so?" asked Maristarre.

"You took away his life."

"He erred in his life."

"His mistake. Yours is the robbery. Now you owe him the debt."

"Then I am to be his slave and he my master?"

"You have seen him as the City saw him, and yourself too, through their eyes. Forget such terms as Master, Magician, Slave. Forget the masks men wear. Go now, and try to see the truth, which is never easy."

So Maristarre ceased gazing far off. She fixed her eyes on Chaquoh and she walked after him. And as she walked, she thought how he *had* written in his life's blood, and said—not *They will die in agony*—but: *They or we will die in agony.* (How much had she misheard as well as mis-seen?)

Dimly behind her she fancied she detected now the shock of war, the North risen, the very shores of the planet, and the City rocking at the blast, blood and soot and violence; tears, courage, songs—till only the weeping of the rain could wash clean the thousand domes of it.

But how far away it seemed.

SOMETHING IN THE BLOOD

by Richard L. Purtill

It is not usual for a person to deliberately decide to become a vampire. Considering the alternative, the young nurse in the following tale did not find that decision especially difficult.

I always arrive at Franco's Bar just after sunset. In the summer there is still light in the sky and on the water; the lights flick on in the town and gleam from the few boats you can see far down the cliff, on the ocean that fills the ancient volcanic caldera. Classical music wells out of the hidden loudspeakers at Franco's, a little too loud but all the more compelling for that.

I sat down at my usual table, and the tall, dark young waiter brought me my usual ouzo and *mezedes* in silence. As I took my first sip of ouzo, I saw her at the next table. The way she was sitting brought her head just in line with the stone harpy on the corner of the terrace, and my first reaction was a purely aesthetic pleasure at the juxtaposition of the soft young face of flesh and the ageless face of stone. Then I realized that the faces were alike in a deeper way. No face that young and beautiful should wear such hopeless resignation, an expression that made her seem as ageless and as alien as the harpy.

When she turned to me and spoke, the expression was gone. Had I only imagined it, was it an illusion born of my own despair? "This must be the most beautiful place in the world," she said, her voice filled with wonder. "It was beautiful in the day, but now it's magical."

"I prefer it after the sun goes down, myself," I said. I couldn't quite keep the irony out of my voice, and she gave me a puzzled look. I had better give her an explanation she could accept. "The sun is my enemy," I told her. "My skin is very sensitive to sunlight. But even aside from that, I find the sunlight on our volcanic rock and ash too harsh. In the day, Santorini seems to me too bleak, too unfriendly to humans."

She nodded with a thoughtful expression. "I see what you mean," she said. "There is something eerie and a little frightening about Santorini for all its beauty. But you said 'our rocks'; are you a native of the island?"

"I've lived here a long time," I said, "and I consider it my home, but the local people still don't really accept me as one of them. Still, I probably know more about Santorini than most of the people born here. Is there anything I can tell you about the island or its history?" It was the first move in a familiar game, a game I had played with many of the young female tourists who streamed through the island every summer, enhancing my life and making the long winter bearable because of what I had gotten from them. But very few of them were as lovely as this girl, or as charming. Had I only imagined that deep sadness in her eyes?

She laughed a little self-consciously and said, "Oh, it's absurd, you'll laugh at me, but I am curious about. . . . Well, do the local people really believe these stories about Santorini? I mean, someone on the mainland warned me about coming here; she was really serious. She said . . . well, she said that there were vampires on Santorini. Now you'll laugh."

I smiled and said lightly, "Oh, no, it's a well-known fact that we have vampires and all sorts of weird creatures. Take the man sitting down there on the lower terrace, the one with the bushy eyebrows He's a werewolf. Only the other day he told me a sad story. He tried to save money by taking the ferry to Athens in his wolf form—he can pass for a very large German shepherd. But a steward saw him and put an iron chain around his neck before he knew what the man was up to. He spent most of the night tied up on deck with no food or water. If a softhearted English tourist hadn't let him loose, he might have been put in the dog pound in Piraeus."

She laughed. "All right, I asked for it," she said. "I guess my grandmother told me too many ghost stories when I was a kid. I still half believe that stuff. You tell a pretty mean story yourself, Mr. . . ."

"Nikolas Tsouras," I told her. "Please call me Niko. And you are . . . ?"

"Ann Morris," she said, "and I am very pleased to meet you. Let me ask you a more practical question, Niko. Can you get anything to eat here? I'm getting awfully hungry; I've been sightseeing too hard to eat much."

I shook my head. "There's a cold plate on the menu," I told her, "but usually they say they're out of it. I often just nibble at the *mezedes* all evening—The little appetizers they bring you with the ouzo. But if you're really hungry, there are several good restaurants nearby. Let me take you to one."

She looked at me for a long moment while I tried to keep the predatory gleam out of my eyes, then she nodded. "All right," she said with a strange little smile. "After all, what did I come to the Greek islands for, if I'm going to turn down an invitation like that from a tall, dark, handsome stranger with an interesting pallor. Let's go."

I took her to Zorba's for dinner; a noisy, lively place where the waiters are friendly and the food is good. Ann enjoyed the food and the wine in a way that seemed to have a curious urgency to it, as if she hadn't eaten or drunk for a long time or expected not to for a long time. But though her enthusiasm was a little frantic, it was also delightful: she seemed charmingly eager to enjoy everything—the food, the night air, the cheerfully impudent little boy who served as our busboy and wine waiter.

"I like to see kids doing something useful," she said. "At home they seem to think the world owes them perpetual entertainment. And of course in America they'd never let a kid this young work in a restaurant where they serve drinks, much less bring the wine and open it for you. By the way, the wine is delicious; I'm really sold on your Santorini wines."

This was my chance. I told her about our Santorini wine industry, about how our volcanic soil gives a special taste to the wine. Then I said casually, "I live in an old converted winery, and have a little cellar of vintage wines that were grown within a kilometer or so of my home. Perhaps you'd like to see my house sometime and taste some of the wines."

She hesitated, and I could see her getting ready to say "No"; she wasn't the sort of woman who'd normally accept an invitation like that so soon after meeting a man. Then she looked at me and gave a strangely sad little smile. "Why not?" she said. "I don't have all that much time left, and after all . . ."

"After all, why did you come to the Greek islands," I teasingly finished her sentence for her. She laughed and rose to her feet. "Let's go," she said. I'll always remember Ann that first night saying "Let's go," to every suggestion, with that strange little note of reck-lessness, almost desperation in her voice.

There were no taxis to be had at that time of night, so we walked to Theotocopolous Square and took the local bus out to my village. At a stop just outside of town, Old Mavrodontes got on, and as soon as he saw me started cursing and abusing me in his high, cracked voice. "*Vrikolakas!*" he yelled, "Vrikolakas!" The con-ductor hustled him to the back of the bus, with an apologetic smile to Ann. If I had been alone, he would not have interfered between myself and old Mavrodontes. But Ann was a foreigner, and in Greece the foreigner is a guest, not to be bothered with local feuds.

"What was that all about?" Ann asked, a little shaken by the old man's vehemence.

I shrugged. "I'm not popular with some of my neigh-bors," I told her. "When I converted the old winery to a home, some people lost jobs, though the ones who really wanted to found work elsewhere easily enough. Some felt injured because they had to go a few kilome-ters to work at other wineries instead of just walking down the road. And some people would like to buy my winery and make money by putting it back into production. The wine business is booming here."

"You seem to be proud of your local wines, but you let me drink most of that bottle at dinner," she said. "Of course you might have had an ulterior motive for that," she added dryly.

"I don't drink much," I said, "not much wine, at any rate." Again I couldn't keep the irony out of my voice, and she gave me a thoughtful look, but said no more. When we got to my little village, we got off the bus to the accompaniment of a last stream of abuse from Mavrodontes and walked up the little lane to my home. I unlocked the door, turned on the lights, and turned to usher Ann in.

She was looking at the little graveyard next to my

house with a strange expression on her face, but when I touched her arm she smiled at me and seemed suddenly full of energy and gaiety. I put some records on my stereo, and we danced and tasted my wine and danced again. At the end of the last record, she put her arms around my neck and kissed me lingeringly. "Is that the bedroom behind that door?" she asked softly. "Let's go."

At first her lovemaking had that same frantic quality that I had seen in her before, but after the first time she grew calmer and it was slow and sweet and good— better than it had been for me for a long, long time. At last she seemed to sleep, but when I raised myself on my elbow and looked down at her face, her eyes opened. "All right," she said, "go ahead." She leaned her head back so that her throat arched, and smiled that curious smile.

"Go ahead?" I said, pretending to be puzzled. She laughed softy.

"Niko, I told you that my grandmother filled my head with stories—not just stories, either; she *knew*. I think she was half a witch herself. From the stories my grandmother told me, you've got to be a vampire. Your face is pale, your lips are red, your teeth are sharp. You don't like the sun, and you come out only at night. You live next door to a graveyard, and the local people all act a little leery of you, except that old man. The name he called you means vampire, doesn't it? I ran across it somewhere reading about Greek legends and superstitions. Except they aren't just superstitions, are they? Go ahead, take my blood if that's what you want, what you need. I don't mind. Perhaps later I'll tell you why."

"All right, my dear," I said quietly. "But I won't mark your lovely throat. It's much better here." I bent over her thigh, found the femoral artery and entered it with one quick bite. She shuddered, and shuddered again when after drinking deep I withdrew. The wounds closed quickly—something in my saliva has that effect—but not before a few drops of blood had trickled out. She looked at them and then at me.

"That was . . . kind of kinky, but I could get to like it," she said. "You really are a real . . ."

"*Vrikolakas,*" I said. "You didn't really believe it, did you? But there's something else hard to believe. You're dying, aren't you? Something in your blood is killing you slowly; I could feel it when I drank."

Tears welled from her eyes; she made no effort to wipe them away, but lay there naked and defenseless with the tears running down her face. "Oh Niko, will my blood hurt you?" she asked brokenly. "I didn't really want that. It was like a story I was telling myself; you were a vampire, but I'd fool you because my blood was . . . bad. I didn't think that . . ."

I shook my head; the familiar warmth was tingling in my body, and I knew that whatever was wrong in her blood did not affect the use my body made of it. There are advantages in being one of the Undead. "No poison can harm me," I told her, "including, it seems, whatever deadly thing is in your blood. But it can harm you, my dear. Now I know why you seemed to be grasping so frantically at enjoyment. How long did the doctors give you?"

"They told me a month before I began to get really sick," she said. "And I felt that I'd never lived at all. I quit my job, sold everything I could sell, even borrowed money. I suppose that's dishonest; I'll never live to pay it back. Then I came here to the Greek islands, the place I'd always dreamed of visiting. If I was going to have only a month, at least for that month I wanted to *live*. Then I met you . . ." She touched the almost-healed wounds on her thigh with wonder on her face. "Will I become a vampire now?" she asked. "What's it like to be a vampire?"

"So long as I only take your blood, no, you will not become what I am," I said. "I would have to reverse the flow and give you some of mine—quite a bit, in fact. Then the parasite that makes me what I am would grow in you, and your body would adapt. What flows in my veins is not exactly blood, but it combines with blood, even diseased blood like yours. The mixture is very powerful. My body heals itself from almost any wound, casts off every disease. And so long as I get new blood periodically, I will never die. There are disadvantages, of course; my skin has no melanin at all, and I could get a severe sunburn from being out in the sun only a short time. But I'm sensitive to cold and damp, too. That's why I live in this climate."

"And during the day . . ." she began, then hesitated.

I laughed, "Lie down in my grave?" I said. "Well, in a way. Even a tiny bit of light or noise can bother me when I try to sleep, and I have a little sleeping room fixed up in a family crypt in the graveyard next door. It has to look like a real crypt in case anyone ever gets in there, but it's very snug and comfortable. Want to see it?"

"Let's go," she said a little shakily, and began to dress. I started to help her, and that caused some delay, but eventually we were dressed again and walked out of the house into the little graveyard. Somebody had been taking out their hostility to me on the tomb that covered the crypt—Mavrodontes or one of the others. The little ornamental chain that made a sort of fence around the top of the tomb had been wrenched from its supports and lay in a heap on the top of the tomb, and someone had battered the little frame that is supposed to hold a picture of the person most recently buried in the crypt. I used to put a mirror in the frame so that anyone looking to see the face of the dead would see their own face. But no one liked my little joke, and the mirror was always broken. I no longer replaced the mirror, but they still battered the frame.

Ann looked at the tomb and bit her lip. "Do the

local people hate you so much?" she asked in a small voice. "Do you . . . ?"

I shook my head. "No, I leave the locals strictly alone," I said. "There are always young tourist girls who can spare some blood and think the whole experience is a rather kinky thrill. Half of them don't even realize what's happening, or what I am. Most of the local people know about us, though some pretend not to. Some are quite decent to me. I'll have to ask Father Athanasius to preach another sermon about the wickedness of desecrating graves—even mine."

Ann was hurt by what I had said about the tourist girls—there was no way she couldn't be. But she said nothing about that, only asked in a steady voice, "You said the local people know about 'us'—are there others . . . like you . . . here?"

I shrugged. "Not so many now as there once were, and some of them have grown very strange over the long years. There are those of them who take no food and drink at all, except blood. If you do that, your body changes in some ways I don't find pleasant. I try to keep at least some hold on humanity. The girls are as much for that as for the blood. But whether you believe this or not, Ann, you are much different from the others for me—very different."

"I believe you, Niko," Ann said quietly. "We have something in common, you and I. We both have something in our blood that's—different. Mine won't let me live, but yours won't let you die. I thought my problem was as bad as could be, but I'm not sure yours isn't worse."

In all the years, she was the only one who had come close to understanding, and my voice was not quite under control as I said, "The loneliness is the worst. I don't dare to love anyone. If they are not what I am, they will go and die and my loneliness would be worse than before. And I could never bear to make anyone else what I am, as some of the others have done. How could they help but hate me when they realized what I had condemned them to?"

Ann looked at me for a long time in silence. Then she said in an oddly expressionless voice, "Show me where you sleep during the day." The little moment of closeness was over; perhaps it never really existed. Her problem gave her some insight into mine, but not enough. To be condemned to death is easier than to be condemned to life.

I led her to the little slab near the tomb that gave access to the crypt. The slab carved with a skull and a motto in Greek. "Vanity of vanity, all is vanity," I translated for her. "Plenty of people believe that now, but they don't dare remind themselves of it. This slab was made by people who still believed in an afterlife; they didn't mind being reminded of their mortality. It's a different kind of reminder for me; I could die, but I'd have to choose to. I've never had the courage, even when things seemed worst. As Hamlet says, 'For in that sleep of death what dreams may come. . . . Must give us pause.' But perhaps someday I'll lose something that I can't bear living with the loss of, and I'll make the choice to die. . . . Sorry, it's chilly out here. Will you step into my grave?"

She gave a shaky little laugh as I lifted the slab and capped my quotation with another from *Hamlet:* "Indeed, that is out o' the air." A wave of desolation swept through me as we descended the narrow steps. I had more in common with Ann than with any other woman I had ever talked with, laughed with, loved with. But she had only a month before the sickness drained her of life. I was at last facing a loss I couldn't live with.

My little crypt is ancient and has some paintings on the wall; strange, wild-eyed saints with golden halos. I had restored them little by little over the years. So long as I am shut away from the sunlight, I can be active for much of the day. Perhaps I am shortening my

extended life span by doing so. Surely the comalike
state we normally enter during the day accounts for
some of our longevity—it is more like suspended ani-
mation than sleep.

Ann was exclaiming over the wall paintings when
we heard a noise from above us. Someone was batter-
ing on the door of my house and shouting. It might
have been wiser to pull the slab down and lock it, let
whoever it was take out their rage on my practically
impregnable door, but this interruption of my precious
time with Ann put me into a red rage, and without
thinking I ran up the stairs with her at my heels.

What we saw when we emerged was like a scene
from an old, bad movie. Hammering on my door was a
wild-eyed young man, obviously an American. Standing beside him with a flaring torch in his hand was
Mavrodontes with a wicked grin on his face. When he
saw us emerge, he pointed his finger at us and shouted
melodramatically, "There is the vampire and his victim!"

"Fool," I spat at Mavrodontes in Greek. "This time
you have gone too far! Have you forgotten that the
house you live in is mine and on my land? Always
before I have thought of your wife and daughter and
left you in the house, despite your mischief-making.
But now I will give your wife a choice. Either you
behave yourself or the whole family must leave the
house. How do you think she will choose, Mavrodontes?
She is as tired of your antics as I am!"

The old man's jaw dropped, and the torch almost fell
from his hand. He was as lazy as he was mischievous,
and his drinking was paid for by what his wife and
daughter earned. Their home was important to them,
and he knew very well that if I threatened them with
the loss of it, he would get no peace—and no more
drinking money—if he made any more trouble. He
took a step backward, and I knew that at the first
opportunity he would slip away, abandoning his American ally.

As soon as I stopped speaking, Ann stepped forward and blazed out at the young American. "What the *hell* are you doing here, Harry? Before I left, I told you I never wanted to see you again! Did you follow me to this island?"

The young man flushed but looked stubborn. "What did you expect me to do when I found you'd sold everything, including some stuff of mine, and told everyone you weren't coming back? Your doctor wouldn't tell me anything, but I know you flew off the handle right after you went in for that checkup. All right, maybe I gave you something; you know I play around sometimes. But I always come back to you, don't I? Damn it, Ann, I need you!"

Ann's voice when she replied was full of honeyed malice. "You *need* me, do you, Harry? Well you're going to have to do without me. Do you know what I got from you, Harry? AIDS, that what. If you were really gay or really bi, maybe I could forgive that, but you don't even really like boys. You just have to show what a big swinger you are, ready to try anything once. Well, you tried 'anything' once too often, Harry. The doctor told me I had only a few months to live!"

Harry's face was paler than mine in the light of the torch, and his voice was barely under control. "Oh my God," he whimpered. "If I gave it to you, I must have it myself. I've got to get to a doctor, to a hospital . . ." He turned and stumbled toward the road, where I could see a car parked, probably one of the rental cars from the town. Mavrodontes called a curse after him, seeing his last hope of making trouble for me vanishing. Perhaps the old man had even hoped that he could egg on the young American to kill me; I saw that in his other hand he actually had a sharpened stake!

"On your way, old fool," I snapped. "And as for that stake, you can take it and . . ." But I had pushed him too far; he was both drunker and crazier than I had thought. He threw the stake like a javelin, right at my face. At that distance he could hardly miss; I felt a blinding pain in my head, and blackness descended on me. The last sounds I heard were Ann's scream and the fleeing footsteps of Mavrodontes.

I awoke in the crypt with an aching head, feeling strangely weak. Ann was sitting on the floor beside my coffin, leaning on the wall behind her. Her eyes were closed, and there was an odd-looking tangle of stuff on the floor beside her; I recognized some old tubing left over from when the winery had been in operation which she must have found in my storage closet.

When I tried to move, a pain shot through my head and I gave a little involuntary groan. Ann's eyes opened, and she smiled at me. "Your head probably feels terrible, but that stake didn't hit you square on, and the gash it made on the side of your head was half closed when I started to bandage it—I've never seen anybody heal so quickly."

She took a deep breath and went on. "If you feel weak, Niko, it's because you've lost blood while you were unconscious. I transfused about a pint of your blood into myself, and probably wasted almost another pint with my makeshift apparatus. I'm sorry, but I didn't think I could persuade you to do it yourself, your way. You said you'd never make another person . . . like yourself . . . because they'd hate you for it. Well, you didn't do it to me. I did it to myself."

I was already feeling a little better, and I raised myself on my elbow to peer into her face in the dim light of the fluorescent camp lantern that lit the crypt. "But why, Ann?" I cried, "why did you do it?"

She smiled at me. "Because I love you, you idiot. I won't say that it wasn't partly fear of dying, fear of the kind of sickness I'd have to go through before dying, but it was mostly because I wanted to be with you so you won't be so terribly lonely anymore . . ." A thought struck her, and she looked at me with panic in her eyes. "Niko, will it work? Have I wasted your blood for nothing when you were already wounded?"

I sighed. "My darling fool, if you took a pint of my blood, the parasite should be well established in your body," I said. "And there's no reversing what you've done. Give me your hand. A little blood from your finger will tell me if the change is complete yet."

It was; the "blood" might as well have been my own, and had as little sustenance for me. "My dear," I said gently, "you've accomplished what you wanted to. I hope you'll never regret it. But now both of us will need blood. I can last for a while on what I took from you last night, and the conversion of your own blood will last you for a long time. But eventually both of us must . . . drink."

She smoothed the bandage on my head with gentle fingers and smiled. "I have plans about that, Niko," she said. "No more tourist girls for you, my lad. I'm a registered nurse—that's why I know how to do the transfusion—and if there's one thing I know about, it's blood. That's why getting AIDS myself from Harry was such a tragic irony. What you and I are going to do is open a blood bank."

I stared at her, speechless, and she laughed at me. "Sounds crazy, doesn't it? Two vampires running a blood bank. But it will work—if you could tell I had AIDS from one drink of my blood, I bet you can detect other things wrong with blood that we get from paid donors. Hepatitis is a real headache, because people aren't always aware they have it. You can screen the blood, and we can take any 'bad' blood for our own use. Brokering blood can be a profitable business anyway, if it's efficiently run. I'll bet we can make a living at it as well as supplying our own needs. There's always a market for a reliable source of blood— and who knows more about blood than a vampire?"

It was utter madness—but it worked. It took time

and a great deal of money to get established. For a while we thought we would have to sell the winery building. We had to take a Greek doctor into partnership to satisfy government regulations, but that gave us valuable contacts in the medical community, and Dr. Elias is too well armored with scientific prejudices to ever realize what we are and what we do with the blood that we screen out.

We have to be in Athens much more than we like, for Santorini of course is too small to support a blood service on the scale we need. With factor-twenty sunscreen and extra-strong photogray sunglasses, we can stand brief exposure to the sun, and we usually take the overnight ferry to and from Piraeus. Our blood clinic in Athens is an old warehouse with no windows, lit by fluorescent lights. When the sun goes down, we enjoy the late leisurely Greek restaurant meals and the nightlife of the city.

But Santorini is still our home. We spend as much time here as we can. Ann has softheartedly bribed Mavrodontes into behaving himself with a "caretaker's" job where he does a minimum of work and earns enough for a maximum of drinking. Perhaps the old fool will drink himself to death soon, but I doubt it—he's too tough. Ann's ex-lover, Harry, was not tough at all—we found out that he had committed suicide when it was confirmed that he did have AIDS.

So we live untroubled by old enemies and have even made a few friends. Ann has hopes for a research program that may someday turn our curse into a blessing. We already can synthesize the substance in my saliva that heals bite wounds, and we use it at the blood bank. Perhaps we will tire of our life, perhaps we will even tire of each other, but I do not think so. There are deep bonds between us. My blood saved Ann from death; her companionship rescued me from loneliness and despair. We do no harm and perhaps a little good now.

For old times' sake, whenever we are on Santorini, we go for an evening drink at Franco's Bar. We always arrive after sunset.

PIÈCE DE RÉSISTANCE

by Judith Tarr

Cooking competitions are quite common in the real world, but very rarely do they appear in tales of the fantasy world. Here is a tale about a contest between a master chef who presided over the kitchens of the King of Jerusalem and a challenger who wasn't really a cook at all but something quite different.

I.

"But," said the king, "I already have a master cook."

His counselor smiled. "Indeed, Sire, you do: the master of all master cooks. And yet even the greatest master is, after all, a man. He grows old. He longs for his own country. He curses the sun and the dust, and sighs for the soft air of Provence. Could he but return there, enriched for life by the bounty of the King of Jerusalem, how joyful he would be!"

The king sighed. "Ah, Provence!" A frown marred his brow. "But, Amaury, Master Folquet is the best in the world. The Greek said so, what was his name, the one from Byzantium. And the Turk from Cairo, or was it Baghdad? And—"

Amaury coughed. The king stopped. Amaury said

very gently, "My lord brother of course is perfectly
correct. And why should the High King concern himself with such a trifle as the wishes of his cook? The
earth here is the most holy in the world; who would
refuse to lie in it for a grave in green Provence?"

The king's frown deepened. Amaury waited. At
length the king struck the arm of his chair with a
massive fist. "All right then. All right! Show me this
genius who'll thrust Master Folquet out of his kitchen."

"Who will help you to grant Master Folquet's deepest desire," said Amaury, not precisely as if he were
correcting the king.

His Majesty glowered and rose. "Of course, of course.
You do all the thinking for both of us anyway. Raymond, tell the groom to saddle my charger. I'll take a
turn or two at the quintain."

He was gone in royal haste. Amaury smiled, not at
all the same smile with which he had favored his liege,
and followed in much more leisurely fashion.

The Mouse swallowed a sneeze. It was infernally
dusty behind the arras, which said nothing at all for
the king's servants. Now if Master Folquet had had
anything to do with them—

He choked on dust and sudden recollection. Master
Folquet was going to be sent away. Back to Provence
with money enough to set him up in his own kitchen,
serving his own dishes in his own time; the dream he
invoked eloquently whenever the purity of his art col-
lided with the reality of his kitchen.

A wave of the king's hand and he would have what
he prayed for.

The Mouse held his breath, listening. Not a sound.
With utmost care he crept to the joining of two tapestries and peered through the gap. The room was empty.
Quick and quiet as the creature he was named for, he
bolted for his hole.

*   *   *

Master Folquet was in a passion. A passion such as only Master Folquet could muster, quiet, restrained, and civilized. Master Folquet was an educated man; he was never uncivilized. Though once, when one of the scullions had dropped a platter with a crash at the very instant when Master Folquet was completing the final perfect curve of a ram's horn in marzipan, he had been heard to raise his voice a full degree. The scullions were still pale with the memory of it, and given to starting at shadows.

This was a less splendid passion. The fourth assistant pastry cook, sent for fennel seed, had returned with anise instead. Master Folquet was flaying him slowly in all the colors of his glorious rhetoric. The Mouse slipped invisibly into the line of scullions scouring pans, every one laboring diligently and listening in breathless awe.

"Provence," sighed Master Folquet. "Lovely Provence! There are fools there; there are idiots; there are mooncalves of truly abysmal stupidity. But none to equal the asses of Jerusalem."

The Mouse set his lip between his teeth and attacked a stubborn stain, and tried to keep his heart from hammering. One did not—if one was a lowly scullion— one did *not* venture to address the Master Cook. One was addressed imperially through a parade of underlings, or one was blessedly ignored. One did not have a mind; one did not have eyes except for one's work; and most of all, one did not have a penchant for prowling hidden passages and eavesdropping on the king.

The Mouse listened to Master Folquet's glorious voice and scoured pans, and wrestled his conscience into submission. After all, Master Folquet wanted to go back to Provence.

The king looked the petitioner up and down. The man bowed low for the hundredth time and smiled.

His face was made for smiling, vast and round and jovial, with a little fringe of black beard and a pair of eyes sunk deep in the pale-brown skin like currants in a pastry. He was huge; he was magnificent; he was the embodiment of a cook. Even his voice was perfect, a warm smooth voice, dark gold and sweet like Hymettus honey. "I am utterly at Your Majesty's service, if Your Majesty should deign to accept one as humble as I."

The king raised his chin a little to a more kingly angle. His eyes were deep and brooding; his face was awesome in repose. "Amaury," he said to his brother who stood beside him, "is this man a paynim?"

The cook bowed even more deeply than before. "Indeed, most puissant lord, this worthless dog was once a slave of Mohammed. But he has seen the light, oh aye, long since; the blessed Christ is now his master."

"As the Emperor of Byzantium will attest," said Amaury smoothly, "along with a truly imperial commendation of his culinary skills. To which also will testify the Doge of Venice, the Lord of the Holy Roman Empire, and"—he paused for an instant—"the lord Pope himself."

The king frowned portentously. "Powerful testimonials. Yes, very powerful indeed. But, Amaury, what will Master Folquet say to all of this?"

His counselor paused. The cook bowed to the carpet. "If Your Majesty will permit—Your Majesty, after all, is the king. But if Your Highness is troubled, perhaps Your Puissance will deign to ask him yourself."

Amaury nodded gravely. "The act of a wise and clement king, to be sure, to grant a faithful servant his freedom and his fortune in one noble gesture."

"Well then," said the king, "send for him."

Master Folquet, sent for, showed no sign of either haste or anxiety. But the Mouse, behind the arras, saw with a shiver that his nostrils were just touched with white.

He did not choose to notice the cook. The counselor won a precise bow, the king one deeper but no less precise. "My lord commands me?" he inquired. The king frowned at him. Beside that magnificent bulk he seemed very slight and very stiff, with a face like a monk's: thin and ascetic and most alarmingly intelligent. He did not look like a cook at all, nor act like one, nor sound like one. And his hair, though beautifully cut, was thin and going gray.

"Tell him, Amaury," said the king.

Amaury bowed and turned his pale wise face upon the Master. "Master Folquet, His Majesty has given long and deep thought to the excellence of your service. What reward, he has asked himself, can possibly compensate such fidelity? What gift can he give to reveal to you his deep gratitude? What recompense save that which, in all the world, you most desire?"

Master Folquet waited and said nothing. His lips had thinned. The Mouse trembled.

"What recompense," repeated Amaury, "but the greatest of them all? Provence, Master Folquet—His Majesty gives you back your homeland, with a barony to set you high in it and a wagonload of gold to secure your place there. Master Folquet, this day is your fortune made!"

It was a ringing conclusion; it rang in silence. Master Folquet moved not at all. He might, perhaps, have been speechless with astonishment.

The Mouse knew better.

At long last he stirred, to bow, to straighten, to say in his precise, trained voice, "I thank His Majesty with all my heart. But I cannot accept his gifts."

The king gaped in most unkingly fashion. The cook forsook his smile. Amaury drew a slow breath. "You . . . refuse?"

"I refuse," said the Master. "With all due courtesy, and with a plea to His Majesty to remember that I am not a baron or a rich merchant. I am a cook. Have I given His Majesty cause for dissatisfaction?"

Amaury opened his mouth. But the king had recovered most of his wits. "No, sir. No indeed! We're perfectly satisfied. But you see, Master Folquet, you aren't getting any younger and Provence isn't getting any closer. And here's this master cook, highly recommended in all the best places, who's ready and willing to take over for you. After, of course, you've gone off to a well-earned retirement."

Master Folquet drew himself up to his full height. "Retirement, Sire?" he asked very softly.

"Riches," said the king. "Leisure. Contentment. In blessed Languedoc."

"Languedoc." Master Folquet smiled the merest shadow of a smile. "I dream of it. However, Your Majesty, I am at heart a realist. A dream gained is a very feeble thing. Nor," he said in the gentlest of tones, "can I be bribed with it. If my lord is not content, he may dispose of me as he wills. He need not wrap his displeasure in gilt."

The king glanced at Amaury, but his counselor was frowning at the floor. "Look here," he said. "I'm giving you your heart's desire. And I've engaged another cook. Or Amaury has. Can't you just kiss my hand and thank me, and let it go at that?"

Master Folquet stood perfectly erect and perfectly still. "Very well. I am dismissed. I shall leave directly."

"Sire!" The cook advanced, bowing and smiling. "Sire, my lord, my good Master, need we part in bitterness? The Master is the prince of cooks, I but an apprentice beside him. Yet if he wishes it, and if His Majesty desires, we may resolve the matter to the satisfaction of all concerned." He beamed at them. "A contest, sirs! Let us have a feast. Half the courses I shall prepare to the best of my poor ability; to half the Master will devote his famous art. And let a court of noblemen sit in judgment upon us. For the victor, the mastery of His Majesty's kitchen; for the vanquished, freedom to go wherever he wills with His Majesty's commendation."

The king's eyes gleamed. "A contest," he said. "A contest. By'r'Lady, there you have it! What do you say, Master Folquet? Would you settle the score that way? Winner take all and Devil take the hindmost."

Master Folquet bowed with perfect correctness. "If so my lord desires," he said. Deep in his eyes a spark had caught, brighter and fiercer even than the king's.

II.

It was a rare diversion between battles and tournaments, invasions of Saracens and invasions of pilgrims: a struggle for the mastery of the royal kitchen. Although the feast would not be held until a fortnight hence, at Pentecost, already the curious had begun to gather and the rumors to fly.

By the grace of the king and the graciousness of Jusuf his rival, Master Folquet held sway in his old domain. Jusuf settled near, yet not too near, in the dusty labyrinth that had served the master cook of the first King of Jerusalem. He asked for no aid and no servants; he had his own, he said with his everlasting smile, and would not presume upon the king's generosity. Later, however, if by God's will he had the victory . . . He smiled and said no more.

Master Folquet said nothing at all. And did nothing, it seemed, but what he had always done. If he prepared any great masterpiece, the Mouse saw no sign of it. His kitchen lay open to any who dared to venture in; he disposed of the inquisitive with a few scathing phrases, and kept his underlings at their usual work.

Jusuf's quarter was shut and barred. The Mouse, loitering about, saw nothing and no one. Sometimes he heard strange sounds or caught a scent as of spices, but that was all. There were no windows to peer through and no hangings to hide behind, and every bolt-hole was most efficiently stopped up.

But the Mouse had one virtue which even his enemies would admit to. He persevered.

Which was why, on a starless night very close to Pentecost, one pillar of the old courtyard had a double shadow. The air was breathlessly warm even so late, but the Mouse shivered in his thin tunic. He hardly knew what had possessed him to leave his bed in the corner of the hearth between Ali and the kitchen cat. If there was nothing to see by day, what could he expect to find in the dark?

He tensed. Lights flickered across the court: torches, leaping and flaring as their bearers moved. They could be guards mounting the walls maybe, or a lord coming late from the city, but guards and lords were noisy with armor or with drink. These made no sound.

A huge shape loomed in the archway. The Mouse shrank behind his pillar; the shape dwindled, became a man laden with a heavy bale. And another came after him, and another, soft on bare feet, flanked by torchbearers. The procession streamed toward Jusuf's door, which opened silently. A gleam of light stabbed the darkness. The bearers passed within. The door shut; the light was gone; the Mouse remembered how to breathe.

His brain shrieked to him to dive for safety. His feet carried him through the shadows to the door. Just beyond it lay an old fishpond, empty now and treacherous in the dark, but railed with stone. The Mouse crouched behind it with every sense alert.

For a long while there was nothing. But the nape of his neck prickled; his lips drew back from his small sharp teeth. The air felt different here. It felt wrong.

It had felt that way when he hid behind the arras and watched the stranger-cook bow and smile and protest his unworthiness. Protest, and propose a contest he could not but lose if he told the truth.

The wrongness was stronger here. Maybe it was the dark and the weed-choked fishpond, and the utter silence.

Again the door opened. The light behind it was red. The Mouse had a brief, searing vision of all within, before a man's shadow blocked it and the door thudded shut.

The Mouse crouched shuddering under a safe, sane, yellow cresset outside of his own familiar kitchen. Within, he could hear snores and the rustling of bodies on straw. Soon the bakers would be up, beginning the day's bread.

He could not stop shaking. If he could just stop—if he could just take the few steps through the door—he would be able to rest.

His feet were not his own tonight. They retreated from safety; they stumbled up a steep narrow stair; they brought him through a curtain and into light.

The scullions were certain that Master Folquet never slept. The Mouse had confirmation of it. For here in the black midnight, he sat in his bedchamber with a book in his hand, no whit less impeccable than he was at high noon. He regarded the intruder with an utter lack of surprise. "Well?" he asked.

The Mouse could not speak.

Master Folquet raised a fine brow. There was a cup by his elbow; he set it in the Mouse's limp fingers. "Drink," he said.

One never disobeyed Master Folquet. The drink was honeyed wine; it warmed the Mouse's cold belly and steadied his quaking knees. He set the cup carefully in its place.

"Well?" Master Folquet said again. "You would be one of mine, I suppose. He of the long elegant name. Abd-er-Rahman Mohammed."

"Mouse, Master," he mumbled. "Just Mouse."

"Mouse, then. It is quite apt. Now, suppose you sit

on my bed, which is a good deal steadier than your
legs seem to be, and tell me why I should not have you
whipped for troubling my peace."

The Master's tone was grim, but strangely enough,
the Mouse was not afraid. Perhaps it was the wine. He
perched on the edge of the narrow ascetic bed, pushed
his tangled hair out of his eyes, and drew a long
breath. Master Folquet waited in awful silence. Gathering all his courage, he began.

He told everything, from that first day behind the
king's arras to the black courtyard and the open door
and the red light in it. "And things," he said very low.
"Things, Master. A cauldron; the red light was under
it, not a comfortable kitchen fire—it made me think of
the one in the smithy. And the—the man, Master
Jusuf, standing by it, and all around him black devils.
They were doing things, I couldn't see what. But Jusuf
was smiling, and stirring the cauldron with a long
white rod like a bone with words written all over it. I
saw them; they moved like bits of fire up and down
the rod. And Jusuf *smiled*."

The Mouse stopped. He was shaking again. Master
Folquet filled the cup and handed it back to him. He
drank deep, until his eyes blurred and his head spun.
Through the fog of wine he heard Master Folquet's
voice. "And you came to me. Why?"

"Why?" the Mouse repeated stupidly. "Why, Master? He's a sorcerer. He's evil. What if—what if he
means to bewitch the king?"

"What if he is only preparing a secret masterpiece
by firelight, with his servants about him?"

The Mouse sat bolt upright. The empty cup slid
from his hand and clattered to the floor; he hardly
noticed. "Master, I didn't tell you everything. There's
something else I saw. The man who came out was . . .
was my lord Amaury. And he said something. He
said, 'Remember. For this, you use only the delights
of the eyes and of the palate. Later, when we are well

rid of that long-nosed clerk who rules my brother's stomach and hence his brain as well, you may work your greater magics.' And he laughed and said, 'Then shall I be king in name as well as in fact, and you my counselor. Cast your spells well for me!' " The Mouse smote his hands together in desperation. "Please, Master. You have to believe me. You have to do something!"

Master Folquet looked at him. Simply looked. The Mouse should have quailed; would have, if this had been daylight and he his usual self. But there was the wine, and he had seen what he had seen. He met the cold eyes with wonderous steadiness and firmed his jaw and waited.

The Master nodded slowly. "You deserve a proper tanning. Spying indeed! And most of it when you were on duty besides. But this—You realize, boy, that if what you tell me is true, our adversaries may be aware of all we say and do here."

The Mouse started violently and stared about, wild-eyed.

"However," said Master Folquet, "I like to fancy that we are protected." His glance drew the Mouse's to the door-curtain. Over it hung a small crucifix carved from olivewood. The Mouse crossed himself quickly.

"A Christian, are you, boy?" the Master asked him.

"My mother was, Master."

"So." Master Folquet nodded again. "Tell me what you would do if you were I."

For a long moment the Mouse was speechless. Master Folquet made no move. The Mouse swallowed and told him.

There was a silence. The Mouse trembled. To his utter and lasting astonishment, Master Folquet laughed. It was an amazing laugh, light and free and very young; it transformed the Master's face, almost made a boy of him. For a few moments only. All at once he was the Master again, calm and austere and terrible. "Do it then," he said, "and tell no one at all. If you fail, I shall have only my poor mortal skill to set against the arts of a sorcerer. If you succeed . . . perhaps, just perhaps—if you swear a solemn vow to curb your penchant for eavesdropping on His Majesty—I shall see that you gain the reward you deserve."

The Mouse threw himself down with bursting heart and kissed the Master's feet.

III.

The great feast of Pentecost found all the High Court in the king's hall in Jerusalem. The gathered might of Outremer was resplendent in the silks and jewels of the East, overlaid with the sweetness of Arabian unguents. Here and there was a darker shape, a priest, a pilgrim from the West come to marvel at the magnificence of this kingdom beyond the sea. The king sat on his throne above them all, gold crown glittering on bright-gold hair, and his robe all of cloth of gold. Close beside him sat his brother Amaury in silk as splendid as his ambitions and as dark as his plotting, and close about him the judges of the feast: the queen enthroned at her lord's side in cloth of silver; the Grand Master of the Knights Templar, all in white save for the scarlet cap of his Order and the blood-red cross upon his breast; the Cardinal Legate of His Holiness the Pope of Rome; and that most celebrated of connoisseurs, the Ambassador of the Emperor of Byzantium, contemplating the scene before him and not quite smiling.

The trumpeters blew the fanfare. A herald advanced, bowed low to the king, and proclaimed, "Your Majesties; Your Excellencies; my lords and ladies of the High Court of the Kingdom of Jerusalem: We gather here on this day of Pentecost to judge a matter of great moment. Master Jusuf of Damascus and of Qum, artist and master cook, has challenged Master Folquet of St.-Géraud in Provence to a contest of skill, the victor to gain the mastery of the royal kitchens, the vanquished to depart and to go where he wills, so that it not be into the kitchens of His Majesty, Guy, High King of Jerusalem. Let this be the way of it, that each Master shall produce three full courses in honor of the perfection of the Holy Trinity; each course shall be constructed about a theme set by His Majesty; and each shall follow the other in due alternation, with first honors to the challenger—unto the culmination, a subtlety which celebrates the glory of the Crusade and the splendor of this eastern bastion of our faith against the foulness of the infidel. Your Majesties, Your Excellencies, my lords and ladies, let the banquet begin!"

The Mouse held his breath. He had chosen an excellent hiding place behind the throne, from which vantage he could see all that the king could. And he had Master Folquet's unvoiced consent for this last and boldest bit of eavesdropping.

The herald had withdrawn. The court waited, murmuring.

Trumpets rang. Drums beat beneath them. The great doors swung wide. Master Jusuf passed through them in flowing white, with a white turban and a wide white smile. He bowed before the king, bowed to all the judges and to the assembled court, and withdrew smoothly to the side of the hall.

All eyes had long since abandoned him. A long line of slaves advanced to the beat of the drum, each in the ancient garb of Egypt, men and women alike bewigged and bejeweled, their long eyes painted with kohl. In each pair of hands or upon each high head rode a platter of bronze worked with strange stiff figures and heaped with the delicacies of ancient Khemet. Rich scents wafted through the hall, strange sweets and spices, fine bread and finer cakes, fishes of the Nile roasted in green leaves, ibis clothed in their white feathers, a gazelle with gilded horns borne before the king. And as the court watched and marveled and the servants moved fluidly among them, the crown of the course floated through the gate as if upon air, drawn and followed by Nubian slaves: a great barge of gold and lapis, laden with sweetmeats, its oars fanning the air as it circled the hall. A soft sound sighed under the drums, a muted "Aaahh" won wonder and delight.

The Mouse hated the sorcerer with all his heart.

Master Jusuf stood aside and smiled, and watched the court partake eagerly of all that the slaves offered.

"Interesting," murmured the ambassador from Byzantium.

At a hidden signal, the slaves withdrew from among the court and departed. The barge followed them, empty now, its oars stilled.

The trumpets proclaimed the second course; shawms and sackbuts joined it in an air as familiar as the stones of Outremer. Here was no magic, no air of mystery, only pages and squires of the king's household, liveried as always, bearing the king's best plate. On it reposed the flower of Master Folquet's art. Lamb roasted on the spit, stewed in fine herbs, baked into a pie with fruits and spices. A compote of fruits from the East simmered in wine and cinnamon. White bread, unleavened as for the Passover of the Jews. And the subtlety, the lamb of sacrifice, each white curl of its wool wrought in marzipan by Master Folquet's hand, and all within filled with sweets and pastries. It was exquisite; it was delectable; it was, said the king, quite as good as anything the Master had produced.

"Quite good indeed," agreed the Emperor's ambassador.

Master Jusuf smiled:

His challenge came with the wailing of flutes and the tinkling of the lyre, a procession of Greek youths and maidens centered about the great carcass of an ox, roasted whole and wreathed in leaves as for a sacrifice and laid upon a massive platter of worked silver; and with it, fish broiled upon coals and roasted birds, olives and cheese, bread and meal and honey scented with thyme. But the subtlety won a sigh which drowned out the flutes. Two and thirty pairs of mules—mules of brass and steel, no larger than the hounds which crouched beneath the tables and howled at them—drew behind them a great fire of gold, the bier of Alexander as it rolled down from Babylon. Every inch of it was wrought of rare and marvelous sugars, and endorsed with saffron that was more precious than gold.

"Charming," said the Greek, nibbling a bit of golden tassel.

Once more Master Folquet sent in his Frankish lads in the same livery as before, but facing the glory of Greece with the splendors of Rome. Pork baked in pastry; chicken flavored with juniper; tunny and other fishes broiled and sauced with garlic and herbs; a potage of lentils and mustard and spices, at which, the Mouse noticed, the queen was seen to smile and to ask for more. But no one sighed or aahed even for the masterpiece, a great wheel of the Zodiac borne by strong young squires. Its fabric was bread baked hard, each sign set in it with colored pastry. And for each sign there was a heap of delicacies: cakes or sweetened fruits or flowers jeweled with sugar, all shaped for the creature of the sign.

The Greek, engrossed in Virgo's honeyed wheaten cakes, had nothing to say.

But the Mouse heard murmurs. "Tastes good." "*Is* good. But not much of a show, eh what? Like a good show, I do." "What's a show if it tastes like spiced straw?" "Straw! Where's your palate, man? In your behind?"

Jusuf, they were saying. And *Folquet*. And *Jusuf, Jusuf, Jusuf*.

Amaury permitted himself a small smile.

A swift drumming, the fierce cry of a shawm, brought more than one war-hardened knight to his feet, groping at his belt for his sword, but no man in the hall bore any weapon. The battle music of the Saracens brought with it a march of slaves in the robes of the desert, bearing their people's delicacies. Young kid simmered in its own milk; lamb stewed with dates; capon stuffed with figs and spices; great bowls of figs and dates and raisins of the sun, with flat bread and sharp goat's cheese and dark olives in their own oil.

The music paused. The drums slowed. All eyes turned to the gate. A new band of Jusuf's servitors bore upon their shoulders a great pyre redolent of spices, cinnamon and ginger, cloves and saffron and cardamom, pepper, allspice, and grains of paradise. Upon this priceless bed reposed a marvelous bird, a creature of flame and gold with eyes like living coals.

The slaves set their burdens before the king and bowing, drew away. The bird stirred and stretched its wings, and bowed as if in homage. And the pyre burst into flame, a blaze of spices engulfing the bird of fire. Its body strained, shuddered, and was consumed.

The flames died. There at the heart where the fire had been hottest glowed a great egg, hot gold. It cracked; a fiery serpent-head wove up through the opening, and a body after it, a snake of flame. It coiled amid the shards of its egg, laying down its head as if to rest.

Suddenly it writhed and swelled and bloomed. The bird of fire took wing from egg and cast-off serpent skin, soaring through the hall in an aura of fire and spices. Sweets fell from its beak into laps and a few bold hands.

The circuit came back to its beginning. The phoenix settled upon the pyre of its rebirth, tucked its head beneath its wing, and slept. The slaves bore it away.

This was no sigh of wonder; this was a full-throated cheer.

Master Folquet's lads gave it time to die down before the foremost sounded a hunting horn. His companions served forth the wealth of the West, the head of the wild boar decked with rosemary, stew of venison thickened with the blood of the stag, pheasant stewed in grapes and herbs, a peacock in the full brilliance of its plumage, small birds roasted and sauced with honey and saffron, a crustade of cream and spices and fruits, and strawberries in sweet cream. And last of all, a unicorn of white pastry collared with saffron-gold, its horn wreathed with roses; and beneath it a bed of rose petals. Yet for all the white beast's flawless beauty, the phoenix had left the court with no taste for any lesser creature. They ate with relish, but they said nothing; their eyes flickered, caught and loosed and caught again by Jusuf's smile. Even the judges nodded toward him as if their choice was made, although the Greek's eye had a strange glint.

The remains of the unicorn departed, the spiral horn, a rose or two, the sharp sweetness of crushed mint. Jusuf advanced to the dais and bowed. "Your Majesties," he said, "my lord judges. We come now to the dénouement. Out of courtesy to the Master who is my adversary in the contest, may I beg that he be permitted to witness its ending?"

"He is here," said a quiet voice at his elbow.

The Mouse had a brief and glorious vision of Jusuf taken utterly aback. But that wily sorcerer was not long or easily discomfited. His smile, which had slipped, returned undiminished; he bowed. "Ah, my good Master! At last we stand together. Shall we stand so until the end?"

Master Folquet bowed his head the merest degree, made reverence to the high ones, and withdrew with Jusuf to the side of the dais. He seemed quite calm as always, quite unperturbed by the whispers that ran among the courtiers. How much like a master cook the stranger looked; and Folquet—why, he might be a clerk or a priest, with no smile to spare for anyone. Now Jusuf was a jovial man, master showman, an artist, one the whole world would envy and Jerusalem could boast of. Who but he could have brought the very phoenix to wait upon them in their High King's hall?

"But," said a lonely voice, "it's all show. Looks good; smells good; but it doesn't taste like anything at all."

The others drowned him out, even as the Mouse braced to leap for his bolt-hole and run.

The court sat with bated breath. Here was the last stroke, the master stroke. The king stirred on his throne; as if that had been the signal, cymbals clashed. Pipes shrilled. Drums beat in counterpoint. Through the gate, stepping to the rhythm, graceful as young deer, came such servants that the knights of the court stretched their eyes and their ladies pursed their lips in delicate disapproval. Houris in veils as fragile as mist, with great dark eyes glowing above them, promising ecstasies. They swayed and swirled down the center of the hall; where their tiny hennaed feet had passed, mists curled and grew. Dark at first, thinning and elongating: the mist became slender shadowy trunks swelling and thickening and raising aloft their branches. Then a shimmer of green as leaves unfurled; blossoms burst there in a wave of sweet scent, a fall of petals upon raven hair and white shoulders, a gleam of burgeoning fruit: orange, lemon, pomegranate. The houris, dancing, gathered the harvest as others bore in goblets of sherbet, snow-cold, flavored with citron. The Mouse eeled toward his exit, running as if the world depended on it.

As the last of the sherbet vanished from the king's cup, hoofs rattled on tiles. Jusuf started a little; Master Folquet never moved. A ripple of notes stirred the scented air. A milk-white jennet stood in the gate with a squire at her bridle, and on her back a figure in extravagant motley, a jongleur from his long yellow curls to his belled toes. As the squire led the donkey forward, the minstrel's agile voice joined his agile fingers upon the lutestrings, singing that song which the troubadour Folquet de Marselha made upon the glory of God.

Nine pages followed the singer, bearing great baskets; nine pages, and a tenth who was somewhat smaller and considerably darker than the rest, breathing hard under the unaccustomed richness of his livery, eyes fixed with great care upon the back of the boy in front of him. But he had a nose to take in the scents of magic and of citrus, and ears to hear the minstrel's sweet trained voice. There was no other sound. The houris had stopped their dancing when the lute cut through the drumming; the drums themselves had faltered and gone mute.

The singer paused between verses. The jennet entered the strange grove. In a single movement the pages began to scatter their largesse, white cakes like manna flavored with almonds and honey, each marked with a small cross. The houris drew back through the trees. Jusuf's smile wavered; his fingers worked.

A gasp ran through the court. For where the manna fell, leaves withered and fruit shriveled and branches writhed and smoked. One small cake, flung by the smallest page, struck a houri's shoulder. She shrieked, piercing and terrible, as hideous as a peacock's cry. Her shoulder was blackened as with fire, a blackness that spread as she stood rooted in her place, overcame and consumed her, till naught remained of her but a faint foul smoke. The pages fanned through the trees, hurling cakes now in handfuls, and the trees wavered and began to fade. The houris ran like deer before the hunters. But the tables of the court hemmed them in and the pages surrounded them. First one, then another and another, blurred and shifted and took wing, black birds like ravens that flapped and croaked but could not escape the relentless assault. The jongleur neither wavered nor dropped a note, even when his

mount stopped full before the astounded face of the
king.

The grove shimmered like a mirage and vanished.
The last black bird fled shrieking into nothingness. The
hall was clean, save for the white drifts of manna upon
the floor. The pages stood in a circle; the singer sang
the last sweet "Amen."

Jusuf smiled no longer. He edged away from Master
Folquet toward Amaury, but stopped, surrounded by
pages. The Mouse stood closest, almost within arm's
reach. Yet a handful remained in his basket; he scooped
it up.

Jusuf's fingers wove shapes of fire in the air. The
Mouse could feel them on his skin, a searing, blinding
agony. He blinked away tears of pain, clamped his lip
between his teeth, and let fly.

Jusuf howled in agony. The honeyed cakes clung to
him, to his face and his hands and his breast. He tore
at them, and tearing, shrank. The noble master cook
had melted away. In his place crouched an old, old
man no larger than a dwarf, swathed in voluminous
white. He shrieked curses in a high cracked voice,
stretching out his hands toward Amaury. The king's
counselor made no move to aid or to hinder him.

The king rose from his throne. But the Grand Master of the Templars was before him with the light of
battle in his eye, thundering in Latin the mighty sylla-
bles of the exorcism. The sorcerer raised clawed hands
as if to counter with a spell.

"Serpent of the Devil," said Master Folquet quite
calmly, "get thee gone." He crossed himself as a proper
Christian should.

The sorcerer's curses rose to a wordless scream, the
cry of a bird; black wings rose out of the white robes.
Before any word or hand could catch him, he fled
through the open gate and was gone.

There was a long and breathless silence. One or two
ladies and at least one young nobleman had fainted;

many another looked slightly ill to have eaten, with such unheeding pleasure, the creations of sorcery.

Very quietly under their Master's eye, the pages began to gather up the cakes which they had scattered. Their movement broke the spell; the court erupted.

Master Folquet stepped into the open space before the dais. Something in his bearing spread calmness. The uproar faded; those whose nerves were steadier sought further strength in wine. Squires moved among them filling cups, restoring a semblance of normality.

The king had not returned to his throne, although he had taken a deep draft of wine. The judges sat on either side of him in attitudes of shock or horror or wide-eyed fascination; save for Amaury, whose face, though drained of color, wore no expression at all. His Majesty ignored them. "What," he demanded of Master Folquet, "did you *do?*"

The Master beckoned. The Mouse left his gathering of manna and approached slowly, eyes down. "Speak," commanded the Master.

The king was awesome and terrible, but Master Folquet was the Master. The Mouse obeyed. In a very small voice at first, hardly to be heard. But little by little it grew stronger, and the court hushed to hear it. He told all that he had seen and heard and done, save one thing only. He did not name Amaury's name. He did not know exactly why, for he hated the schemer with a fine fierce hate, but he was glad after all. For Master Folquet's glance flickered at the omission, and he nodded very slightly, with the suggestion of a smile. Amaury relaxed by slow degrees; a ghost of color returned to his cheeks.

"So," said the Mouse at last in ringing silence, "the Master gave me what I asked for, a bag and enough flour to fill it and a man to help me carry it. We went out into the city to a place I know. A church, my lord, very small and very old and almost forgotten, exactly like its priest. He's nearly blind, too. He was glad enough to lay a blessing on our bag, even without the bit of silver we paid him for it and the napkinful of food that the Master himself had made.

"We brought the flour back, and the Master took it and made it into cakes. If it's blasphemy, my lord, it's my fault, not my Master's, and you must punish me. But it did what we meant it to do." He ended on a note of high courage, with his chin up and his shoulders back and no tremor in him anywhere.

The king stared at him. The Cardinal Legate was frowning; the Grand Master gnawed his lip. But the Greek grinned in his curled black beard. "Magnificent!" he cried. "A tale worthy of an emperor's court. Your Majesty, this boy deserves his weight in gold at the very least, for his wit and his courage and his utter loyalty to his Master."

"Well," said the King, "yes. Yes, I suppose he does. It was a splendid thing to do. Splendid!"

"And," the Greek said, "as for my judgment, even without the *pièce de résistance*, I would accord Master Folquet the victory. Do my lords agree? My royal lady?"

They nodded. Even Amaury, quickly and without looking at the Master.

"Of course," said the king after a pause. "Of course. Amaury, shall I give the boy a barony? Master Folquet of course has his kitchen back, which was what I wanted in the first place."

The Master stirred. "Your pardon, Majesty, but I think perhaps, after all, I shall take what first you offered and return to Provence."

"And I," said the Mouse, "will go with him. Begging your pardon, Sire. A barony is very pleasant, but I'd rather be a cook. Master Folquet has promised to teach me," he added with great pride.

"But you can't go," the king protested. "Who'll be my cook?"

"There are cooks enough in the world, Your Majesty," said Master Folquet.

"But only one like you." Amaury had mastered himself at last and risen, smooth and urbane and wise as ever. "Who else could have defeated that monster who would have cast his spell upon the High Court? Master, we beg you. We beseech you. Do not abandon us now. Remain with us and continue to delight us with your consummate artistry."

For a long moment Master Folquet was silent, pondering, holding Amaury's veiled stare. "Suppose," he said, "that I agree. Another plausible stranger may come. Another wizard with designs on His Majesty, or a true master cook who longs to challenge me. What then?"

"Then," said Amaury, "we send him on his way and sit down to one of your inimitable feasts. What else could any wise man do?"

"Nothing, perhaps," conceded Master Folquet.

"So stay," the king said, "and stop this nonsense. Thibaut! Wine for the Master, and a toast to his victory!"

"To victory," said Master Folquet, raising his cup; and with a deep sigh: "To my dear lost Provence."

But the Mouse had seen the glint in his eye. Triumph; relief; and a flicker of laughter.

LONG, LONG AGO

by R. Chetwynd-Hayes

The great road was straight and long and apparently endless, at least for one who was dead and been walking along it for two centuries. Occasionally he would catch up with another traveler, exchange a few words and move on. Then he encountered a young woman who convinced him that they should try to find a way off the road. Their efforts were successful, resulting in something totally unexpected.

Long, long ago I died, just how I cannot remember, but I think as the result of a natural illness. There is the faint memory of a good wife, plump, cleanly and obedient, weeping by my bedside and I believe two or three smaller editions of myself, who neither wept nor smiled, but looked—if I again remember correctly—rather frightened.

Be that as it may, I found myself walking the great road, feeling much younger than I had for many a year, presumably enjoying that perfect health which is the body's birthright.

I assumed I'd walk it for all eternity, only of course there was no means of measuring time, there being no sun, moon or stars in the cloudless sky, and the sameness of the landscape, the straightness of the road, rather gives the impression all this walking was getting us precisely nowhere.

No—that is not quite true. Sometimes one saw a dim figure in front, which after maintaining the same distance, despite my frantic efforts to catch up, suddenly appeared walking but a few paces away. A man or woman with whom one can converse, discuss the barely remembered death day, the adventures encountered on the road. Presently, (if that word has any meaning) after perhaps a long and enthralling conversation, that particular fellow traveler disappeared and became again a dim figure in front or far behind until a new one came into being—or perhaps not.

More often than not, one walked alone on the great road.

I believe that this strange world in which the road exists (or does not exist) is a creation of a great mental force, that might be the source of all creative thought. But it must be confessed that I—and the other travelers—rarely bothered ourselves about such complicated matters, it is sufficient to know we still lived, after a fashion, and maybe one day (strange how these valueless expressions survive) will reach some kind of destination.

Mostly rolling, lush meadow land bordered either side of the road, broken here and there by small woods from which came strange sounds, that may have some connection with the weird shapes that can, on occasion, be seen flitting from tree to tree. Once, in a long while, I saw through a gap in the trees, standing on a low mound, a white building that had no windows, doors or chimney pots, but when I took the trouble to leave the road and trudge seemingly countless miles to examine one of these structures, I could in no wise determine its purpose.

Although I could not detect the slightest sign of an opening, there were faint lines traced on the rough white surface; some straight, others twisting and coiling into an intricate pattern. Furthermore, when I placed my ear close to a whorl, I detected a muted humming sound that seemed to originate from deep within the building. The phenomenon caused me some distress, for the only sounds heard on the road were those that came from the woods and an occasional sigh that may have been caused by a gentle breeze, which was, in turn, the only manifestation of movement, apart from those made by the weird shapes and, I might as well confess, that they might have been the result of imagination toying with light and shadow.

One could never be certain of anything on the great road.

Then came that memorable occasion when I caught up with, or she dropped back with me, Movita, which is as pretty a name as one could wish for, but certainly no more pretty than its alleged owner. I say alleged, because I had never met anyone of either sex who confessed to a name before. One addressed a traveling companion as "you" and referred to oneself as "me" and I never felt the need to identify myself by a more positive label. But Movita—remembered name or invented—looked as someone called Movita suggested, having a mane of thick black hair, matching large eyes, white oval face and full red lips. Desire and, for that matter, any fleshly appetites were a ridiculous anachronism but I felt an urge to place an arm around her shoulders, press lips to her white forehead, then hold her hand as we continued the endless journey.

She spoke with a soft lilting tone.

"I see you wear mid-eighteenth century costume. Did you die on some battlefield?"

Both statement and question puzzled me. I frowned and asked:

"Mid-eighteenth century? Battlefield? I do not understand."

She expelled a deep sigh. "None of you remember.

I thought as you looked—well—almost young—you might remember. Tell me—do you realize we have what they used to call—died? Kicked the bucket? Pushed off? No—I see you don't."

I felt a surge of rising indignation. "I remember much that is beyond the comprehension of others."

She giggled, an enchanting, youthful sound that I *had* forgotten. "You sound like someone out of the Ark. OK. What do you remember?"

"I think . . . I believe . . . maybe there was a good wife, plump, cleanly and obedient, weeping by my bedside . . ."

Her giggling grew up and became choking laughter.

"Oh gosh! Honestly . . . ! Oh, my Gawd!"

I assumed an outraged mien. "I see nothing to laugh at, young lady."

"There you go again."

"What is so comical? I speak as an honest man should."

"Maybe so. But square as a window pane. But seriously, is that all you remember of pre-death? A good wife, plump, cleanly and obedient, weeping by your bedside?"

"There were, I believe, children but it all seems to be a dream."

"Oh, no. If there's any dreaming, this is it. The trouble is, I can't get the hang of what it's all in aid of."

"You speak so strangely."

"I speak strangely! Pardon me while I blush. But what really bugs me is how everyone on this bloody great road takes it all for granted. I mean, walking, walking without getting tired, hungry or thirsty. It just doesn't make sense."

After some consideration, I decided she was right and wondered why I hadn't thought along the same lines myself. It might be reasonable to assume that the road was purgatory, or even a branch of hell. It most certainly was not paradise. I put this notion to Movita. She made a sound that I have not heard since my arrival on the road.

"Balls! I know you lot way back in the year dot believed in hell fire via harp playing heaven but that would be as non-productive as all this walking. I mean, as I see it, there must be—but must be—a reason for everything. Otherwise the entire bloody universe is nothing but a shambles."

I could no less than rebuke her for this gross blasphemy, although up to then I had not given religious matters much thought. The mind was apt to shy away from the subject.

"It is wrong of you to speak so irreverently of God's work. His unfathomable creation."

She held out a slender hand and I had to subdue an urge not to grab it.

"God! I mean—what—who is He? As I see it, God is not a person, but a power—a source of unlimited energy from which we all sprang. The spoonful that is our share, won't let us die. OK, so we go on and on, but there should be a purpose."

My ire grew stronger and so did the desire to defend the faith which had been mine since the beginning. "God is the King of Kings, whose will cannot be questioned. Now you have raised the subject, I am certain that we are condemned to walk this road as punishment for sins committed in another place."

She shook her head violently and now I had to subdue an urge to strike her.

"Only man punishes without reformation in view. How can a never ending walk atone for sins that some of us never had time to commit?"

"It is not for us to question . . ."

Again that beautiful head was shaken. "That spoonful of power I mentioned demands we never cease questioning. I'm so certain of that, maybe that's why I remember more of pre-death life than the rest of you."

My mind grew tired of arguing about such matters that I only dimly understood and I really did not want to discuss. I entered a black period when one is only aware of slow moving feet, the steel blue roof and gray floor, that is the road; all else is swallowed by an ever moving mist. Maybe these non-aware periods are the equivalent of pre-death sleep, when we are permitted to recruit our strength without the need of food or rest.

Be that as it may, when I again came to myself, Movita was some way ahead, apparently deep in conversation with a gaunt man dressed in black and wearing a tall hat. I did not try to catch them up, knowing that such an effort would be futile. Instead, I fell to thinking of her outrageous ideas and the notion that she might remember more of pre-death life than others who walk the great road. A disturbing person to talk with and one capable of arousing even more disturbing thoughts.

Why had I never tried to remember more of my pre-death life? I suppose because it did not seem worth remembering. Or, maybe, it could not be recalled without either great effort or some exceptional gift that had not been granted to me. The only event that stood out was that brief memory of what must have been my death bed. Yet—how old had I been? Whatever, the age at death was frozen for eternity, for I had seen seemingly young, middle-aged and old walking the great road. Although all appeared to enjoy never failing good health and the ability to walk without food or rest.

Movita had said I looked young, so it would be reasonable to suppose I had been thirty or perhaps a little more. Young to leave time and join eternity. But it was all so long, long ago.

Then I saw Movita leave the man wearing the tall hat and begin to walk extremely quickly across the fields to another white structure standing on a hill. As this would be a chance for me to join her again, I too left the road and trudged (speed seemed to be beyond my powers) through lush grass, until I reached the slope and was able to clamber up to the building. Movita smiled a welcome over one shoulder.

"Hello, I thought I'd lost you. Suddenly found you were miles behind and I was walking beside an old boy who looked and sounded like Abraham Lincoln. He'd got some antiquated ideas. Ever had a close look at one of these things?" She pounded the wall with a clenched fist. "Must have a purpose. But be damned if I can see what."

"There's a faint sound coming from all those I've examined," I said. "You have to press your ear to the wall."

She nodded impatiently. "I know. Listened to it often. And you know something, it sounds uncommonly like traffic. You know—motor cars. But of course you wouldn't. Horseless carriages driven by a machine—lots of little explosions. Oh, hell! Anyway, I was killed by one. Knocked me flat into the next world while I was crossing the King's Road. There must be a way into these things if one could only figure out how."

I frowned. "But there is no opening of any kind."

She wrinkled her nose and I felt really ashamed of my need to embrace her.

"There's a way into and out of any place if you really think. I mean really think. Those lines—they must be there for a reason. Maybe if you push them in a certain way an opening will appear. I've tried all ways. Every blockhouse—that's what I call 'em—I see, I have a go at it. Well, it's better than that continuous walking. And you never know—maybe I'll hit the jackpot."

"But should you find a way in—and that I cannot believe to be possible—what would you do? Surely not enter?"

She looked at me with an air of comical surprise. "But of course. What a cautious little man he is. You know those lines have a familiar look. I'm sure they're the answer. Let's examine this thing separately. Back and front." She gave me a smile that caused my heart to race. "This is the first time I've had anyone to help me. No-one else seems interested."

"I never thought of getting in, only wondered what they were for. What do you want me to do?"

"Look round the back. See if you can find out where those lines start and if they point in a particular direction."

"But they wander around all over the place."

"They might appear to, but if you look carefully, several lines come together to form a kind of rough arrow."

"That's true! I never noticed that before."

Movita patted me reassuringly on the shoulder. "It takes a long time to train yourself to see the obvious. Never take anything you see for granted. Especially on the road."

I blazed a trail through the tall grass round the building until I reached that part which could be designated the back—according to which direction one was facing. Certainly it looked no different here than the front, the intricate pattern of fine lines having a similarity with those that decorated—if that was the right word—the other three walls.

The longer I stared at them, the more complicated they seemed to become. The mind reeled when confronted with that maze of whirling, twisting, vaguely arrow pointing lines. After a while it seemed as if I was wandering amid an intricate maze of tall white-bricked walls, each one surmounted by arrow-shaped iron spikes, and there was that feeling which first came to me when I found myself walking the great road. Black despair, the knowledge that one—the ego—was cut off from all human contact and I would never

again see a human face or hear a child's voice. In fact,
I never have heard a child's voice, possibly because a
child has never merited being here.

But now, while in this dream within a dream, I
tasted again the dregs of black despair, for it would
seem that I had exchanged a broad highway for an
extremely narrow one that curved left, then right,
twisted upon itself like a writhing snake and led me
precisely nowhere.

Shut in, running between towering white walls that
permitted but a narrow strip of blue sky as a roof, this
could well be a passageway in hell, and most probably
was.

Suddenly I heard Movita's voice speaking to me as
over a long distance.

"Keep at it. Thinking as you are—as we are. I'm
pretty certain that is how it happened. The two of us
must have the same thought waves or something and
by concentrating together on those lines have pro-
jected ourselves on to another dimension. Haven't you
read Von Holstein? Of course you wouldn't have. He
was after your time. Never mind, follow the lines—I
mean the alleyways—they're bound to lead somewhere.
And spare me a thought now and again. It will help us
keep in contact."

I began to walk quicker and a panic feeling of being
shut in grew and threatened to swallow whatever stock
of courage I had.

"I am . . . I am not very happy here."

A chuckle came shuddered across non-existent time
and space.

"Me too. Never mind—yet again—this too will pass.
The main thing is to keep moving and thinking—well—
brave thoughts. It's like crawling through a pipe. So
long as you keep calm and concentrate on reaching the
ring of light, you're OK . . . I mean all right."

"Can you keep talking? The sound of your voice
helps."

"Surely. You know something? I believe that when we stood on either side of that white building, a universe separated us. Perhaps it still does. I wouldn't know. Say, what can you see on your side? I mean in your alleyway?"

"If you mean the passage down which I am walking—nothing. Just tall white walls surmounted by arrow spikes. Above the blue sky—what there is of it—and under my feet a smooth gray floor."

A deep sigh shuddered across my brain. "Same here. And there's a feeling we've swapped the road for an alleyway. Imagine walking through an endless alley for a few million years."

"Million—years? I'd forgotten such terms."

Movita laughed softly and I wished I could hold her hand.

"Maybe I'm a misfit. Not really supposed to have come to the road. I remember too much. On the other hand perhaps people like me are necessary. I mean you would never have made anything out of those lines without me. Perhaps now you're free of the road. Me too."

Her voice did comfort and I was able to concentrate my thoughts wonderfully.

"The passage—alley as you call it—is turning continuously and I keep expecting to see something unusual round each bend. So far that's proved to be wishful thinking."

"Maybe I should tell you all that I remember about myself. It might help you. I was born in 1965 and died sometime during September 1985. I know I'd just celebrated—if that's the right word—my birthday, which was on September 7th. Therefore, I guess that car bumped me off around the 14th. That made me twenty and a tiny bit. That's what I'll be for all eternity, I suppose. Twenty and a tiny bit. I was roughly—in every sense of the word—educated at a private school near Brighton. They chucked me out when I was sixteen, the direct result of losing my virginity in the potting shed. Well, it had to happen somewhere. My parents did their proverbial nut . . ."

"Proverbial nut?!" I queried. "I . . ."

"Got agitated . . . angry . . . excited . . . Oh, my Gawd! Any road, I vacated the ancestral hall and got myself any number of dead-end jobs, until I met Anthony, who was not only as dishy as a well-cooked casserole, but also owned Heywood Motors. Well, to cut a long story short, he set me up in a flat in the Old Brompton Road, brought me a nice little Aston Martin and altogether behaved like a millionaire with a non-understanding wife, is expected to behave. Maybe I'd have ended up as Mrs. Anthony number two, if I hadn't been so careless crossing the King's Road. Have you understood any of this?"

I followed the passage round a pronounced curve, before sending my brief answer to wherever she continued the long journey.

"No."

"I thought as much. What's the use? We're worlds apart, in every sense. Still we've somehow come together on this crazy jaunt and have got to help one another in some way. Is your passage twisting like a corkscrew?"

I nodded vigorously, then, remembering she could not see me, said:

"Yes."

"So is mine. Maybe we'll get somewhere any time now."

Looking up I saw that the sky had become tinged with pink, as though way up and beyond, the sun was setting. This also meant visibility in the passage dimmed every ten paces, so that eventually I moved through a multi-colored gloom that reminded me of a cathedral, lit by stained-glass windows. I reported this change to Movita.

"I'm in the same state," she said. "It would seem we are both walking on parallel lines and will doubtlessly come together when they reach infinity. But I think the change in light must mean we are entering a different—what? I don't know. Dimension?"

"My soul shakes . . ."

"Well, keep it still. Soul-shaking is the last thing we need now. And keep your eyes open. Anything could happen and that soon."

The passage seemed to turn into a complete circle, before I all but ran into a green painted door.

"A green door?" Movita questioned.

"Yes. With a large glass handle."

"Same here. Have you tried to open it?"

"Yes. But I can't grip the handle."

A contented little chuckle came rippling along the passage, seemingly quite near now.

"That proves it. We're in another dimension. Strangers in a strange land. Wait a sec . . ." A slight pause, and then . . . "I've just had a go. No joy either. We'll have to find another way to open our communal door. Blow on it . . . will it to open . . . imagine it open . . . and know it was never closed . . . Come on. Thinking cap on or we'll be marooned in front of a green door for all eternity."

Feeling like a puking schoolboy who cannot solve a problem set for a junior form, I stared at the unresponsive portal, while making some completely ineffective jabs at it. Then a simple solution slid into my mind.

"Wait for someone to open it."

A slight pause, then: "You may be right. Yes, that might well be a possibility. Which means we are standing in some room, cupboard, even on a front doorstep, although it doesn't look like a front door. However, as I can't think of anything better, let's wait a while. I'd say one thing is certain, we'll never see the road again."

I nodded in agreement. "I'm almost sorry. After all, I'd got used to it. And it might have one day led to somewhere."

"I don't think so. I'm certain now its only purpose was for a traveler to get fed up and work out those squiggly lines. Perhaps the dim ones will wander it forever."

"That would make stupidity a cardinal sin."

"Could be, only I don't believe in sin. Just right and wrong. The law of cause and effect."

I growled a protest. "You speak so strangely. I am tired of trying to understand you. As though I have not had enough to contend with. It could be that your sinful thoughts contaminated me, and hence we have both wandered from the road that would have finally led to redemption."

"Don't be such a bloody idiot. I'd say you've been walking the great road for around two hundred and fifty years, and if you haven't found redemption in that time, you never will."

"More blasphemy. I will . . ."

At that moment the door flew back and for a moment I was face to face with a young person attired in a blue garment that covered her from neck to just below the knees. A young person with corn-colored hair, large blue eyes and a rose-bud mouth. For a short while we stared at one another, then she opened that pretty mouth and screamed. It was a very loud, drawn-out scream, such as I could never remember hearing before, and most certainly had no desire to hear again. Then she turned and ran from me with all her might, not without, however, casting one terrified glance over her left shoulder.

After some hesitation, I stepped out into a bright room, that was pleasantly decorated in blue, furnished with a large desk, some strange looking chairs and a carpet that covered the floor from wall to wall. As I moved forward I gradually came to realize that my feet hardly, if at all, touched this carpet and progress could be obtained with the maximum of ease.

It was rather like floating, even if I had never experienced such a phenomenon before, and not at all unpleasant. I all but glided to another door and emerged into what looked like a small hall that had a glazed door at one end and a curving staircase at the other. These surroundings were such a welcome change, I did a little dance of joy, by now fully convinced that far from being led into hell, I had by some miraculous means reached at least the outermost regions of heaven.

My job received its crown when Movita came gliding down the stairs.

She greeted me with a cynical smile.

"Why are you prancing around like a deprived goat?"

I expressed surprise. "In the name of sanity, girl! Why aren't you giving thanks for our deliverance. These surroundings suggest to me we are in a mansion. . ."

"Come off it. Mansion! I'd say a semi-detached in Wimbledon. Or maybe Slough. And we are a couple of spooks haunting it."

"Spooks? I don't understand."

"Ghosts . . . specters . . . phantoms. We have returned to the dimension of the so-called living, equipped to put the fear of the uncanny up anyone who sees us. There's a guy upstairs laid out on the bedside rug. He saw me glide out of a built-in wardrobe."

"And a young female screamed when I came out of a kind of cupboard. Then ran away."

"That's what we've got to expect from now on. Always supposing anyone sees us. I've got an idea we won't be visible all the time and to some people never. Which will be a relief."

I nodded vigorously. "I second that. I can't abide screaming women."

"Who can? But now we are up against the same old problem. What is the purpose of two ghosts haunting a semi-detached? There does not appear to be rhyme or reason but I'm sure if we watch and listen, truth will come crawling out from behind the wainscoting, sooner or later. But let's find out what period we've landed in."

"How?" I inquired.

"You are dim. Calendar, or newspaper. Or maybe someone will have the telly switched on."

I decided to ignore the strange words she used, for when she took the trouble to explain their meaning, I rarely understood what she was talking about. But in some mysterious way she had got us off the road and into these far from unpleasant surroundings. I followed her to a doorway on the right of the stairs and into a room from which came sounds of feminine lamentations. My attention was immediately drawn to a plump middle-aged lady who was engaged in bathing a young man's forehead with a wet towel, then to another, who had to be her slightly younger sister, who in turn was ministering to the young female who had screamed and bolted when observing my sudden appearance.

The plump middle-aged lady was speaking with a carefully controlled voice.

"I know such an appearance can be extremely disturbing to anyone not accustomed to psychic phenomena but you must have been aware of the history of this house. Those who have passed over often drift in—so to speak."

The young man—red hair and a matching nose—brushed the towel to one side and expressed an opinion.

"Any house that allows the ghost of the niftiest number I've seen in many a long year, to come out of a bloke's wardrobe, should be knocked down. Better still—blown up."

The young female abruptly terminated the ministrations of the younger sister.

"And I almost died when I . . . when I opened the

shoe cupboard and found myself staring into the face of a man—with long hair, a beaked nose and glaring eyes. And . . . and I could see through him."

"I know, it must have been distressing," the plump lady agreed, "but really interesting, if you get my meaning. Great-Uncle Manley will be tickled pink. He'll have a seance going here before you can say Jack Robinson."

"You can count me out," the young female retorted, jumping to her feet. "The only spirits that interest me come in a bottle."

"But you can't go out yet, dear," the plump lady protested, "you haven't had your tea."

"I've lost my appetite."

"Never fainted before in me life," the young man informed the room in general. "But when I saw that nifty wench, a cold wave came up from my feet—and out I went. Like a light."

Movita nudged me in the ribs—and I felt it.

"That newspaper—oh, my Gawd! That sheet of paper on the table. There's a date on the right-hand side. Can you read it from where you are?"

"No. The young female is in the way."

"Then go through her. Go on, she can't see you now. No, I don't know why. I suppose the atmosphere isn't right."

I could not nerve myself to go through a solid being, so eased my likeness round the female and peered down at the broadsheet and after trying to make some sense of the printed text (and failing) finally read the date.

"November 27th 1990," I announced.

Movita whistled. "Five years after my departure for the Great Road. To think I've been walking that damned road for five years."

I believe I did sort of slide through the right shoulder of the young female as I returned to my companion, for I must confess to a feeling of renewed excitement when confronted with the knowledge that this room was a fragment of a world which had not come into being until two hundred and fifty years after my death.

From beyond the windows came the humming sound I had first heard when my ear was pressed to the white wall of the mysterious building. Back in the mists of time, two hundred and fifty years, or a million—or maybe only five seconds. I tried to explain this miracle to Movita, who regardless of her sharp and shining wisdom, had not been reared in an age when the marvelous had been accepted as commonplace.

"Time did not exist on the great road, no more than it does here. I believe what we are observing here, either took place long, long ago, or has yet to happen."

I expressed surprise when she nodded. "You may well be right. Or maybe it is pure imagination. But let's enjoy the show, no matter how it is presented."

"But," I protested, "would it not be more enjoyable to venture out from this place and fully experience the world which has come into being since my death."

She shook her head. "Even if it were possible, you wouldn't like it. That humming sound is merely a reflection of a mighty roar of a million engines that drive vehicles along highways that would make the great road look like a country lane. No, my handsome man from yesterday, here we stay to haunt a semi-detached in Wimbledon—unless the powers that rule the universe decided to reveal the reason for our existence."

We drifted from the room—it was so easy and almost sleep-provoking—and, after some little hesitation, for we had the normal honorable reluctance to eavesdrop or invade that privacy which is every civilized person's birthright—ventured to glide up the stairs to those upper rooms, which from time immemorial have been designated as sleeping chambers. Here, after wandering round the landing for an unaccountable period of time, we were disturbed by the sudden passing of the young female, who fled past—or through us and entered a bedroom.

"That one is not my cup of tea," Movita stated with apparent sincerity. "I think we should see what she gets up to in her spare time. It might be interesting."

"But," I objected, "she has gone into her bedchamber. No gentleman . . ."

"I know, but in our present form, I cannot believe we qualify for the title of lady or gentleman. So let's pop in and see what she looks like without her stays on."

In fact she looked very good, having a figure that would have been exciting to behold, if I had been in a condition to appreciate it. She lay down on the bed as naked as the day which had seen her birth and began talking aloud.

"Me seeing spooks! Not as though I'd been smoking grass. Maybe I'm cracking up."

"I wouldn't mind having a body like that," Movita observed. "I mean a real flesh and blood body, not this thing I'm lumbered with now."

"What's wrong with it?" I inquired.

She raised her eyes ceilingward. "How long 'as he been dead? It's all right to go walking with and that's about all. You can't eat with it, shag with it, put it to sleep or present it to living company. Not without screams all round."

The young female's voice again attracted our attention.

"Maybe it's sexual repression. Could be. Not getting it regular could result in a kind of sex DTs. I must ask Mark about this." She turned over and presented us with a superb back view. "But wait a minute. That clot Maurice saw a wench spook! He's sexually repressed? That must be true. I mean, first cousin notwithstanding, he's a drip. But nobody would drop the essentials for him."

"The lady hasn't a kind heart," Movita said quietly.

"A spot of walking the great road would do her no harm."

"One feels," I said after some thought, "that after a period spent in this world, the great road might not be such a bad place."

"That's the kind of cynical remark middle-aged people usually make, then sit back and wait for the applause. Believe you me, the twentieth century world is not half bad, so long as you are born in the right place. OK. It's a bit like Rome in the fourth century. Surrounded by barbarians who have to pay tribute, but I guess the average Roman citizen didn't let that worry him."

"I'm getting out of this house," the female on the bed announced, "or as soon as maybe. Trouble is I mustn't upset the two dotty aunts, or that perfectly mad Uncle Manley, for all three old dears are loaded and my share is worth waiting for. But if it's haunted. . ."

"Strange," Movita yawned, "for the first time since my death day, I feel tired. Feel sleepy. Do you suppose this wench is draining me?"

I shook my head. "I'm in the same condition. Maybe it's the change of atmosphere. Neither of us is used to being shut in."

"I wonder," the girl on the bed looked rather fearfully round the room, "if those spooks are here now. Sort of watching me?"

Movita grinned. "You're not so dumb after all. My nameless friend has been suffering from bulging eyes for the past ten minutes."

I laid a hand on her arm and felt some substance under the thin material of her dress. "Let us retire to some secluded spot and at least pretend to sleep."

She yawned again. "There's no need for pretense so far as I'm concerned. You don't suppose there's anything we can do to scare young Fanny there, before leaving?"

I tried to pull her toward the door. "Forget her for a bit . . ."

To my great alarm, she broke away and floated over to the dressing table, there to grab a hair brush of respectable size, being made of some material to resemble walnut, then move in like manner to the bedside where she raised the implement and after a pause, during which she appeared to concentrate her entire powers—resulting in gleaming eyes and glowing skin such as I had never seen before—she brought it down with a resounding smack on the white posterior.

The young female released a piercing scream which, no doubt, was the result of pain and fear, then leapt from the bed and still yelling in a most disconcerting fashion, ran from the room.

Movita laughed immoderately and for the first time I experienced a certain amount of irritation at her irresponsible behavior and wished I could treat her shapely rear portion in a like manner.

Then tiredness struck me like a billow of warm, gray mist and I longed for a vast green field where I could sink into lush green grass, and sleep forever under a warm benign sky. Instead, a laughing Movita led me by the hand out on to the landing, up another flight of stairs to a large attic which sprawled under the tiles. On the floor lay an old mattress, which when I lay upon it felt monstrously hard, until Movita whispered: "Think of soft—soft swan down—anything comforting you will—then call upon the god of sleep, who must obey your will."

And so it was. For the first time since my death day I slept and dreamed of a faraway planet where beings with white skin and wonderous black hair danced under a silver moon and there was a glorious feeling of peace, such as my soul had hungered since the cosmic-second of its creation.

And in that dream a tall man with a terribly beautiful face came up to me and said: "To be an intelligent air-breathing creature is a miracle that occurs rarely in the universe, and each one is an embryo god."

And I asked: "What of me and Movita, who do not breathe?"

He replied: "You are gods. Pray that you never know your power."

And I awoke . . .

I awoke in a room that, from any point of view, was luxuriously appointed, having well-padded sofas and chairs, light blue walls and matching carpet which covered the floor from wall to wall. Light was provided by a softly glowing white bowl, suspended from the ceiling, and this amazingly seemed to burn without the aid of either candle or oil, a fact that attracted my attention for some considerable time.

A number of people were seated round a circular table, their hands outstretched on its walnut surface, their eyes closed, while a white-haired, excessively fat man at the head intoned:

"Are there any spirits present? Are there any spirits present?"

Movita peered up into my face. "So you've come too! I thought you had died a second time."

I cleared the lingering mist from my awareness.

"I think I slept, which is most extraordinary. What are these people doing?"

"Holding a seance. Trying to contact spirits like us. They're not very successful so far. I've felt no urge to join in."

I gazed upon the gathering with some disfavor. "Witchcraft! I thought there was the stench of evil about this place."

Her bubbling laughter came about within six inches of my left ear. "You really are something. Lots of people play at this sort of thing, mostly kidding themselves. But a few have the gift. A medium once got my mum on the wire. She warned me of what was to come. 'You've got a long walk in front of you, my gal,' she said. Course, at the time I didn't know what she meant. But I can't think this lot have much going between them."

"Yet," I said with trepidation, "I find myself drawn to that fat man. It is strange and rather fearful."

This was true. It seemed as if the fellow were seated in my brain and addressing his bizarre remarks to me.

"Both of you have been seen in this house and one manifested his or her presence in a most . . . eh . . . striking way. It could be that you are lost, require help. If so, manifest, enter one of those seated here and speak with their tongue."

"Movita," I pleaded, "I feel an urge to slip into that fat man. May I be damned if I'm not positively drawn to him."

Movita shrugged. "I should fight him off if I were you. I mean to say—suppose you were stuck in him?"

I examined the fellow before replying. I judged he had reached middle life and would have been a fine figure of a man, had he enjoyed the pleasures of the table less, but that could be rectified. If one was looking for a body to possess, one could travel farther and fare far worse.

"It would be a means of living again. At least for a time."

Movita's eyes sparkled. "You could be right! Perhaps that is the meaning I've been looking for. Maybe some people are given a second time round, particularly if they have walked the great road and acquired . . ."

"Humility," I suggested.

"No—confidence and humility. We know man is immortal and if that knowledge is passed on, it must eventually change the mental outlook of the entire population. And you know something—I bet it has been going on for a long time. People coming back from the dead and taking on another body. Great guns! It probably happened to you. That's why we walked the great road. Some returning spirit took over our last bodies and chucked our souls out."

"You have a terrifying imagination," I protested. "To take over another person's body must be classed as stealing in a really big way."

"You thought of it first. Why don't you have a go? Go on. Slip into old fatty and see if you can stay there."

I shivered. "I don't think I have much choice. It's as though invisible ropes are round me, pulling . . ."

"Get in What'syername."

The fat man had his eyes closed and his voice seemed to whisper in my brain.

"Come in . . . come in . . . the vessel is waiting . . ."

I went in. It was so ridiculously easy. A small hole appeared in the center of his forehead, and I felt myself gradually floating up into a perpendicular position, then—while not shrinking or losing my feeling of being less than normal size—slid into what appeared to be a large room lit by two blue-glazed windows. Suddenly I expanded—and instantly I became aware of pounding heart, blood racing behind eardrums, an ache in the right knee and elbow, a rumbling in the stomach—and four startled faces staring at me.

The body was mine for a few seconds, then a voice screamed: "Get out . . . get out . . ." And I heard myself—using an alien voice—reply: "No . . . you get out. This carcass is mine by right of conquest."

I found myself being ejected through that little hole, but was heartened by hearing—feeling—Movita shouting: "Fight back. Go on. Get the bastard out. He's had that body long enough and look what a mess he's made of it."

I re-entered the large room but this time deliberately expanded my ego until I felt certain I was crammed into every microgram of space and there just could not be room for another being to exist. It was rather like holding your breath under water, while a parasite that insisted on clinging on to you slowly drowned.

A voice that became fainter by the second, pleaded: "Please go away. I did not really believe in an after life, but now I do . . . I do . . ."

It was then that I *knew* he—the one time tenant-fat-man—would find himself walking the great road, not remembering who he had been.

Sound exploded in my eardrums, consisting mainly of babbling voices demanding to know if I—the late occupant—was all right. It took me some time to acquire control of my new voice, then to think up words that would deal with a fantastic situation.

Unless one has actually experienced this phenomenon, the details are rather hard to explain. Firstly, I came to understand the shell I had inhabited on the road, could hardly be classified as a body—as Movita had so shrewdly surmised. Feeling, pains, real breathing, hearing, seeing instead of a—facsimile of the real thing—had to be accepted. Speaking became a disaster until I remembered how to coordinate brain-control to vocal chords. Then there was the matter of the brain. What I can only describe as memory patterns, formed by the previous tenant, interfered with the memories I had brought with me and, until experience enabled me to sort out one from the other, I was, at times, two people. So it was when the plump lady—Aunt Matilda—inquired as to my well-being, I replied:

"As well as one fresh from the great road can be, Miss Brightridge."

A bald-headed man, who I afterward found answered to the name of Reg Parkinson, inquired—somewhat hesitantly:

"Did . . . did the lost spirit attempt to take control?"

"I'm doing my very best, Mr. Parkinson. I wonder how this will all end?"

This question and answer game went on for some time and it became apparent that the assembly were not all that happy about some of my replies. Neither was I all that happy when I realized that Movita was no longer visible (or audible) and I was alone in this new environment without her support. Presently, I got up and (feeling a trifle light-headed) made my way to the door, not all that certain if this house was the late Uncle Manley's natural habitat, or if he lived elsewhere.

In the hall this problem was temporarily forgotten, when a loud screeching argument, or the kind of argumentative hysteria which usually takes place when two females fall out, came from above stairs. The only words I could distinguish were: "Get out . . . I won't . . . you cow! . . . No . . . no . . . please." I believe everyone accepts the unacceptable when faced with a session on the great road. But with great reluctance.

Presently the corn-headed female appeared at the very top of the stairs, which she began to descend with the dignity of an empress making an entrance.

Aunt Matilda pushed her way through the little crowd congregated in the doorway and inquired anxiously:

"What's the matter, Lucy? Have you seen another manifestation?"

Lucy's smile was all but obscene and she gave me an elaborate wink.

"You could say so, Auntie dear, and Uncle Manley and I are going out to talk it over."

In passing she grabbed my arm and began to drag me toward the front door, while ignoring my protests and the company's demand for information. Not until we were out on the pavement, which bordered a road where strange vehicles roared back and forth at terrifying speeds, did she reveal the truth.

"You half-baked idiot. It's me—Movita. It's amazing what you can do when you really try. I pushed the cow out—and now I'm in. For good. Gosh! It's good to be alive. Now we can really have fun."

But I could only stare at the passing traffic, then

look up at a mighty flying machine that marked its passing by a sound not unlike thunder.

"Well," Movita demanded. "What do you think of it all?"

I stood on that strangely constructed pavement and shook my head, as I uttered a plaintive cry.

"I want to go back to the great road."

THE OLD MAN AND THE CHERRY TREE

by Kevin J. Anderson

Through no fault of his own the old man had been confined to a Buddhist monastery for most of his life, a life which revolved almost entirely on his skill at gardening. His crowning achievement was a re-markable cherry tree—how remarkable even he didn't realize.

He had lived almost his entire life within the walls of the Buddhist monastery. The priests there told him the Shogun would cut off his head if he ventured outside ever again.

Many years before, his father had been a powerful lord, a *daimyo*. But the Shogun had gone to war with the *daimyo*, ordering that all the lord's family be executed. On the final night, while the father sat bemoaning his imminent loss of life, the boy's mother had managed to steal away to the nearby monastery with her dearest son. She begged the head priest to save him, to secretly give her some other boy to be executed in her son's stead. The man told her it would be improper for a priest to undertake such a task; but after she offered large sums of money, the priest admitted that the monastery was sorely in need of a second golden image of Amida for the altar. Besides, the boy he had in mind for the exchange was a mere foundling anyway, given over to the care of the monastery however the priests saw fit.

They struck the bargain. The mother kissed her son, then gave him to the priest as he emerged from the monastery with a second boy who somewhat resembled the *daimyo*'s son.

Before the priest could take her son into the monastery walls forever, she reached into her robes and carefully withdrew a package wrapped in fine silk. Upon seeing the silk, the priest's eyes opened eagerly. "This is for my son," she said, handing it to the child. "Your father's blade—the sword of a great *daimyo*." She unwrapped the silk to reveal a lovely jewel-encrusted short sword. Gold covered the grip, and fine characters danced on the blade. "You must keep it always by you because it will bring you good luck. When all else has been forgotten, still it will tell you the name of your father—see, it is engraved on the blade. You will learn to read it after the good priest has taught you the characters." The priest's eyes reflected the gold of the sword, and he fervently promised to care for the boy. The mother bowed and disappeared with her false son into the night shadows from which she had come.

The boy grew up in the monastery. The priests soon stopped trying to take his father's sword from him when they realized they would never be able to sell it, not with the name of the rebellious *daimyo* engraved on the blade. And they never made the effort to teach him to read, considering themselves safer if the boy was not constantly reminded of his true identity.

The boy took his pleasure in gardening, caring for the plants and trees in the monastery's beautiful garden. He was especially captivated by a single cherry tree which had been planted by three novices the very morning the Shogun had cut the heads off the rest of the boy's family. The small cherry tree had stood so frail and frightened in the garden, reminding the boy of how he must appear to the other monks.

As the boy grew older, he never shaved his head, or took the vows, nor studied the sutras as did the other novices. He planted and tended his flowers and trees and shrubs in the garden, until the monastery became known for the beauty harbored within its walls. But above all, the boy—now a young man, actually—tended the single cherry tree with all the love he possessed, until it became the glory of the entire garden. In spring the cherry tree would explode with pure white flowers, as if a sweet-scented winter had dropped gently into the monastery garden. At the time, it was said that the blossoms lingered longer on this cherry tree than on any other in all of Japan, and people traveled great distances to gather up some of the fallen petals, which they used for curing the sick and for making love potions.

Sometimes, in secret, the *daimyo*'s son would climb up into the tree and look out over the monastery walls which kept him imprisoned. None of the priests had bothered to tell him that the old Shogun had died, nor that the new one did not care about the young man's family name. Instead, he sat up in the boughs under the silver moonlight and looked out to see the wide world he would never be able to explore, listening to the wind in the leaves of his tree and the faint sounds of snoring from the monks' sleeping quarters.

In time, he came to consider the cherry tree his closest and dearest friend. He talked to it as he tended the rest of his garden, and the other novices began to snicker and laugh among themselves about the strange gardener who talked to trees.

So the years passed. The tree continued to grow, and the gardener continued to grow older. Year after year the white blossoms came, and the *daimyo*'s son—

now an old man—took no greater joy than in watching the petals drift in the wind. He wept for those that caught like kites on an updraft and escaped, floating down on the other side of the monastery wall.

Each spring many people came to see the blossoms, some even making grand processions all the way from Kyoto. The pilgrims talked among themselves about the exquisite beauty of the delicate white flowers, and of the glowing, honest satisfaction in the face of the old gardener who stood so proudly beside his tree.

And then one year the tree did not blossom.

The other plants in the old man's garden launched forth their leaves and flowers as always, but day after day the cherry tree remained barren, as motionless as a stillborn babe. The people who came to see the tree departed in disappointment—it had once been magnificent, they said sadly, but the old cherry tree had died, and they would have to go elsewhere from now on.

The monks began to talk that they would soon cut down the marvelous tree, and burn its wood in the fire.

The old man could not bear to hear this and, recalling the days of his youth, he somehow managed to climb into the tree, searching the branches for buds, any small flickering of life. But the branches were as dry and as barren as the paper on which the monks copied their sutras. The old man saw other cherry trees in the distance, gleaming with their white flowers and scattering petals into the wind. Then his heart knew for certain that the old cherry tree had died, and he threw his arms around the lifeless bole of his only friend, weeping until the curious monks came out and called for him to come down. His legs were weak, but he managed to descend the tree and stood shaking. The monks left him, whispering among themselves, and went back to their work.

As he looked long and hard at the lifeless branches

of the cherry tree, the old man decided what he must do. That night, when all the monks slept, he crept out into the darkness of the garden and lifted up one of the flat rocks he had long ago placed around the cherry tree. Under the rock rested his father's jeweled sword, glinting in the light of the dying moon—the colorful silk wrappings had rotted, but the sword was untarnished and as sharp as ever. The old man looked grimly at the blade.

There was one way to show one's utmost devotion, to remove grief and end this life of confinement and pain. Brave warriors followed their lords to death, committing *seppuku* to show their absolute loyalty no matter how their lord had died. And if the warriors could slit their bellies in an ecstasy of pain and honor, couldn't the old man do the same at the death of his dearest companion, his cherry tree? His father's sword was a special sword, the sword of a great *daimyo*, perhaps even containing a little magic. This act would be his final gift to the tree he had loved for so many years.

The old man loosened his robe and squatted down as near as he could to the dead cherry tree. He held the sharp point of the *daimyo*'s sword against his stomach, looking down at the engraved characters signifying his father's name—but he still could not read them. The night was cold and crisp, probably the last such night in spring. The noise of the rustling barren branches above sounded to him like a death rattle.

Done properly, *seppuku* would have been a grand occasion—with many priests and faithful companions. But the old man did not have even so much as a white cloth to sit upon. Tradition required that once he had slit his belly, once he had proven his devotion and bravery, his closest friend was then permitted to strike off his head to end the pain. But the old man had no best friend, and so after he made the deep thrust and long sideways cut, he was forced to bear the pain as best he could, until he could bear it no longer . . . and then it made no difference. His blood spilled onto the earth.

The next morning the monks came out into the garden for their tea and found him there. They shook their heads, muttering at how the lonely old man had finally ended his life, but that he had not even done *seppuku* properly. The old gardener had become well known, and many people—bringing many donations—would have come to see the death ceremony. The old man had been very inconsiderate not to let them know of his intentions. Some of the monks came to carry him away, and marveled at the beautiful sword they found upon him. No one knew where he had gotten it, and none of them recognized the name of the long-forgotten *daimyo* written on the blade. The monks cleaned the sword, and placed it in their treasury.

But that morning, when the sun rose high enough that its rays struck the old cherry tree, something wondrous happened. The wind picked up. A shiver ran through the ground as a silence descended on the garden. Some of the monks dropped their tea, burning their fingers, scowling at each other. Then they all looked at the dead cherry tree.

The barren branches trembled, as if the old tree were straining with all its might . . . and suddenly every branch, even the smallest twigs, brought forth a deep red flower, as scarlet as fresh blood. As the monks watched, gaping in amazement, the tree covered itself with flowers, more than it had ever borne before.

One brash novice crept up to the new flowers in wonder and touched them. He cried that the petals felt wet, then yelped in pain. "It burns! My fingers!" He tried to wipe the moisture off on his robe, then ran to hide inside the monastery.

Word spread quickly throughout the land, and people flocked to see the Blood Tree, as it had been named. The Shogun himself came to see the miracle, and when the monks told the story of the old man who had tended the tree, and of the mysterious sword he had used to commit *seppuku,* another old man from the vicinity recalled the name of the rebellious *daimyo* and how a previous Shogun had executed the entire family. Then others remembered how at the same time the monastery had received a generous donation from the wife of the *daimyo* . . . and although they could not be certain, many guessed the identity of the gardener.

The Shogun commanded that the monks bring him the ashes of the old man, and they carried out a simple clay urn, bowing their heads in embarrassment that they had not given the ashes a more ornate resting place. The Shogun spoke in his most respectful voice so that all could hear. "If this old man was truly the son of a rebellious *daimyo,* trapped for all his life in the sanctuary of the monastery walls for his own protection, long after it was necessary, I . . . I, the Shogun, now pardon him. I set him free so that he need no longer remain inside these walls."

So saying, the Shogun reached into the urn and flung the ashes high in the air, watching as they drifted out to explore the world on their own.

The Blood Tree shuddered, and, with a cracking sound, collapsed into a heap of charred splinters, burned from the inside out. The people gasped, and even the Shogun was amazed.

Many years later, wandering peddlers could sometimes be seen at night, keeping to the shadows and entering houses where the seeds of dissent had already been sown, secretly offering to sell splinters of the

Blood Tree which would cause almost-instant bad fortune and possibly even death to one's enemies.

The Shogun caught several of these peddlers, and executed them.

PHONE REPAIRS

by Nancy Kress

*Most of us have at one time or another been sub-
jected to wrong numbers. It's very unlikely that we
have ever received calls that were intended for an
unassigned number in a home that did not yet exist.*

When the phone rang, Dave Potter seized it with a
desperate relief he tried not to let Caroline see. From
the way her face froze and she turned her back away
from him and toward the sink full of dirty dishes,
Potter knew he had failed. She had seen the relief. It
would only make worse the fight that was already
bearing down on them, inevitable and dreary, like one
of those unstoppable cold fronts picked out on weather
maps in little blue spikes.

The phone call was from his son Brendan, sixteen,
whom Potter had not seen in three days. Their hours
at home barely overlapped since school had let out for
the summer.

"Dad. I wrecked the car." And—belatedly, laconi-
cally—"Sorry."

"What do you mean, you wrecked the car?" Potter
said, his voice scaling upward in some subtle combina-

104

tion of fear and outrage. Caroline stopped clattering dishes. Her green eyes widened. "Are you all right?"

"Sure," Brendan answered.

"He's all right," Potter said to Caroline at the same moment that Brendan said, "Why the hell were you on the phone so long? I've been trying to get through for forty-five minutes."

"No one was on the phone. Look, what happened? Is anyone hurt? Did you hit another car?"

"Nah. Telephone pole."

"Was anyone in the car with you?"

"Nah. Look, Dad, it's no big deal, all right?"

"No big *deal?* What shape is the Buick in?"

"Well . . ." Brendan said, and Potter heard the drawn-out reluctance and clamped down hard on his temper.

"Where are you, Brendan?"

"Cathy's Towing. Corner of Elm and Hackett."

"I'll be right there. Stay put."

"Can't. Kelso's already here to pick me up. We got the track meet in fifteen minutes. Why were you on the phone so goddam long?"

"No one was on the phone!" Potter yelled. "Stay put until I get there!"

"Hey, I said I was sorry!" Brendan snarled, the snarl now justified by Potter's yelling, by Potter's unreasonable order, by Potter's failure to be an understanding parent.

"Just stay there," Potter repeated. Caroline, tight-lipped, began running water into the sink. On the other end, the phone clicked dead.

When Potter arrived at Cathy's Towing, Brendan wasn't there. Potter's Buick was symmetrically caved in on the passenger side in a deep U. Raw metal gleamed like fangs. Cathy, a beautiful mid-thirties blonde in the dirtiest overalls Potter had ever seen, regarded the car with something close to artistic satisfaction. "Been the other side, your kid've been a goner. If he hadn't of been belted in, even." Potter turned his back on her.

At home, Caroline was on her hands and knees, scrubbing the kitchen floor and crying. Potter put a hand on her shoulder; she shrugged it off so violently that Potter nearly slipped on the soapy Congoleum. "Don't touch me!"

"All right," Potter said wearily and went into the living room to make himself a drink. Caroline scrubbed more savagely; he could hear the stiff bristles of her brush rasp across what was supposed to be an E-Z-Care floor. The blue spikes moved closer.

Money. Sex. Kids. In-laws. Those were supposed to be the big four, but Potter knew that this was something else entirely, something both less visible and more pervasive, like lethal radiation. His and Caroline's marital rage seemed to come from everything and nothing, a melt-down at the core, beyond the puny fire-fighting of mere words. It had been going on for months now. Potter saw that it would go on for months more, while both of them watched helplessly, until at some point it no longer did. His hands shook as he poured himself a J & B.

The phone rang.

"Hello?" Potter said.

"Bill!" a woman's voice cried, low-pitched and husky with warmth. "Just a minute—*now*, kids!" Children began to sing "Happy Birthday."

"This isn't Bill," Potter tried to say, but was drowned out by the song. All the children—it sounded like three of them—stayed in tune, their voices high and sweet. When they had finished, the woman's voice returned; Potter could hear the laughter in it.

"And from me, too—happy birthday, darling. You don't know *how* I wish we were home with you!"

"This isn't Bill. You must have the wrong number," Potter said. He felt a perfect fool.

A pause at the other end. "Isn't this 645-2892?"

"No, I'm sorry. This is one digit off that number."

"No, *I'm* sorry," the woman said, a little stiffly. Stiffness didn't destroy the husky timbre of her voice. "I must have dialed wrong."

"I'm sorry," Potter said again, inanely, and hung up. In the other room, Caroline scrubbed and cried. Potter drank off the J & B and poured himself another, staring at the phone.

Potter's daughter Melissa sat cross-legged on the living room floor, scissors in her hand, bent over paper dolls. Her dark hair, a little too long at the bangs, fell in a shiny, tangled curtain over the shoulders of her yellow pajamas. Saturday morning cartoons blared from the television, mindless and irritating as blowing sand. The faded rug bore the wreckage of a Friday night at home: spilled potato chips, sticky glasses, Potter's unopened briefcase, the discarded sections of last evening's newspaper mixing with the discarded sections of this morning's as Potter tossed them down from the sofa.

Caroline, bare-footed, padded in from the bedroom. Potter glanced at the smooth line of her thigh beneath her short summer robe, and looked away. Caroline began shrieking.

"Damn it, Dave, why the hell are you letting her cut those up!"

Potter raised himself on one elbow. What he had assumed were paper dolls were in fact photographs, all the family pictures kept in a red-topped dress box which Potter had failed to recognize because the red top was removed and upside-down. Melissa had methodically sliced into at least three dozen of the photos, cutting off all the people's heads. The little girl's eyes, raised suddenly to Potter's face, horrified him.

"Can't you watch her while I at least get some sleep on a Saturday morning? Can't you at least do that?"

Caroline shouted, her voice gone shrill with hysteria. She grabbed for the scissors in Melissa's hand. Potter saw beheaded pictures of Caroline waving in front of the Washington Monument, of Melissa and Brendan at the beach, of a dog they had owned briefly three years ago. He saw his wedding pictures.

"That's not too goddam much to ask!" Caroline shrieked. Melissa moved her gaze from Potter, still stunned by it, to her mother's contorted face. Eluding Caroline's grab for the scissors, she twisted her small body to plunge them into Potter's briefcase. The leather released air and a pungent smell like riding tack.

Caroline gasped and seized Melissa. Her eyes met Potter's over the child, their green wiped perfectly blank by shock. Melissa wrapped her legs around her mother and began to sob into her neck. Caroline carried her into the bedroom and closed the door. Potter heard it lock.

On his knees he sorted numbly through the photos, looking for some clue to what Melissa had done, some of the reassurance that might come from finding a pattern to the pictures she had chosen to destroy. There was none. Pictures of relatives, friends, people Potter no longer recognized—all had been equally defaced. In the wedding photo, Caroline, Potter, the best man and maid of honor had each been decapitated. Caroline's white gown floated around what was left of her, tight at the waist and a billowing cloud below, a silk so light and delicately scented that it had once seemed like mist against his hands.

Potter squeezed his eyes shut as tightly as they would go.

The voice on the phone was deep, with a reckless lilt of gaiety. "Connie? Listen, darling, we finished up early here and I'll be coming home on the 8:45 flight TWA tomorrow night, and wait till you hear the news I've got for you, you lucky sexy broad!"

"I'm sorry," Potter said, a little resentfully. He knew his voice was pitched a little high for a man and the husky-voiced woman's was low, but there was still a difference. "I'm sorry. You have the wrong number."

Silence, and then the man said in a changed tone, "Is this Dave? At 645-2872?"

Surprised, Potter nodded, caught himself, and said, "Yes. How did you know?"

"We've been getting your phone calls for a few weeks now. The lines must be crossed. Have you been getting our calls?"

"When you all stay home long enough to get any," Potter said, out of a sudden spitefulness that took him by further surprise. The man's—Bill's—voice hardened.

"I'll call the phone company. Don't sweat it. Sorry for the inconvenience."

"Yeah," Potter said. "Me, too."

"She needs therapy," Caroline said to Potter during a commercial for laundry detergent. They had been watching TV in isolated silence for two hours, only one dim bulb left on in the shabby living room. Both children were asleep. Potter had gone to check on them during the previous commercial: Brendan scowling even in sleep, his ungainly adolescent face a clenched fist; Melissa's features so smooth and soft that Potter's heart had clutched in his chest.

"She should go at least four times a week, Dr. Horacek says," Caroline continued. In the semi-darkness Potter could not see her face, was glad of it. "That's at first. Maybe more, maybe less after he gets a feel for her disturbance. That's what he said: 'a feel for her disturbance and what might be causing it.' "

"Four times a week. Jesus, Caroline, the company insurance only pays half of any non-physical therapy. I checked today."

"Yes," Caroline said. She didn't sound surprised.

The TV commercial ended and the program, whatever it was, resumed.

"Look at it this way," Caroline suddenly added in a hard voice he didn't recognize but knew immediately had carried them over some border, into a new descent in terrain, "now I couldn't divorce you. We can't afford it."

She jack-knifed off the sofa and went into the bathroom. Potter sat there, reaching for the drink he had already finished. The phone rang.

"Congratulations, Mr. and Mrs. William Boylan!" said a professionally cheery voice. "Your entry has just won an all-expense-paid trip to Hawaii."

Potter said nothing.

"Hello? Is this the Boylan residence? Hello?" The voice sounded a little less professional.

"Yes," Potter said, "but which Boylan did you want? There are a lot of us, and the listings in the phone book are wrong."

"Let me see," the voice said uncertainly, "Mr. and Mrs. William Boylan at . . . I have it right here someplace, here . . . at 5542 Lapham Park Road."

"No, I'm sorry," Potter said, "this is James Boylan on East Main."

"Oh, I *am* sorry," the voice said, all professionalism restored. It added roguishly, "Especially for you!"

"Happens," Potter said. He hung up and went back to stare at Melissa's sleeping face.

There was no 5542 Lapham Park Road. Potter, driving out after work in Caroline's Chevette, which he knew she needed that evening, followed the street from its origins at a city park out to its last suburban house, 5506. The builders had not yet put up the rest of the development, although there were signs they might: a half-finished road, red X's on certain trees. The finished houses were big, surrounded by healthy mature trees left standing during the building process, and sparse new lawns. There were in-ground swimming pools, bay windows, twin chimneys, landscaped lots large enough for that urban luxury, privacy. The smells of summer evening hung in the air: cut grass, warm asphalt, overblown roses, the sweet sweat of healthy toddlers. Lawn sprinklers whirled.

On the way home, Potter stopped at a restaurant with a public phone and directory. There was no listing for William Boylan.

"I needed the car," Caroline said stiffly to Potter when he returned. Her green eyes sparkled with resentment. "You knew I needed it tonight."

Potter didn't answer. Anything he said would only make it worse. Sadness welled up from his belly to his throat, choking him.

"I *told* you," Caroline said. Melissa, standing beside her mother, looked at him flatly. When he reached out to smooth her beautiful hair, she flinched.

Brendan slouched into the living room. It was the first evening he had been home in over a week; more and more he stayed at his friend Kelso's house, with Kelso's family. Potter had at first protested this, but Caroline had said wearily, "Oh, let him stay there. Why would he want to stay *here?*" and Potter had not fought her. He knew he was losing some quality essential for fighting, some fundamental vigor.

"Phone, Dad."

"For me?"

Brendan's face twitched in disgust. "No. For Superman." He slouched out.

Potter walked on trembling legs to the extension in the bedroom. A girl's voice said, "Daddy? It's Jeanine." He recognized the voice; it had last sung "Happy Birthday" to him, sweet and tuneful. How had Brendan come to pass on the call? Whom had she asked for?

"Daddy?"

Potter closed his eyes and heard himself say, "Yes."

"Guess what? I won!"

"You did."

"Yes! You sound funny, Daddy. Are you okay?" The young voice radiated concern.

"I have a cold, Honey."

"Oh, I'm sorry. Anyway, I won! I played a wrong note in the first movement, you wouldn't believe how dumb, but I didn't let it rattle me and I played the second movement like we rehearsed, and I won! And one judge said I was the youngest to win in the violin division *ever!*"

"That's wonderful."

"Yes," the voice burbled, "and you should have seen Gary and Susie, they were jumping up and down in the first row and clapping like crazy, even Susie. Mom, too. Here she is."

"Bill?" said the voice Potter remembered, its huskiness and warmth as full of light as the child's. Potter could *see* it, that light: shimmering auroras, silver and pearl, behind his eyelids. He hung up.

For a long time he stood there, finally whispering, "No," but so softly no one else could hear.

"No what?" Melissa said. She had unaccountably appeared at his elbow. He looked at her, at the horrible flatness in her eyes that had drifted there out of some imbalanced chemical weather in her brain, out of Potter's and Caroline's misery, out of some unknown country that, Potter realized, he did not really believe Dr. Horacek would ever map.

"No nothing, baby," he said, and reached to gather her into his arms. Melissa kicked him and squirmed away, running from the bedroom. At the doorway she turned, her little face full of the anguished and pointless fury which modern medicine said was part of her illness, and spat.

"Don't touch me! I wish you weren't my Daddy!"

She whirled and was gone. Potter grabbed the phone and yanked the cord from the wall. With all the strength he had left, he hurled it across the room at the mirror over the dresser. Glass shattered and flew wildly in silver splinters of flashing light.

AT&T Subsidiary Repair Operator Number 21 claimed that the company had already acted on Complaint #483-87A, cross-wired phones in the same digital decad, but would look into the situation yet again. Potter said that the address on file for the other digits did not exist, and possibly the digits did not either, and there would be nothing to look into. Repair Operator Number 21 did not reply.

Potter took to calling 645-2892 from his office, from the kitchen extension when there was no one else at home or the bedroom extension when there was, once from a pay phone outside Melissa's therapist's office. He never called twice at the same time of day; he never spoke. Jeanine or Connie or Bill or Gary would answer, and Potter would listen a moment and hang up. Susie never answered; Potter guessed she was too young, perhaps even a baby. Gary's voice had the huskiness of his mother's. Only Bill Boylan ever reacted with suspicion to the silence at the other end of the phone, and Potter imagined his suspicion to smell of protection, not fear. Connie and Jeanine answered liltingly—"He*llo?*"—Gary with offhand confidence. Often there was laughter in their voices, as if the phone had interrupted some blithe conversation or on-going family joke.

On a Saturday night in late October, calling at 10:30 P.M. when Caroline had stormed out after a fight and Brendan had not been home for two weeks and Melissa had gone on one of her increasingly frightening rampages and then, exhausted, had fallen asleep, Potter heard two receivers lift simultaneously. Bill's voice said, "*Hel*lo," the first syllable heartier than the second, and Jeanine said "Hi there!" and then burst into laughter that echoed from what sounded like a dozen feminine young throats. A slumber party.

"Get off the phone, Honey," Bill said. "I got it."

"Yes, Daddy."

"Hello," Bill repeated to the silent Potter. And then, "Now you listen to me. I don't know who you are or what you think you're doing calling my family every few days like this, but you better cut it out now, buddy, or you'll wish you had. The phone company can put a tracer on this line. I've already spoken to them about it. Do this again and you'll be in deep shit. From both them *and* me, if I find out who and where you are. Got that?"

"Yes," Potter said, not caring if Boylan recognized his voice, if he connected the crossed-wires malfunction with this newer, less mechanical one. But apparently Boylan did not make the connection. In his world, Potter thought, malfunctions were separate, manageable. They did not mutate and cross-breed and turn cancerous, feeding on their own deformed tissues until the center itself could no longer hold.

"Scum," Boylan said, and hung up.

Potter put his own receiver down gently, as if it were alive.

He gathered together all the photographs Melissa had decapitated, and put them into a 9 × 12 manila envelope. With them he folded one of Melissa's therapy reports, a heartbreaking document in prophylactic prose: "Subject systematically destroys toys in playroom environment. One-to-one observation reveals no symbolic preference in plaything destruction." Potter put into the envelope a notice from the bank stamped INSUFFICIENT FUNDS. He added a torn piece of foil from the packet of birth control pills he had found in Caroline's drawer and had left there, after a long sightless moment in which he felt the knife he had not minded at his actual vasectomy. He even put in a paint flake from the Buick.

He addressed the envelope in clear block letters:
MR AND MRS WILLIAM BOYLAN
5542 LAPHAM PARK ROAD
WINTHROP, NEW YORK
At the Post Office, he looked up the zip code for such
of Lapham Park Road as existed. He was careful to
include his return address. Five days later, the manila
envelope was delivered to Potter's mailbox, stamped
NO SUCH ADDRESS—RETURN TO SENDER.

So it would have to be the phone.

He stayed home from work on a Tuesday, when
Caroline was at her part-time job and Brendan and
Melissa at school. Just before he picked up the receiver, Potter had a moment of clarity, unwelcome as
sudden nakedness. Why had he mailed the envelope?
What had he hoped? To somehow poison the other,
luminous world he could not have, or to send a cry of
help for his own? He hated both alternatives, writhed
in humiliation just thinking of them. Boylan's voice
saying "Scum. . . ."

But as he had hoped, it was Connie who answered.
That husky voice, vibrant with warmth. "Hello?"

"My name is Dave Potter. Listen, please don't hang
up on me, Connie. You don't know me, but our
phone lines were crossed a few months ago and I
spoke to you and your family. Since then things here
have just fallen apart, you can't know, I don't know
how or why but I'm about at the end of my rope and I
need to talk to you for a while. Just talk. I'm harmless
to you, I swear it, and your house doesn't exist anyway so I couldn't come there to—" Potter stopped,
appalled. What was he saying?

Connie was silent. Potter felt her bewilderment,
coming over the phone line in waves. He clutched the
receiver tighter.

"Please don't hang up. Please. I know how this
must sound to you, but there isn't anything here like
your family, your marriage, *nothing*, do you hear me,

we can't do it anymore—" He realized he was shouting, made himself lower his voice.

"Connie—"

"Please leave me alone," she said, and even through her fear and his grief some part of Potter's mind still registered that "please," a grace note grown so alien that it stunned him and he groaned.

"Connie—"

"I'm sorry," she whispered, "I can't help you," and hung up.

Potter remained standing in his bedroom, listening to silence. After a while, it was replaced by a dial tone, and then by a high whining drone like wind in dead trees.

In January, after the holidays, Caroline asked Potter for a divorce. He didn't contest it; in New York State, there would have been little point. He and Caroline argued bitterly over financial and custody arrangements, but by Valentine's Day she was gone.

Potter moved into a two-bedroom apartment, to which he brought his children every other weekend and Wednesday nights.

Shortly before his share of the furniture arrived but after his phone had been installed, Potter surrendered to impulse and dialed 645-289 . Standing there in the bare wooden box with its sterile walls and cheap Scotch-guarded carpet, Potter felt his heart begin a slow hammering against his ribs, which kept up even after a voice answered.

"The number you have reached has been disconnected. The new number for that party is unlisted. Thank you for using AT&T."

In June, Melissa was taken off Ritalin by her doctor. Without the medication, her rages increased for a brief time, but then began to subside. It was decided at a tense conference of Potter, Caroline, Dr. Horacek, and the clinic staff that Melissa should repeat kindergarten at a public school. This announcement did not seem to upset her. "Okay," she said, not looking up from dressing her Cabbage Patch doll.

On a Friday afternoon the following October, Potter was driving in an unfamiliar part of the city. He had had a business appointment that had taken far longer than it should have. His watch said nearly 6:30, and he still had to pick up the circus tickets before the Ticketron closed and get to the bank before. *it* closed. He needed a hefty wad of cash for tomorrow. Early, before the bank opened, he was driving Brendan upstate to visit two community colleges that were supposed to have strong programs in mechanical arts. The colleges were two hundred and fifty miles apart; they had appointments at the first one at 10:00 A.M. and the second at 4:00 P.M., and would spend Saturday night at a motel somewhere. Sunday afternoon was the circus for Melissa, and Potter hadn't gotten around to doing any laundry in two weeks. It would be tight, very tight. He drove with one hand drumming on the dashboard, leaning forward over the wheel to arrive at the Ticketron three inches earlier.

He passed the intersection of Lapham Park Road.

Potter wrenched the wheel to the right. Before he had time to think about it, he was driving east on Lapham, away from the city park, past the row houses separated by narrow concrete driveways, past the 1950s ranches and split levels, to the old trees and new development where the road ended.

The builders had done a lot in fifteen months. The last house was now 5573. Beyond it, bulldozers and backhoes stood yellow and silent against the bloody Indian summer sunset, looming over stacks of lumber and bags of cement and spools of cable. Kids climbed on the bulldozer, shrieking at each other in delight. As Potter watched from his parked car, one of them, a small boy, climbed off the heavy equipment and wandered down the street to stare at the moving van in front of 5542.

The new owner was carrying in furniture himself, along with the uniformed movers. He balanced a hall table, silky amber-colored wood with a matching chair upholstered in rose, against his muscular chest. The chair, upside down on the table, slid a little. A woman ran lightly down the steps, smiling, and steadied the chair. She had sleek chestnut hair, bright blue eyes, and long slim legs in crisp jeans. Behind her a child appeared in the doorway, waddling on bare legs beneath a plastic diaper; an older girl dashed up behind the toddler and grabbed her before she could try to navigate the steps. The older girl grinned and shook her head, her long hair cutting the air. From around the corner of the house, Gary tentatively approached the neighbor boy and smiled shyly.

Potter started his engine, made a three-point turn, started back up Lapham Park Road. The hall table had had an underslung, open shelf instead of a drawer. He wondered if the table would stand in an upstairs hall or a downstairs one, and if the phone placed on it would be a desk model, a slimline, or some fancy custom job to match whatever the Boylans' idea of home decoration might be.

Potter pushed his foot down on the gas pedal. The bank closed in half an hour, the Ticketron an hour after that, and if he didn't get to the bank before it closed, he wouldn't be able to be on time for his trip with Brendan tomorrow. He stopped thinking about the phone. It had nothing to do with him; it never had.

THE TALE AND ITS MASTER

by Michael Rutherford

In the land of the Six Kingdoms the fine art of storytelling was highly regarded, and its practitioners could be rewarded with fame and fortune. Remus, a young storyteller, had been given the opportunity to achieve his utmost dreams. Unfortunately his lack of humility and gratitude was more than made up for by his overweening ambition and pride.

Once upon a time, in the small town of Smunsk, during the reign of Cinnabar the Second, a baby was born into the Guild of Seers, Speakers, Dreamers, Storytellers, and Non-Fanatical Prophets. As the midwife drew the caul from the infant's head, the wind rose and shook the small house like the beating of great wings. The night itself seemed dissolved in the dark rain that flooded the streets. The old woman tied the cord, snipped it with rune-etched scissors, and passed the child to its grateful, weary mother. His loud cries and florid face augured well for his future.

On the tenth day of life, Simon the fat Guildmaster came and crumbled the eggshell of an evening thrush over the boy's lips, so he would sing with limpid clarity. Then with a feather dipped in the blood of a

Stygian ox, the Master drew a mystic character on the child's cheek, so he would be capable of bellowing great distances. Finally the Master tickled the boy's left foot and twisted the baby's right ear, so the child might move listeners to tears and laughter.

"May your son bless the Guild as we have blessed him today," the Guildmaster told the new parents.

Johan shook his superior's hand. His pale face flushed with unavoidable pride. Rose, his wife, was bent over the street pump in front of the house, washing chicken blood from her hands. The child had leached some of her meager beauty, but her blonde hair still shone with the luster of pregnancy.

"The entrails of the chicken were most propitious," she told the two men. "Ann of the Shadows said they were some of the most gaseous she had ever seen at a Guild birth-blessing."

"May the gods be generous to your son and to our Guild," Simon said.

"Amennn," the parents answered together.

After hours of festivity, the last pitchers of harvest beer flowed down the practiced throats of the Guild members and the celebration tables were cleared of food. It had been a joyous day and, given the modest means of Johan and Rose, a robust celebration.

Finally the whole Guild of Seers, Speakers, Dreamers, Storytellers, and Non-Fanatical Prophets and their families left the narrow, thatched house and ambled to their more substantial residences. As was the custom, Simon the Guildmaster brought up the rear. When he turned from Sparrow Alley to the Boulevard of the Muses, he heard the strident, powerful cries of the baby. Simon took it as good omen and smiled.

Remus, as the child was named, rapidly outstripped his father's abilities. Johan was a second-level singer; the Guild used him for Informal Gatherings, Name

Day Celebrations, Duck Pin Tournaments and the like. Though his enthusiasm exceeded his skill, the Guild made good use of Johan with serfs and artisans. Suffice it to say that Johan was not accredited for Large Public Gatherings or Castle Entertainment.

Already, in the Guild pre-school, Remus displayed remarkable voice and, despite his youth, was an admirable bearer of tales. His robust frame and black spiky burr of hair were in marked contrast to the frailty of his blonde parents. The malicious whispered about the barbarian mercenary levy that had taken place in Smunsk some months before Remus' birth, when Johan left his young wife to go on a tour of yak drivers' stations in the provinces. But most shared the attitude of Simon the Guildmaster, who saw the first wisps of shadow-making skills in the boy and knew the deep love Johan and Rose had for the child, whatever his earthly (or as some whispered) daemonic origins. And Simon also saw in the child the possibilities of fame for the Guild and his own reputation as a teacher. In the puffed ambitions of the good Guildmaster, we now recognize the power of dream-planting that Remus could work at even this young age.

One summer evening, Johan and Remus sat on the stoop of the house telling stories to the urchins of Sparrow Alley. Tongue work, Johan called it and knew it good practice for his teen-aged son. Caught up in the potent focus of their unlined faces, the gray-haired little man sketched fairy tales and mild hauntings for the generous currency of their attention. At last Johan blew the candle out, ceased his finger pictures of ogres, birds, and rabbits, picked up the candle holder, and went inside.

"Might I stay out and practice on the children?" Remus asked his father.

"Practice WITH the children," Johan corrected, secretly pleased at his son's request. Johan understood the boy's desire to work without his father present.

"As you wish, Remus. But I'll call you in soon. Don't start an epic."

Remus and his audience sat and listened as Johan went upstairs. Some nights the old man feigned his departure and listened to his son from the hallway. Those nights Remus had to watch what stories he told, staying with the stale, moralizing fables that the Guild ordained as proper for young audiences.

But tonight Remus was free to experiment.

"He's gone," Remus said, "now I'll tell REAL stories. Pay."

The children on the stoop began emptying their pockets: coins, small bits of jewelry from the back drawer of a mother's dowry trove, silver forks, even a tiny cured ham. Remus looked over the gifts, put them smoothly into his leather study sack, eyed the uneasy children.

"Some of these are cheap offerings . . ."

The children shivered.

". . . but I'm feeling kind."

They let their breath out in relief.

"If you want to hear more, next time I expect greater reward," Remus told them, shaking the sack for emphasis. "Do we understand each other?" A mewing sibilance of agreement from the children. "We'd best start; the old fool will call me in a minute. So listen to me now."

The children, who had been fidgeting in anticipation, froze. Indeed they had no choice. The nights Remus spent on the stoop with them had gradually revealed some of his powers to himself. Remus slipped into each mind with tendrils of command as soft and binding as root filaments. He found the stagnant pools, the cellars, keeps, and closets within each child, and he let some of their denizens loose. Just enough to make each listener vulnerable. Remus judged his control now by the drawn bows of parted lips.

Remus smiled in faint scorn and began: "Once there was a frog who hoped to be a prince and there was also a cruel princess who had heard of the frog's dream . . ."

Remus drew an emerald tree frog from his jerkin pocket, pulled a long steel needle from his belt. He held the supple frog by its feet; the frog jerked in futile parody of jumping. Though he never needed them, Remus had a fondness for props.

When Johan finally called Remus to bed, the children stumbled home, their faces drained and flat. The images faded from their memories; the fears that Remus had released drew slowly back. Though they stayed out beyond bedtime when Remus told them stories, their parents never complained: the children slept like the dead. Upon waking, all spoke of the beauty of Remus' stories, though none could quite remember them. And other than this just appreciation, there were no effects that any noticed. Just the waxing vague hunger that in the evenings drew more and more of the children of Smunsk to Sparrow Alley to hear the stories that Remus told on the stone steps of his father's house.

At sixteen Remus was a rangy, handsome youth with a studied sullenness. In the Guild Hall, Master Simon had taken over his exclusive instruction. Remus had sped through the minor orders of memory, gesture, improvisation, and flattery and now stood just two ranks below his father, an unprecedented achievement that gave the older man only pride.

Simon sat at the stained carved lectern that loomed over the Guild Hall like the figurehead of a spectral ship. From this eminence, he oversaw the day-long classes that filled the immense room, bellowing out corrections through the din and gabble of voices. Classes were taught simultaneously, the Guild instructors agreeing that any speaker must be capable of conquering the noisy distraction of other raised voices. Now at twilight, the final class of the day, the politicians, strove to hone their slippery craft. These students were, for the most part, talentless adolescents from wealthy families, whose instruction produced an embarrassingly large portion of the Guild's income.

As a class-ending drill, Tipple, the Master, was putting his charges through the daily Broad Gesture exercises.

"Watch me," he commanded, "it's a wide sweep, not a mincing hack."

Tipple swung one meaty, beringed hand and accidentally hit a student bent over in ursine Erstwhile Listening. The rest of the class guffawed and choked on their cigars.

Simon shook his head and walked out into the evening. The pathetic nature of the class accentuated the gifts of Remus, Johan's son.

And what would the boy become, Simon mused. His skills were so prodigious that the future shot out in countless arcs. Remus' natural artistry made him shun politics. But Simon had also seen the hunger that Remus had for an audience, a hunger that completely counterfeited what all true storytellers possessed: the urge to speak and share; to fuse tale, teller, time, and listeners in one ephemeral union.

Sometimes Simon himself was disconcerted by Remus, the youth seeming to mock him without actually doing so. Perhaps Remus' glib, arch manner came from never being extended or challenged. But Simon sensed in an inchoate, disquieting way that there was a coldness in the marrow of this almost too talented stripling. Too often, Simon had heard Remus shift the focus of the listeners from the story to himself, watched as in barely perceptible ways the boy eased communication to control. The Master had tried to inculcate Remus with the classic lessons of the seduction of power, of the gifted and the fame-graced brought low, robbed by indolence and adulation of the very talent that had raised them. But Remus parroted back the morals of these illustrative fables with an oily comprehension that bespoke only understanding.

Simon wandered through the marketplace, where the farmers packing their unsold produce back into the ox carts grinned as they saw the old man gesturing into the darkening sky. The artist snared by a story. And indeed he was, though the story in Simon's heart grew more and more disturbing: Remus a Leader, a Major Entertainer, or even a Mesmerist.

Fortunately, Mesmerists only appeared once or twice a century. The last had led the youth of the whole Six Kingdoms in a weaponless crusade against the Insatiable Trolls of the Icy Moors.

Simon's immediate concern was the boy's forthcoming public examination by audience. To be admitted as a full member of the Guild of Seers, Speakers, Dreamers, Storytellers, and Non-Fanatical Prophets of Smunsk, a candidate must entertain an audience drawn by public crier and move them to applause. Never had a candidate so young been offered to the fickle reception of the crowd.

And the story itself that the candidate told was the deeper part of the test. For each candidate must go out into the wide world and find a new story or a shining variation of an old one. Thus the Guild itself was enriched and the trove of its spoken knowledge increased by each successful applicant. Though Guild members learned hundreds of stories throughout their careers, it was this quest story that truly defined each artist, that each became known for. It was Guild Law that name credit be given whenever a quest story was told by another.

Listeners were always hungry for unheard adventures, fairy tales, and fantastical diversions. Some few times, a quest story became the immediate fortune of its discoverer. Word of the story's beauty, power, or vision would spread in a fever throughout the Six Kingdoms, and only the tale told with the integrity of its master's voice would satisfy the munificent curiosity of even rulers and their courts.

In its own way, the search for a new story was as arduous or dangerous as the trial by audience. Some candidates vanished for years before returning with stale limericks; some gave up and took their revenge on listeners by becoming salesmen. Though the times were relatively tranquil, some died in the course of their travels from hunger, ill-health, or banditti.

Often, the quest itself became fabled and was told with the quest tale or even supplanted it. So it was that the delicate myth of the elves and how they came to forge the snowflakes was incomplete without the preface of how Zubon had heard the story through the gossamer walls of a Lutner bawdy house. All that was remembered of Glagno's story was the search itself: the oar-bondage for twelve years in the benches of the Choline Pirate flagship, the mermaid's love for him, and how the waterspout drew the two of them up to reign in the Mistral until the final drying of the seas.

With like tales, aphorisms, and nuggets of sleep-inducing advice, Johan prepared his son that rain-soaked, mist-bedraggeld morning when Remus set out in search of the story that was to be his fortune. Remus lolled with undisguised boredom as his father gave him the last words of paternal advice:

"And never begrudge listening to the poorest, most unlikely speaker. Some of the finest stories in the Guild's history have come from toothless mouths and vacant faces. My own story I found by listening . . ."

". . . to a leech-gatherer who mumbled it to you from the mud of a bog in a thunderstorm," Remus concluded, having heard the story of his father's story innumerable times.

"I know you've heard it all before, Remus," said his father, "and that's the lot and bane of all sons."

He clapped him sharply on the shoulder. "Be gone, boy, be gone and be well. Write to your mother, if you get a chance. And remember to display the seeker's Medallion on your chest. It'll guard you from harm and draw those who would speak to you."

Remus tapped the Medallion on his son's cloak with reverent nostalgia. A tongue of fire embroidered with gold threads, Rose had spent hours making this emblem of her son's quest. The medallion was mark of protection; anyone in the Six Kingdoms harming the tale-seeker would be killed with leisurely, agonizing torture by the local Guild. Many miscreants committed suicide rather than enduring the torment of listening to a Guild member chant the genealogy of famous pig breeds or the coronation speeches of their monarchs. But while the badge shielded one from physical danger, it also drew drudges and bores to the Guild candidate, those who were full of private wisdom, family japes, and bathhouse-wall canards.

"Good-bye, father," Remus said with transparent eagerness. "I'll return with a story that will bathe me in jewels."

They exchanged the secret handclasp of the Guild and Remus leaped down from the steps and walked through the stale shadows and dripping eaves of Sparrow Alley. He swung onto the Boulevard of the Muses and headed swiftly for the city gates, for the wide world beyond the walls of Smunsk.

Without looking, Remus sensed Simon the Guildmaster quietly gazing from a rain-streaked window of the Guild Hall. Simon had awakened hours before class to watch his prize student depart. Remus reached the strong gaze of his mind-sight into the old man's soul, laughed to himself at the ambition and affection for him that fused in the old man's heart, and sent a prickly, hobbling gasp of arthritis through the Guildmaster. With a jaunty lope, Remus passed through the city gates, nodded graciously as the guards saluted the Guild Medallion glowing on his cloak. He walked off into the distance, the muddy road sucking at his boots.

Though he was but sixteen, Remus was broad-shouldered, strong, and confident, wise beyond his years with the pilfered wisdom of the many whose memories he had slipped into without their knowledge. The power of his thought-thievery had grown mightily in the last months. Only his parents and a few others had thwarted his inner prying. There was a kindness to Rose and Johan that was repellent. Some fewer were opaque with the sheer force of their thoughts. Already he could read the eyes of women, and he sought behind the eyes with the mind-vision he exercised with such power. And contrary to Guild custom of poverty for story searchers, Remus carried a weighty store of coins frightened from the hordes of children who had begged his stories each night in Sparrow Allcy.

Remus pulled the Guild Medallion off his cloak. With his powers he didn't need it. He'd sift through those he met until he found a story dazzling in its invention and take it as his own without its possessor's knowledge. A week or two to gain the tale, a month or two of pleasure in the towns and then he'd have some wench sew the Medallion back on his cloak and he'd return to his Guild fortune. Remus walked on, oblivious of the rain, spending the wealth of his fabulous future, warmed by the certainty of his triumph.

After a month of drunken dalliance, of utter confidence in his thought-thievery, Remus realized that he had found nothing worth repeating. He was cautious of openly cheating those he met, of mentally forcing them to give him money. His fortune of childbooty melted away. He began to search in earnest.

While he was by no means humbled, Remus had been brought to a grudging admission. The Guild quest was a greater challenge than he had ever imagined.

His mind-reading had almost worked against him; it had brought an almost immediate recognition of how rare a truly original story was. Every story that he sapped and fleeced from an unsuspecting mind was a variation of ones he had heard spoken in the Guild many times, had learned in the simplest classes.

With deepening worry, Remus realized that all the stories might have been found, that he might be living in a barren, lightless age in which conventional wisdom had driven out the capacity for wonder that made stories possible. That there were no new stories left. There were many tale bearers, but no tale crafters. And Remus did not desire a mere minor myth, some tiny cameo of elvish magics; he desperately sought something beyond mere uniqueness: a work of such chilling originality that it would be a miracle that it not be known.

He finally moved out of the cities, the villages, and hamlets, where true story-speaking had slipped to gossip and listening was unheard of. If there were any tales left, Remus knew he must find them in the countryside, in superstition-tainted hollows, around the fires of wanderers and nomads, for whom the sun still had a name and the wind a voice. With these people, he could prompt a rude bed and a simple meal as he mined their pagan thoughts for that rarest jewel, a story of magnitude and undiscovered brilliance.

It was a bitter day at the end of the third month of Remus' quest. The ground was hard with frost. It had been five days since he left the piled turf lodges of the wolf-hunters, two days since he had exhausted the store of jerky and flat bread they had given him. He was numb from the impassive roof of gray winter clouds, the ceaseless, leaching wind, from probing the minds of the hunters. The hunters had had no myths or stories, barely thoughts, only a savage and precise series of sexual fantasies, some of which involved women. The unrelenting weather had an elemental purity that he found almost preferable to the hunters' dreams.

Remus saw smoke rise from deep within the winter-barren forest and be torn to nothingness by the wind. He stumbled into the nameless woods and dreamed vaguely of thawing himself and mind-tinkering a meal from whomever he met. He found a faint trail that seemed to bend toward the smoke. He hoped it led to whatever tended the fire and the warmth it promised. Be it troll, brigand, or simple woodcutter, Remus was beyond caring.

Hunger stitched pain in his belly. Jackdaws and ravens flapped away as he followed the suggestion of the path, were snatched away by the gusts like leaves of a black autumn. The trees stood closer together and the stony halflight of the day darkened. Remus stumbled on, wished blankly that he reach the fire and whatever fate awaited before night left him blind and alone for the prowling beasts of the forest. Remus' ambitions had simplified to a steaming bowl and the mindless company of dancing flames.

Remus was about to throw himself on the ground and become one more lost story when he cleared a rise and, with night seeming to pause for a moment on the spikes of the bare treetops, looked down into a tiny clearing and saw a hearth fire winking through the walls of a glass house.

"Welcome, storyteller," a caressing, cinnamon voice said barely above the wind. "It is time that we finally meet."

A small, humped figure stepped out of the twilight. It was a hunchbacked crone, the hollow socket of her left eye sewn shut with golden thread, thread like that of Remus' mother-sewn Medallion. She reached out a withered hand, took his arm and led him into the shining rooms of the glass house.

Remus awoke in the middle of the night. The bowl of venison stew and the warmth of the fire had melted him to weariness, and the crone had led him to a small room where he had fallen asleep on a simple, sumptuous pile of furs. Now he lay awake and watched the stars winking through the clarity of the glass roof. Remus rolled over and saw the fire in the hearth fallen to a red honeycomb. A soft, strong light rippled from a corner of the living room beyond the fireplace. Remus stared and in the cold radiance recognized the old woman's face, saw how light issued from her open mouth as she slept, broke like silent water over her knees, and gradually faded across the floor.

Remus realized that he slept in the house of a witch, a storyteller whose very breath was luminous with soul-shivering power. Such were the legends that he had laughed at in the Guild School. Only exhaustion let him regain sleep. At that moment Remus knew he had found his story and his fortune.

Rain bathed the glass house the next morning, gave way to broken clouds and finally an austerity of winter sun. The crone quietly went about her household tasks, as she watched him devour the elegant meals that she materialized with slashes of her crabbed hands. Remus smiled back winsomely and tried to pry inside her mind. The first feathery attempt to slip into her thoughts drove a spike of pain through his forehead. He recoiled and knew that he must wait.

The shadows of the bare trees crept in long fingers through the transparent walls before she finally spoke. Once more Remus was startled by the contrast between the limpid, effortless beauty of her voice and the ruin of her body. She sat down on the opposite side of the crystal table, glanced at him with the disconcerting nakedness of her one maelstrom eye.

"Enough hesitation and sparring, my dear," she

said soothingly. "My name is Mali, Mali of the Moonfire Tongue. I know of your quest and your vaunting ambitions. I too have needs and desires. Rarely have I met one so young with such mind force. So young and so handsome."

"Thank you," Remus said politely, "I wait on your words, oh paragon of beauty and kindness."

Her dry lips twitched in an unfortunate display of her gums. "I am happy that fate conspired to unite the two of us. You see, I am dying."

"I'm sorry," Remus volunteered with admirable sympathy.

"And before I die, I would pass some of my craft to one worthy of receiving it."

Remus tensed involuntarily as a foxfire of eagerness played over him.

"Or more honestly," the crone continued, in the honeyed youth of her voice, "I would trade with you. I offer you a story, a story that is my heart's essence. A never-heard story that would be the making of your glory. I know you saw the light well from my mouth last night. You sense the core of my being. And in your marrow, you know I speak the truth."

Remus quickly bobbed his head, leaned forward on his elbows. "It is no belief I have in you, it is certitude," he said. Then he pulled out his dirk, pinked his little finger. "Make what trade you will. I offer my blood."

The two watched the blood pool on the icy table. Then the hag laughed. "Dying, I desire not your death, manling. I want less than your blood. Less and more." She touched his finger and healed it.

The anticipation of his future dragged Remus headlong to words. "I agree to your terms, oh fey and generous lady."

"I am glad that we avoid unseemly haggling," she said softly. "There are but two sticking points. The first is that you must whisper thanks to me three times before each telling you make of the story. These small thanks will sustain my soul in its lonely wanderings after death."

"Most readily, willingly agreed," Remus hastened.

"The last condition is simply this: you must sleep with me this night and love me to my satisfaction. If my tongue is quickened to joy, I will give you my story at night's end."

The crone finally broke the lingering silence.

"Brave words you spoke before you heard my price," her shining voice quavered. "I do not hold you to your too-eager promise."

Remus suppressed a shudder before his hand stroked her dank hair. He bent across the table, pulled her face to his and felt her tongue slide between his lips.

The moon rose and fell, the stars spun in their courses, and Remus watched them slowly toll the night away through the crystal thatch of the glass house. His senses blurred to nightmare. Remus slid down the glistening cries of her voice and finally ceased to wonder at the voracious fecundity of her desire.

Somehow through the wall he heard the bird cries that presage dawn. He found himself on the floor, awakening at Mali's feet. Every joint ached and his mouth tasted of compost. The old woman rocked gently in her rocking chair, humming to herself, beams of light breaking through her gape-tooth smile like stalks of golden wheat.

"Well and most prodigally done, my final love," the beautiful voice purred. "Bargain made, price paid. Rest your head on my grateful thighs, and I will give you the story that is my life."

And she rocked and stroked Remus' head as it rose and fell on the withered sea of her thighs. And the voice, which held all the beauty that the woman's body lacked, lulled him and loved him again. Light fell from her mouth like a dazzling rope, like the cord between mother and newborn. The light fell from her mouth and flowed between the narrow parting of his lips and filled Remus with the heady distillation of dreams. And this is the story she told him: the Tale of the Dragon.

In those august years, when the air itself was more substantial and supported them more easily and the stronger darkness gave richer contrast to their flames, a dragon of promising wing span, potent breath, and teeth of admirable sharpness was born in the high peaks of the Dolorous Mountains.

Her parents watched the pearly egg crack, saw the ruby eggtooth pierce the opalescent shell. Balog, the male, breathed spurts of smoke as Falla, his mate, crouched over the emerging dragonette. Falla's neck snaked back and forth as she cocked her python head. Her crystalline eyes throbbed jade to ruby, fear to love. It was their first hatch.

Two hundred yards below the eyrie, wedged into a narrow fissure of the adamantine cliffs, Kazan the thief heard the signals of breath, spied the gouts of fire and steam that broke across the upper ledges. He realized that his agonies of preparation would soon bring him wealth or death. No man of the Shattered Coasts had ever stolen a dragon chick.

Her scaly udders distended with mother's magma, Falla dragged herself to the nest of gold coins, jewels, and men's bones that she and Balog had fashioned from the heaped store of their cave. As she fell to her side, Falla drew the wobbly newborn to her teats with a gentle wing. Balog licked the tender scales of his mate's neck, and Falla lifted her wing to show the fierce nursing.

Balog growled with satisfaction and turned to the mouth of the cave, his claws striking sparks on the stone floor. Twelve leagues distant, there was a village of Amazons that Balog had spared for this event.

Tonight he would return with some of the tender warriors in his craw for Falla. Balog flapped open the leather of his wings, blew one spurting triumph of conflagration, and sprang from the cliff into flight.

The vast cold shadow passed over Kazan as he crouched against the cliff, his face and hair darkened with ashes to the complexion of the rock. He watched the male fly with baleful swiftness away, away. After five still minutes, Kazan gently opened his pack and readied himself.

In the cavern above, the dragon nestled against her mother's breasts, her small snake head shiny-scaled. Faint rings of smoke broke over the perfect daggers of her teeth. When her daughter fell asleep satiated, Falla drifted to shallow, grateful rest.

At the top of the rock chimney, Kazan pressed his feet against the far wall and wedged himself cautiously. He flexed his bruised hands over and over until they felt supple again, drew five deep, silent breaths, and flung himself up.

As he cast himself over the rim of the cliff, the smouldering half-closed eyes of the mother beast flared open, the cleft wet whip of her tongue flickered out, and she bellowed to her feet. Kazan yanked the horn bow from his shoulder, notched the silver-headed arrow, in a heartbeat drew it back and shot the cured thornwood shaft through the fiery left eye and into the abomination's brain.

Falla blasted one wail of fire over the small figure, but Kazan had turned his back and the wizard-blessed leather singed, cracked, and held. Falla's stubby feet scrabbled at the rock, and she died before her head thudded at Kazan's feet. Her tail slashed three times, flung treasure and bones against the walls of the cave. Kazan turned slowly as the dust of the lair settled on him. There were only two sounds: his breathing and the puling, urgent cries of the baby dragon.

Kazan unwrapped the drugged goat's heart and forced it between the jaws of the monstrous infant. She swallowed it in one frightful bite. Kazan watched the lump slide down the amber throat. The baby's eyes glowed at him with predatory affection. As Kazan returned to his pack at the edge of the cliff, the dragonette waddled after him, nuzzling his legs and hissing for affection. By the time Kazan had uncoiled the vine rope, the tiny beast had curled in leaden sleep, her head pointed toward her new parent. Kazan stared fitfully into the sky. He needed another hour. Tying one end around the dead beast's neck, Kazan played the thin, steely rope down the long rock face until he felt it slacken.

Using catgut thongs, Kazan bound together the legs of his prize. With the tenderness of all thieves for priceless goods, he slid the sleeve of dragon skin over the sleeping chick, drew his steal-sack barely shut to admit air. Kazan forced the bag into his pack, squatted to pull the straps over his shoulders, wobbled to his feet. The months of exercise had strengthened him; though the dragonette was almost his weight, Kazan could carry her.

The rope cinched around him; Kazan stared for the last time at the dragon's lair, at the mounds of jewels and coin, at the skulls studding the floor. The great scales of the mother dragon were already beginning to darken and fade. He thought of her mate, shivered, and began to rappel down the grim precipice. By the time he reached the base of the cliff, his hands were bloody from the speed of his descent. Kazan ignored the pain. The sure knowledge of his fate if he were caught spilled through his thoughts. He tightened the straps of the pack and set off at a desperate trot for the tiny mouth of the Endless Caverns. It was a league and a half away.

*   *   *

Even before the proof of sight, Balog felt there was something horribly, inexplicably wrong. The sky itself stank with the treachery of humankind, and when he saw the awkward cast of Falla's body at the mouth of their cavern, he knew the tragedy as he skidded across the floor of their nesting place. He swallowed the now-bitter bits and blood of the Amazons that he would have coughed down his nursing wife's throat, saw the serpentine glory of her body stiffened, their firstborn gone, stolen, seized; the hateful shaft in his mate's once-burning eye and, most sacrilegious, the mother used as anchor for the violator's rope. Later he would eat her body, as blood and love demanded, but now Balog was lover and father-avenger. The flame of his hatred blackened the cave, and he turned in cold, fiery wrath to the rescue of their firstborn. Balog hung steel-taloned on the brow of the cliff, and his keen nostrils defined the smell of the thief. He glided swiftly to the base of the mountain, caught the scent again, rose relentless and inexorable to skim the rock barrens, massive and deathgrim, to rescue his child, to rend the murderer and thief of his happiness.

Moments away, he found them: the wretched little figure bent beneath a burden that must be his daughter. The creature turned a frightened, white face as Balog swept down with spread claws. And then it vanished into a tiny hole in the rocks. Balog's talons scored the opening, and he crashed and scrambled to the hole, thrust his snapping jaws in as far as his neck could reach, heard the thief scuttling deep away, the baby's scales too soft for him to use flames.

His claws were blunted; blood from his foot pads seared the cave mouth. It was a day and a night before Balog admitted her loss. His heart was as bitter and black as the taunting darkness of this thief's entrance. Balog spread his wings and flew to wreak his woeful vengeance on men and all their works.

* * *

Blind hours of stumbled tunnels, of the way anxiously divined in the flicker of a sputtering torch, Kazan's attention fixed on the smears of glow-worm paste that marked the single proper path in the labyrinthine confusion of the galleries and tunnels of the Endless Caverns. A misstep, a false turn, and Kazan and his prize would be forever lost in the lightless gullet of the indifferent rocks.

But as his legs trembled with exhaustion, the pack squirming on his shoulders, Kazan recognized the quartz knob at the entrance to his refuge and stumbled into the perpetual light of the vast gallery. Slipping off the pack, he gently drew the mewing dragon from its sheath, clamped the twice-forged manacle about her neck, and, shielding his face from the sear of heat, led her to the great chain anchored in the living rock. He fastened her manacle to it with a troll-proof padlock whose key hung from a leather strap around his neck. The chain was long enough to reach to the cleft deep within which throbbed the magma that gave the huge gallery its constant illumination. Here the dragon could feed on the fire-milk that would nourish it in the weeks of solitary training that lay ahead. The beast rasped Kazan's face once with her tongue, then ambled off to feed at the end of her chain.

Spent, Kazan stumbled to the far side of the chamber, unfolded the dragon-skin suit that he must forever wear to mask his man-scent from the dragon's natural appetite for humankind, slid into its stiff folds, pulled a goat bladder of Scythean honey wine from his pile of stores, and drank a self-satisfied toast to his audacity and glittering future. He fell into the first untroubled sleep he had had in months.

Kazan named her Almara. As goslings will bind themselves to a dog or a man in the absence of true parents, so Almara clove to Kazan. In the three months in the cave, the she-dragon grew rapidly. Kazan raised her with calculating kindness, preening the strengthening wings, polishing her scales with fleece, and trimming her nails with great armor files. Occasionally he fed her bits of the dried corpses of the three beggars he had hired so stealthily to carry his provisions into the depths of the Endless Caverns. To keep his scheme secret, Kazan had killed them when they reached the gallery. Almara gnawed their hacked limbs with ravenous alacrity.

The dragon's love for him waxed and deepened as she grew. She never questioned their disparity. The last month in the cavern, Kazan could control her with his voice. She was flying now, swooping through the harsh, lava-lit heights of the gallery in the newly discovered pleasure of flight. They had taken to sleeping beside each other, Kazan awakening to find himself blanketed with the velvet stretch of her wing. He found that he enjoyed grooming her and was faintly puzzled at this slight softness in the splendor of his great and greedy scheme. Almara took well to saddle and bit; she seemed more eager to fly with him astride her neck than to fly alone. Kazan sighed in a surfeit of ambition as he stroked the warm muzzle, watched the steam of her breath break between the fingers of his blacksmith gloves. One week more of flame practice on the mannikins hung from the stalactites and they would be ready for the sun, for the kingdoms of men, for Kazan's ascension to wealth, more rightly, for the glint of sunlight on gold and a nest of bullion and jewels for Almara.

She followed him faithfully through the dark leagues of twisted caverns as Kazan obeyed the glowing trail marks he had left long months ago, the daubs of faint luminescence that led beneath the raw-edged snow-crested mountains that separated them from her long-forgotten parents' lair. Hopefully he was beyond her father's wrath. When at last the dragon and her master stood at the cavern mouth, each rejoiced at the sweep of the verdant fields and tiny order of the villages beneath them. Almara bent her head to Kazan's face, saw the avid hunger there and took it as her own. He scratched the tender scales above her eyes, tightened the saddle on her lowered neck, took the reins in his hands, and together they leaped into the waiting sky, the bountiful horizons of their future.

After five years of fighting dour battles, of crushing insurrections, scattering invaders, or simply leveling recalcitrant villages and obdurate castles, Kazan was rich. His coffers were full, his tables groaned, his lands produced plentifully. He had a grim castle, his own wizard. Kazan was bored.

Kazan the King-Maker, Worm-Lord, and Fire-Wielder listened with faint interest to the proposition of the emissary of Udo the Malignant. The round, sweaty man spoke with a sincerity that testified that his life was forfeit if he could not enlist the infallible assistance of the Dragon Master:

"And in his further generosity, Lord Udo offers the hand of his only daughter to the wondrous Kazan, most glorious wreaker of havoc, army destroyer . . ."

"Cease," Kazan ordered from his winged throne. "Grolsch, what is the measure of this Udo?"

The desiccated wizard stepped from behind the throne and spoke in a bored voice, "A poisoning, cutpurse, whoreson greedy rogue who usurped his father's throne and mounted his mother to have this daughter."

"Not another," Kazan sighed in disgust. "Away, serf."

"And Lord Udo begged that you peruse this limning of Princess Fiona," the little man wheedled as he drew an icon from his diplomatic pouch.

The small picture glowed less from its artistry than

its subject. Perhaps it was the golden sheen of the hair, but Kazan leaned forward with a certain hunger. The messenger stammered up the steps, handed the picture to Kazan with abject hope.

"Is this a true likeness?" Kazan asked the wizard, passing him the image.

Grolsch twisted the picture in his taloned hands, held the painting close to his hard eyes, seemed to peer down the maiden's bosom.

"Strangely enough, yes," he said. "There is a certain timid magic to the colors, but this truly is the girl."

He handed it back to Kazan, who studied the miniature a long moment.

"She's a virgin," the messenger added redundantly.

Grolsch snorted. Kazan glared at the little man, then turned the picture face down in his lap.

"We'll subdue Lord Udo's populace," Kazan said abruptly. "Fifty per cent down, fifty per cent upon completion, the Princess on my arrival. Grolsch will draw up the usual contract with you."

A bellow of scorching longing surged from the courtyard, shook the tapestries along the high walls, thrummed through the stones of the castle.

"Gentlemen, you must excuse me. My mistress calls." Kazan gave them both an ironic bow, strode through the great hall, his dragon livery creaking.

As she always did when Kazan walked into the courtyard, Almara squealed joyously and blew flame into the evening air. In the intervals between battles, they flew daily together at dawn and dusk.

Almara was fully grown now, the length of twenty tall men from black snout to lashing tip of her arrowhead tail. Her scales were darkly iridescent, her wings had the sheen of a dark lake, testimony to her health and the delicate, exclusive care that Kazan gave her. The Dragon Master himself still groomed, polished, stroked, and preened her.

And Kazan still wore the dragon-skin suit. He was weary of its stiff embrace. He even slept in it. But Grolsch had confirmed for him its absolute necessity. Kazan himself had eye-proof of Almara's appetites as he watched her take her bloating fill of the race of man after each conflict. Fortunately, she was fastidious, and as was her gentle wont, licked him only after cleaning herself of the scraps of her meals.

Almara lowered her great head to have him scratch behind her ears. Her lambent eyes glittered; she allowed no one else near her. The months of training in the cavern had made her Kazan's. Kazan sensed more and more in those first turbulent years, as she protected her frail rider from arrows and lances, that Almara regarded him as hers and fought with even deeper fury the few times he had been wounded. Even the treachery, machinations, and intrigues of the jealous were forestalled by the knowledge of the dragon's wrathful affection.

Now as they mounted the evening sky, Kazan saw the first stars glinting to light and thought of Fiona, and dreamt, as even rich thieves do, of marrying a princess. A cold wind buffeted the dragon and Kazan slid a little in the saddle. Almara looked back quickly, saw his hand wave assurance. Satisfied, she blew one long gust of fire into the rising darkness.

Singed, smoke-soiled and sweaty, Kazan slid from the dragon's back and strode wearily across the jousting field in front of Udo's castle to the waiting awe-struck crowd and the cluster of ermine-clad nobility drawn apprehensively before them.

It had almost been too easy. The small village had withered beneath the torch of Almara's breath; the men had put up a desperate momentary resistance, and then Almara had eaten, barely staunching her hunger. Apparently the villagers had refused to pay

Udo's last usurious tax. The collection of Udo's levies would be much smoother now, Kazan thought.

The band struck up a disjointed march, the ranks of ragged soldiers snapped to attention, and Udo the Malignant waddled out to meet Kazan. A small, veiled maiden followed in his wake. Grolsch walked solemnly behind the pair.

"Well done. Oh, most completely, horribly successful," the greasy little man gushed, adjusting his coronet. "My deepest, most heartfelt thanks, oh mighty Lord Kazan. Even now the other villages hurry their late taxes to our humble gates."

"Grolsch," Kazan asked, "has our fee been paid?"

"Loaded into your coaches and sped to Castle Kazan," bowed the wizard.

"Even so," said Udo, his eyes shiny with porcine hospitality, leading the girl forward. At Udo's nudge, she dropped her veil. A blush suffused her flawless face as Kazan stared in disbelief at the palpable innocence of her.

"We have prepared a modest feast in your honor and that of your bride," Udo said, with a bow, "and have laid out the wedding chamber."

The child blushed even deeper, seemed on the edge of tears.

Kazan looked at the wizard in mild confusion.

"The fat wretch wishes to be able to say that you are his son-in-law," Grolsch explained. "We can take her now without further delay."

The beautiful child began to cry.

"It is as your wizard says," Udo agreed. "My daughter is yours to do with as you please. I merely suggested the marriage vows to make her more compliant to your wishes."

Castle Kazan was not a particularly festive place. Perhaps it was best to have their first night here, Kazan thought. He shrugged. "If it will put the girl at ease, we will have a marriage ceremony."

Without speaking, the Princess Fiona reached out and took Kazan's smoky hand in both of hers.

Across the field, the dragon Almara suddenly bellowed and tore the earth as the girl touched Kazan. Udo, Fiona, and Grolsch stepped away from the Dragon Master.

"Ready the marriage feast, Lord Udo," ordered Kazan. "I will settle the dragon for the night and then return to minister to my betrothed."

All hastened into the castle. Kazan hurried to the restive dragon, stroked her hot muzzle, took the saddle from her neck, led her into the depths of the granary under the castle walls, chained her to the thick millstones. Almara threw herself on the cobbled floor with a clatter of scales and watched Kazan with a fitful flickering in her jeweled eyes.

"Still hungry, sweet friend?" Kazan asked.

He scratched behind her tiny, tufted ears. The dragon growled faintly.

"It's away tomorrow, you and I, back to our castle. I weary of these pitiful escapades. We must get out of politics and back to honest thievery."

The dragon gave him a brief nuzzle, rolled away. Kazan stroked her neck.

"Good night, faithful beast," he said as he walked out. He remembered the face of the princess and lengthened his stride.

Despite the slight smell of decay in the chapel of the local deity, the wedding had been moving. After they had exchanged vows, Princess Fiona, now wife to Kazan Dragon Lord, slipped the bridal veil from her face and let it drift to the floor. With fervent simplicity, she turned to her new master and embraced him. They were strangely matched: the child-bride in her white, intricate lace and the battle-lean thief in his hacked and worn dragon skin. The company cheered as the two walked out of the chapel to host the wedding feast, the bride's hair like beaten gold in the light of the ceremonial torches, the dry lisp of the groom's steps as he walked in his scaled boots.

As they sat at the high table of the feast, to see and be seen, Fiona kissed her husband before the well-wishers.

"Thus I begin my thanks for saving me from that woesome beast," she told Kazan.

"The dragon is total servant to my wishes," Kazan assured her.

"Not the flying worm, dear husband. My father." She squeezed his hand with small, sharp-nailed fingers.

Fiona steadied her husband as they followed the wavering torches up the twisting staircase to the bridal chamber. Kazan had been obliged to drink numerous toasts. But he drew himself up when the castle steward opened the burnished door with its intricate castings of intertwined couples. The steward bowed to the bride and groom, handed Kazan the key to the door, and took himself away with discreet dispatch.

Kazan bent down in smirking bravado, caught the beauteous Fiona in his arms, and carried her across the threshold into the perfumed chamber. As her arms slowly tightened around his neck and he felt the petals of her breath, he glanced about the circular room. With its confection of white sheets and heaped pillows, the massive four-poster bed glowed in the swaying light of priapic candles set on high stocks of ebony. A ceiling-to-floor mirror doubled the bed and candles in its silvered depths. And beyond the bed stood a black cast-iron tub with four clawed feet and steam rising above its dark rim. Plush towels and fragrant soaps rested on a small table beside it. Kazan stopped his kiss, stared momentarily. His bride caught the direction of his eyes, turned in his arms, and looked over to the tub.

"I ordered the servants to prepare these ablutions,

my sweet lord," Fiona explained softly. "Before we attend to our mutual pleasure, I want to bathe your winsome body and myself wash the battle sweat from you. Would you love me like a lizard all in your scaly skin?" She laughed and began to undo the dull ivory dragon-tooth buttons that bound the suit to Kazan.

Kazan had taken his sporadic dalliance in brief interludes away from the dragon. His reservations died when Fiona put her mouth to the blanched skin of his chest as she slowly peeled the dragon garb from him.

"My lord tastes bitter," she said through puckered lips, "but I will sweeten him."

She drew the naked thief to the steaming tub, led his hands to the fastenings of her wedding gown and after the two stood bare as peeled sticks, they stepped together into the slow roiling of the scented waters. With wanton, blissful hands, Fiona washed five years of muck, dragon oils, and battle drear from Kazan's skin and made him smell like a man again.

The candles had guttered down to waxy fists when Kazan woke in those darkest moments before first light. Fiona, his wife, clung to him with tender possession as she slept, her hair snaking across the bed like rolling lava. During the night, his future had narrowed to the exquisite figure that lay beside him. His glance drifted over the mirror: the two languid bodies, the pillows tossed about the samite sheets like heaped clouds, the crimson swatches of his wife's virgin blood scattered across the milky, four-posted firmament.

His ear throbbed. Kazan reached up and felt the sticky warmth of his own blood on his fingers. It had passed without notice in the tumble of their lovemaking, but Kazan realized now that she had bitten through the lobe of his right ear.

Like the disquieting aftertaste of a troubled dream, Kazan sensed the dragon stirring, heard the low, demanding growl of his charge, lonely and hungry in the damp granary. He rose and silently pulled the dragon-skin suit onto himself again. After the bath and the gossamer pressure of Fiona's hands, his second skin had a chafing stiffness.

Heavy with wine and the fumes of love, Kazan stumbled down into the bowels of the castle, found the dragon crouched on her haunches, sheathing and un-sheathing her claws. Almara flared her nostrils as he walked close, her eyes vortices of fire in the dark room.

"It is I, Kazan your Lord, oh worm of my heart, beast of my fortune," said the thief with a dull heartiness.

He picked her saddle off a pile of wheat sacks, threw it over her rigid neck, cinched it with practiced craft, tugged her reins lightly to lead her out. For the first time in Kazan's memory, the dragon resisted. He pulled harder, slipped, and almost fell in a puddle of her drool. Kazan lashed out with the reins and whipped her snout. Almara scuttled back, whimpered, and Kazan dropped the reins in embarrassment.

"Forgive my sharpness, dear Almara. My thoughts are elsewhere," Kazan apologized, stepping closer and scratching behind her ears.

After ten minutes of strokes and soft whispers, the simmering burble of Almara's breathing eased and Kazan led the reluctant dragon outside. Despite Almara's waking cries, Udo's castle remained silent. No doubt it was the earliness of the day and the effects of the wedding feast.

Almara and Kazan stood in mute appreciation of the morning. The sun glowered at dawn's edge and the low sanguine beams pierced the ground fog in harm-less mimicry of the dragon's battle wrath. Kazan swung into the worn comfort of the saddle, swayed in mo-mentary giddiness. The dragon garb scraped against his flesh. The odor of the skin suit and the lucent soaps and rich oils of the nuptial bath mixed unpleasantly. The dragon glanced back at Kazan, wrinkled her nostrils, and turned away, a curious glimmer in the low embers of her eyes.

Kazan flicked the reins, and dragon and man mounted the air in swoops of her velveted wings. The castle of Udo the Malignant fell away, as in voiceless understanding they flew into the incarnadine simplicity of the rising light.

They soared for hours before returning so that the spirits of both man and dragon were once more in harmony as they wheeled above Udo's demesne. Suddenly the dragon drew its wings back and, stooping like a falcon, dove toward a milky flag flecked with a multitude of roseate butterflies, a flag that snapped above the castle's single tower, a tower that Kazan, clinging in numb confusion to the pommel of the dragon's saddle, realized held in its highest story the bridal chamber.

Almara tore a great swatch from the banner, worried it for a moment, swallowed the rag. Kazan pulled harshly at the bit, wondered anew at the antic behavior of his beast, and finally guided the dragon to a gentle landing at the far end of the jousting field. As Kazan sprang from the saddle in anger, Almara bowed her great head in contrition, a nervous slaver dribbling from her jaws. Kazan caught himself, eyed her with concern.

"Are you ill, my steed, my flying fortune?" Kazan asked brusquely.

He touched her face, gave her ears a soft buffet. Almara licked his face, her black, cleft tongue rasping his skin.

Kazan stumbled back.

"Great clumsy beast," he cursed.

He touched the side of his head, stared at his bloody fingertips. The dragon had stripped the scab from the love bite Fiona had given his ear. Only the thud of the drawbridge falling across the moat drew his attention away and prevented him from berating his monstrous charge. The dragon herself crouched stolidly, the meek blaze of her eyes reflecting the image of Kazan.

Made familiar by Kazan's familiarity with his daughter, Count Udo walked with Grolsch and Fiona at the head of his festive court.

"A most sublime jest, Dragon Lord, a marvelous caprice," Udo told his son-in-law.

"You have my advantage," Kazan replied, with a flat courtesy engendered by Fiona's presence.

"Surely you were aware that the banner you directed your firedrake to rend was your wedding sheet, displayed by the bride's family as custom demands, fit testimony to her purity and your so-potent affection."

Kazan's silence was washed away in the jocund laughter of Udo's retainers. He glanced up to the torn sheet gaily flapping its speckled shreds from the flagstaff atop the wedding chamber, then looked with small embarrassment to his bride. Fiona wrinkled her nose, stepped to Kazan's side, and put her arm around his waist.

"Let us leave swiftly, beloved liege and husband," she said.

Kazan noticed Fiona's attire for the first time. She wore a tight all-covering garment of sea-mist velvet, its surface lightly sketched with an intricacy of scales.

"My daughter heard of your dragon dress, Lord Kazan, and tormented me to have this likeness made for her once she knew her future was yours," Udo smiled indulgently. "We come out to bid you adieu and farewell. Your wizard says your services are bound already to another kingdom. And of course, farewell to a daughter, welcome to a new son," Udo bowed obsequiously to Kazan.

"Wholesale rates in the future," Grolsch said dryly.

Kazan kissed Fiona over and again, held her at arm's length, admired the fit and sheen of her reptilian fashions. He led Fiona to the wizard, "Grolsch will speed you to the castle in his charmed carriage, my sweetest love."

Grolsch took her by the elbow as Kazan turned to the dragon.

The girl held her lover's steps with her voice, "May I not fly with you this once and only once?"

Kazan looked in bewilderment to the wizard, to the beseeching, heart-wrenching face of his bride, to the blue feather of a night heron plaited into her hair.

"The beast is tamed to your desires, my Lord," Grolsch volunteered. "Let the Lady Fiona ride only this one time. And besides," the wizard's face creased with an unexpected smile as he looked at the girl, "Love has its own wisdom."

Hand in hand, the Dragon Lord and his bride walked up to the dragon. Kazan studied the creature's flat, expressionless face. Almara blinked at the tiny, golden-haired figure, then bent her great head for the girl to stroke. Kazan breathed again, sighed thanks.

"Oh dear and mighty Almara, you will carry my bride and me together to Castle Kazan. This is my wish and my command."

The dragon raised herself, enveloped them once in the dark shadow of her unfurled wings, and bowed her neck.

Kazan swung into the saddle, lifted his wife to sit before him, patted the glistening scales of his steed. Fiona waved a final time to the crowd and the dragon rose with awful majesty, left the groundlings in dusty turbulence.

When all could spy them again, the three were almost between clouds, a distant fabulous puppetry against the lighter sky. And then the tiny dragon shrugged and the lovers fell from their seat and a second, brighter sun novaed above Castle Udo. When the halos and furred light cleared from the vision of the momentarily blinded watchers, one smoking dragon-skin boot fell to earth, the blackened plume of a night heron drifted down in the warm drizzle of white ash.

Only a few had the presence of mind to follow Grolsch the wizard as he careened into the dank granary and burrowed deep into the mounds of unsavory grain. For Grolsch was the only one to realize that the fell dragon, grieving and heart-shattered, would return to feed.

Dawn's rosy fingers plucked at the cabin of glass. Mali's voice rustled and cracked, narrowed to a trickle, "Some say it was the bridal bath that washed the dragon scent from Kazan and that when Almara tasted the blood of Kazan's love bite and smelled him for the first time as a man, the fate of the thief and the princess bride was sealed. Others feel it was the inevitable jealousy of the beast; that as long as Kazan shared himself with no other, he was the dragon's master. They say simply that having bound himself to a dragon, he must life-long keep faith with it. That love consumed him in the end."

What light there was left in the witch's voice fell splintered into Remus' dark hair.

"Remember the promise," she coughed, an autumnal gust through dry nettles. "Whisper thanks to me three times before each telling."

There was a rattle in her throat like dried beans spilled on stone. Her head fell against the back of the rocker and the only light in her gaping mouth was the glare of the rising sun.

Even as he slit her throat with the dagger drawn quietly from his boot, Remus knew she was dead. Steam hissed from the gashed neck, a sudden cloud of gray moths spilled out and dissolved in the air. Remus heard for the last time the ghost of her voice's beauty, "Remember my name, remember meee . . ." And then the frail words followed Mali into whatever darkness held her.

As Remus wiped the dust from his blade, the crone's body withered to the husk of a shed snake's skin.

"That's that," Remus said to himself.

He felt the story curled and powerful within himself, held his hands to his mouth, blew, and laughed as he saw phosphorescence splash into his palms.

Then the glass house began to crack. It seemed to wait for Remus to escape and then collapsed with a melancholy tinkling. The splintered pile blazed like a jagged, brittle rose bush and then softly fell to dust.

Funereal wails rose from the depths of the forest and blended into a ululating dirge. Remus felt the trees lour over him. The forest shifted its shadows to reclaim the witch's glade. With the sound of vellum pages turning in a grimoire, ravens flapped down and lit in the stark branches. They cocked their heads and watched Remus silently with their bright, black eyes. The wails grew louder, closer. Remus knew it was time to leave.

He pulled his cloak around him and threw himself down the path that led out of the forest. There was a crinkle of reflection. Without breaking stride, Remus saw that Mali had sewn his Guild Medallion back onto his cloak with golden thread. The Medallion was melted inextricably into the fabric. Remus didn't care. If it was the dead woman's fancy to remind him of his art, he was indifferent. Remus had what he had wanted, what he needed to transcend mere storytelling.

When he reached the edge of the forest, Remus looked back. Winged shapes drew to a pillar of luminous blue smoke; mournful, howling cries saturated the wind. But no eldritch forms flitted through the trees behind him, and Remus knew that the witch's final rites held no danger for him. He turned away from the forest and walked in the direction of the morning sun, for the weed-split stone of the Old Road, to retrace the journey of his quest and vault himself to the stage of his first triumph, the public telling of the story that he had found.

There was a harsh rap at the door and Johan opened it narrowly, to keep the deluge from flooding the hallway.

"Let me enter, old man. It is I, Remus, your son."

Johan swung the door open, and the hooded figure strode into the house, seeming to bear the storm in with him. Johan caught the blaze of the Guild Medallion with its strange gold thread, and then Remus threw back the hood and looked around the small house with disinterested remembrance.

"My son, my child," Johan said with tearful concern, "the quest has made you a man."

He looked into Remus' drawn face.

"A man and more," said Remus, blowing on his hands.

Johan stared as the pulsating radiance in his son's breath outlined the bones of Remus' fingers.

"I can see that you have found more than a story, Remus," Johan said, aghast. "It's late and your mother sleeps. You can greet her in the morning. Rest now. Your room is as it was when you left." He led the gaunt stranger to his son's room and took his cloak. Remus stumbled in and fell on the narrow bed.

Light geysered from Remus' face as the weary, hypnotic voice commanded his father. "Display my cloak and Medallion in the Guild Hall tomorrow as proof that I have returned. Tell them that I am ready to face the public trial of my story." Remus' voice slurred and his father heard the soft cadence of sleep and saw the rhythmic flash of his son's breath in the dark bedroom.

Johan quietly closed the door, hung his son's cloak on the pegs in the hallway, wondered at the preternatural effulgence of his son's voice. He stood for a moment in the hall, staring at the Medallion that throbbed on the damp, stained cloth like a salamander in the heart of a furnace.

When Johan awoke the next morning, he told Rose that their son had returned and must not be disturbed. Then he walked to the Guild Hall as soon as it opened, hung the cloak with its golden Medallion on the door in display, and with an uneasy satisfaction, announced to Simon the Guildmaster that Remus had returned bearing a story and demanded public trial.

In secret Guild Council, the dice were thrown, the lots drawn, and the time of the telling of Remus' story chosen. Although the speaking platform was immediately erected in front of the Guild Hall, it was four days before Remus was summoned to try the mettle of the story he had found.

In Johan and Rose's house in Sparrow Alley, Remus waited hungrily in his shaded bedroom for the moment when he would unleash his story. He barely deigned to speak to his parents, asked them to leave him to prepare his spirit for the ordeal. They respected his wishes, took his inclination for nervous anticipation. They did not see that it was a profound and total scorn for the simple people who through some accident had honored themselves with his birth.

Throughout the city, the Guild itself spread rumors, suppositions, and expectations for Remus' public trial. While no one in the Guild had seen Remus or talked to him, these rumors served to guarantee a large audience for Remus and to publicize the Guild. It was late fall: the harvests had been brought in. Throughout the city, the adolescent, the jaded, and the curious gathered choice selections of fruit and deliquescent vegetables to pelt Remus with, should his story fail to hold interest. Such was the fickle temper of those times.

And so it was, that at the second hour of the night watch, on a cool and bracing autumn evening, the brass trumpets of the Guild of Seers, Speakers, Dream-

ers, Storytellers, and Non-Fanatical Prophets summoned
the populace of Smunsk to judge the Quest-Tale of
Remus.

Remus commanded that the torches in the square
be extinguished, and the resinous, winy odor of their
smoke swam through the night. Remus turned from
the crowd and spoke softly to the vacancy between the
rowels of the stars: "Thanks to you, old witch, for the
gift of story and the strength of speaking." Remus
whispered Mali's name three times into the sere, chill
wind and felt his thanks spin away to feed the darkness. Angry voices rose at this unexpected delay.

Remus pushed the hood of his cloak back, turned to
the crowd, and blew a plume of dragonish fire out
over the fractious faces which stilled the murmurs of
impatience. He cast his mind out and felt the angry
strength of the mob. Though there were too many for
him to command, like a skillful wrestler Remus used
the impetuous rush of their anger to throw them into
the Story of the Dragon.

Since Mali's gift of eloquence, his mind-force had
not increased, but had grown infinitely more delicate.
Now when he rode the story as Kazan himself had
ridden Almara, Remus realized that he had only to
tell the Tale and the listeners themselves would toil
like monks to illuminate its borders. He knew (and
perhaps this was the lunar enchantment that Mali had
chained to his breath) that the most binding seduction
lay in this participation, where without thought, each
listener sketched the faces of Fiona and Kazan with
those they adored or scorned, filled the infinite details
of scene and setting with their own lives.

As he chiseled the crowd with his fancies, Remus
fed on the sobbing awe of their faces. When he was
done, and the sucking, tidal adulation began to break
on him, Remus staggered away in the darkness, dripping gobbets of light, stumbled home to his room in

Sparrow Alley and barred the door to family and sudden friends. Weakness loosened his joints, and he faced the price that all who burn with a true story pay. Exhaustion rose from the bed and engulfed him.

The crowd in the square stood clotted with amazement, stood until their voices had gone hoarse and their hands swollen with applause. At last some of the less giddy Guild members relit the torches, and all the listeners weaved home, fuzzy with the lateness of the hour and the downslope of exhilaration.

The Guild of Seers, Speakers, Dreamers, Storytellers and Non-Fanatical Prophets held the Guild Admission Celebration posthaste. In Remus' absence, all toasted Johan and Rose, and Guildmater Simon, whose protege Remus had been acknowledged. After an hour of flagons and songs, no one missed Remus. Indeed, all were more comfortable in honoring his antecedents than in actually facing the possessor of such daunting talents.

None noticed the silence of Remus' parents, who sensed that while raising a Guild-Legend, they had also witnessed the transmutation of their son into something of more than mortal stature.

Mindless of the wind's increase and the churning approach of the first winter storm, a figure that had stood at the back of the crowd vaulted onto his horse and spurred its flanks. Casio, knight of the White Eagle Couriers, galloped down the wide road to the storied walls and stalwart gates of Datal, castle of King Cinnabar the Second. Casio knew that his rank was assured if he were the first to bear to Cinnabar's ear the word of the eruption of such a storyteller. The knight also knew that the King was chary of all those capable of stirring the populace. Cinnabar was well aware of the difference in regard between those who raised taxes and those who raised spirits. Down the hard, cold road Casio raced, with the news that secured Cinnabar's gratitude, and, as all the stories tell, the final fortune of Remus the Light-Spiller, Master of the Tale of the Dragon.

Two months passed before Cinnabar invited Remus to court. The King sent out spies to watch the story-teller and attend his performances. Ostensibly, it was to assure himself of the propriety of having Remus exhibit his skill. But behind it all was the King's concern for a being whose word-power created so many instantaneous admirers. Meanwhile, as the word of his debut in Smunsk sizzled about the kingdom, Remus plotted with deliberate caution. He had already begun to receive offers from fairs, nobility, and certain religious orders, the acceptance of which would assure him mere wealth.

On the strength of his reputation (and some thought-twisting), Remus rented a beautiful estate outside of Smunsk and lived a life of such luxury as he felt would further his fame. He insulated himself from his parents and the Guild. The few times he appeared in public, Remus confirmed the noble and worthy arrogance expected of such a talent.

Remus finally accepted a commission from the Barbers, Bleeders, and Surgeons to provide the final entertainment at their annual convocation. Though it was a smaller audience than Remus might have commanded, his choice was a wise one. By the time the plump members of the audience had been washed with Remus' light and rose in a havoc of applause through the cunning cozening of his mind-bonds, Remus knew that his name would echo back to all the villages these healers served. And that each listener would celebrate Remus' tale-spinning to his patients. For the entertainments of healers are the thoughtless aspirations of the afflicted.

Remus' next appearance was for the assembled multitudes of the Fire-Fall Celebration. As the first meteors sang down in their lucent cat scratches, Remus stood on a high mound at the end of the Valley of Watchers and threw the flash and splendor of his voice out over the breath-hitched thousands who sat on the dark grass giving thanks for the falling stars. Throughout the lives of all who heard him that night, Remus' memory and the refraction of his words were bound forever to the heaven-sent wash of the Fire-Fall, that most joyful and beauteous of annual occasions, the divine shower of stars. Small matter that some were trampled in the rush of ecstatic pilgrims who surged up to touch this singer whose voice itself mirrored the prodigious sweep of the night's sidereal pageantry.

After this spectacle, a troop of cavalry rode up to Remus' estate and, with a swoop and flourish of plumes, gave the major-domo the tiny folded invitation sealed with Cinnabar's signet.

"Our Royal Master here signifies his pleasure and asks that the most illustrious Story-Wielder Remus perform for us a month hence."

From a high tower window, through a slit in the sable draperies, Remus saw the confirmation of his triumph, heard his servant's rehearsed reply.

"When my master ceases the mystic toils and communion with spirits that are daily necessary for the maintenance of his gifts, I will present him with this token of his signal honor."

The courtier bowed from his horse and gestured at the bullion wagon lumbering up to Remus' door.

"The benevolent and generous Cinnabar offers this small token of his artistic appreciation," the knight said, drawing the canvas cover from the wagon's bed.

The mound of gold coins glowed like a dragon's hoard.

Remus watched from his window as the King's emissaries clattered down the cobbled road. The heaped dower of his story-prowess glistened like the sun's blood. He stared at this reflection of his heart's fire, smiled, and began to make his plans.

*   *   *

The palomino had almost pranced by the two drab figures before Remus recognized his parents. They stood under the trees that overhung the curling ironwork of the gates to Remus' estate. The coaches of the mummers, the minstrels singing on their sturdy ponies, the ox-drawn carts with their oiled canvas shielding the folding scenery; all these had contributed to the dust that clung to Johan and Rose.

"We heard of your royal commission and came to see you off," Johan said.

His parents stood together and looked up at Remus with affection that turned his stomach. Their son knew that they might not have spoken if he had not seen them and stopped. His horse danced impatiently.

"I am off to make my fortune," Remus told them, looking into the humid air, off toward the High Court of Datal. "I will return and raise you two from the squalor of Sparrow Alley."

"Spare those who love you false promises," Rose told him. "You leave and would forget us."

"Dear mother, I pass from a feeble and benighted profession to the pantheon. I am beyond mere stories. I am past words. I am the voice made light. I . . ."

". . . have forgotten that the speaker is not greater than his story or the story greater than its teller. That we speak to move and not to control." Against his wishes, Johan had risen to anger.

"My weak-skilled father," Remus replied, his voice corroded with pity, "as I ascend from your narrow world, remember how I have dwarfed the stunted, carping tenets of your beloved Guild."

Remus drew a weighty purse from his brocaded jacket, threw it at his parents' feet with contemptuous largesse. He whipped his horse once and cantered away.

"Blasphemer," the old man spoke, choking on his

spittle. He picked up the purse and threw it with feeble violence at the vanishing horseman.

"Sweet fool," Rose told him and walked to retrieve the gold.

Remus led his caravan slowly down the long road to Datal. His ponderous retinue prevented speed. And Remus knew that it was better to let word of his coming precede him. They camped outside towns, never stayed at inns, knowing that mysteries gave greater aura than the taint of facts.

When they did proceed through villages and small cities on the way to Datal, it was at midday, so they could clog traffic and the curious hordes could marvel at the numbers of Remus' host, at the massive black wagons carved with fearsome imps and crawling symbols of a nameless zodiac. Within his own great coach fashioned like a dragon with folded wings, Remus fed on the whispered speculation and superstitious fear. As they dragged the monstrous coach with its lapis lazuli scales, the albino dromedaries spat with ungainly malevolence on all who came close. The very animals added to the imperious air of Remus' nobility with their random, violent tempers.

When he received the royal invitation, Remus had gathered to him the itinerant painters, mummers, actors, musicians, and minstrels, of whom there were the usual hungry superfluity. At his command, they had begun the majestic labors which Remus deemed necessary to stage the Tale of the Dragon before Cinnabar, his court and the populace of the royal city of Datal. For while Remus had absolute confidence in the naked power of his telling of the Story, he was succumbing to a self-importance that demanded embellishment. With his hirelings, the artisans of art, and the physical trappings of spectacle, Remus was trying to provide a gaudy frame for the vitality of his beaming speech and the stern enchantment of his story.

The witch had faded to a distant, insubstantial memory. More and more, Remus believed that the story was his and that by tricking it out in this impressive artificiality, he had tamed it. Soon, with the subtle powers of his mind-force and the hypnotic fire of his voice, Remus would move to subjugate Datal and then the remaining Five Kingdoms and the wide world beyond. And perhaps later, he could speak the sun to rise and fall.

The woesome dragon's head on Remus' coach bobbed up and down and the brazier of charcoal cast refracted flames through its garnet eyes as the sentry called to the caravan from the high walls of Datal: "Who would enter the fortress of Datal, seat and treasure of mighty Cinnabar the Second?"

From the belly of his dragon coach, Remus heard his page's reply: "We come at Royal Command to perform for his Majesty. We are Remus, Lord of Light and Master of the Tale of the Dragon, and the performers and possessions of his company."

"You are awaited and expected by our most interested King. We will lead you to your quarters in the palace."

At the captain's order, the grim brass gates swung open and Remus and his procession made their torchlit way to the opulent chambers of the East Wing of the palace. Even at this late hour, clumps of citizens stood and gawked at the passage of the fabled speaker and his fantastical equipage. Remus made a quick mindcast. Datal was ripe with his rumor and reputation. Even the dreams of the sleeping city were tinged with his name.

"We are well pleased. Pleased and greater than pleased." Cinnabar held out his hand for Remus to kiss.

Remus lightly brushed the King's knuckles with his

lips, avoiding the beetle-backed ring that held a cache of poison. "Your thanks is my greatest reward," Remus answered traditionally.

The King's family stared slack-mouthed at the story-teller. Though Remus had reined his powers in for this private presentation of the tale in the royal chambers, the low flicker of his speaking had rendered all in the small room speechless.

"Nevertheless," the king said, "I can tell from my daughter's eyes that I will have no peace until you are fitly rewarded."

The fair girl blushed in her gilt chair as her father laughed. Then from behind his long silver beard, Cinnabar drew forth a leather pouch and handed it to Remus.

"A token," the King apologized.

From mind-theft of Cinnabar, Remus knew the pouch contained a plum-sized ruby of the first water. "My most unworthy thanks," Remus replied.

"Our appreciation again for this private performance, Story-Lord. I know the anxious details of preparation you still must attend to for the public performance before all our subjects."

Remus took the cue and bowed to them again. "Your leave," he said, "to provide for the entertainment of your loving subjects."

"As you depart," Cinnabar smiled gently, "let us walk with you and exchange a few pleasantries."

With silent humility, Remus followed the King to the archway at the far end of the chamber.

"If you charm our assembled subjects in your public performance tomorrow night with the same majesty you brought to this private display, we will find a place for you at Court," the King promised, blandly stroking his beard.

Seemingly tongue-tied with joy, Remus nodded his gratitude. He had read the King's mind all evening, knew that assassins lurked behind the arras, knew that if the city of Datal was as moved as the King's family had been, the King would put him in the damp, sweat-stone depths of his stronghold and he would end his life strangled with a greased bowstring.

"I wish you could read the joy in my heart," Remus told the King.

The rivet-studded door swung to let Remus pass, and the King again gave Remus the benison of his smile.

Without thinking, Remus whistled the Guild Song of the Stalker as he made his way back to his troop. Tomorrow night he would make the crowd worship him, then blast the King with a spasm of light as he sat in his royal box. The guards would side with Remus, with some thought coercion and slight gold. Then he would marry the Princess and rule the kingdom that would be the foundation of his conquests.

Later Remus puffed wreaths of light into the dim corners of his chambers as he oversaw the painting, sawing, and hammering of his minions. Tomorrow night, he would allow the King to crown him Lord of Datal, Ruler of the First Kingdom.

The crowd gathered in the great square of Datal, a host worthy of a coronation or a royal funeral. Its size was not lost on Cinnabar, nor the perfunctory interest they displayed for one of his rare public appearances. If the storyteller lived up to his promise, it would be death for the radiance-spilling sorcerer.

Cinnabar looked on his daughter with barely controlled disgust as she joined the chants of "REEEM-UUUSS, REEEMUUUS" that rolled back and forth across the square.

Finally, as night settled on Datal like a raven's belly, minstrels stepped from the shadows of the stage and soothed the crowd with recorders, finger drums and the uncanny drone of bagpipes. Smudge pots were lit by unseen hands and smoke rolled in slow thunder-heads over the audience. Mummers rose and fell, ca-pered and sprang across the boards in eerie pantomime of souls who had lost the darkling path to salvation. And in a moment of hesitation and frozen gesture, the ropes and silent pulleys of the scene painters spread the huge dragon wings of canvas that had been folded at the sides of the stage. At staggering expense, the wings had been edged with the star-silver of the last elven chromatic dreamers, and as the starlight hit the blessed tinctures, the scales of the false dragon's wings burned with lunar, sympathetic brilliance.

In this hiatus of breath and thought, Remus stepped forward into the wavering glare of the smudge pots at the edge of the stage. He raised his arms and the false, glittering scales of elvish paint shone against the black goatskin of his costume. The crowd teetered on the brink of worship, and Remus felt Cinnabar's serpen-tine thoughts pronounce his doom. Remus tasted the diapason of brilliance welling within his throat and knew that after he had seduced the crowd with The Tale of the Dragon, Cinnabar himself would fall from power.

With his trappings, his hirelings, the orchestration of this stupefying stagecraft that forged these listeners to such malleable anticipation, Remus knew that he had finally gained control of the story that he had received months before in the glass cottage from the dying witch's lips.

So it was that Remus, in his overweening joy, did not thank Mali three times for the boon of the story.

"Once upon a time," Remus began and saw the spellbinding radiance break over the crowd and rush to the far walls of the royal square, splash, and return in a luminous seiche. Never had he such woesome power, never had the light raced in such a cataclysmic torrent.

He held the crowd in such sway that they did not

hear what drew near, until the end. Remus was taken with himself, savoring his word-mastery, the reflections and refractions he gave his glistening voice, slavering at the submission of so many hearts. So taken that he did not notice how a single great cloud sped over the night, blotted constellations dark for a moment and drew swiftly closer.

Remus looked up when he felt the buffet of wind, heard the deep, almost apologetic cough from the living darkness above him. It was not until then that his control faltered, that the light broke, and the whole crush of upturned faces saw in terror what Remus saw and not what he willed.

In huge concussive gusts, the dragon lowered herself into the glare of the smudge pots and hovered above the storyteller. No sophistry of elvish paint, stagecraft, or fable could approach the glittering, molten presence of the flying worm. And though none such beast had been seen in over four centuries, the crowd's recognition was as instinctive as its fear.

The dragon bent her head down from the darkness and if such a creature can be said to smile, she smiled. The smudge pots and torches around Remus paled in the seething glare of her one huge eye, and their weak fire played on the corded golden cables that bound shut the hollow socket of her other eye.

For one crisp moment, man and dragon shared recognition. Then with a grievous, grieving bellow, the dragon incinerated Remus, the stage, the royal box, and the immediate listeners with the virulent sear of a comet's tale.

So many in Datal had come to hear Remus that even the voracious appetite of the dragon was slaked. Some few remained cowering in basements and cisterns to flesh the deeds of the night to story. Finally the abomination threw herself into the depths of the firmament and flew with black, sure strokes back to her lair in the high cold peaks of the Dolorous Mountains, from where, centuries before, Kazan the Thief had borne her to the world and ways of men.

In the narrow house in Sparrow Alley, Rose and Johan looked up from their supper and sat with twisted mouths as the stacked coins their son had thrown them smoked and fell to cinders in the table's center.

"Our son has died," Rose stated.

"His body followed his heart," Johan amended.

They daubed their eyes as they stared at the fire's ruin.

"He finally broke faith with his story," the father wept.

"Perhaps he betrayed love," Rose hoped quietly.

For as usual in marriages, they spoke the same thought in different words.

SANCTUARY

by Kim Antieau

Kiri Marlin apparently suffered from a severe case of agoraphobia. In her case, however, her unwillingness to leave her home was not a phobia at all.

I went back to the house yesterday. At first it seemed too different. The long twisting drive was almost overgrown. The lawn was covered with weeds; Kiri's flowers had all since died. Then I looked up at the pine trees swaying in the wind and heard the gentle noise of the sea air winding through them. My chest tightened and the memories came rushing back. I wondered, as I have wondered nearly every hour of my life for five years, how I could have done what I did to Kiri.

In the summer before my last year of college, I came to the tiny coastal town of Canyons to work in my uncle's store. I accepted his offer of work because I wanted to experience smalltown life. I had spent most of my life in cities and, as a future psychologist, I thought I should learn to deal with all kinds of people. And I needed a job.

My uncle's store served as a food, drug, and feed outlet for the town. Everyone knew my uncle Bob and within the week everyone knew me. First suspicions appeared to be instantly allayed when people were told: "This is Bob's nephew Jason." For the first week it seemed my entire name was "Bobnephewjason."

Since I served as delivery person as well as stocker and cashier, I was able to see most of the town and some portions of the beach within the first week. I began to learn what home belonged to which people. Most of the houses were single-story frames, bent and crooked, as if shaped by the constant sea wind.

There was one house, however, that stood out among the others. I spotted it on a delivery run one afternoon. I stopped the car and looked up the drive. The house was built on a hill overlooking the beach and town. Tall evergreens shielded the wooden and stone two-story building from the winds. To one side of it was an enclosed greenhouse, and when I squinted, I could just make out a figure inside, bending over. Someone honked behind me, and I started up the car and left. Later I asked my uncle about it.

"That's the Marlin home. Kiri Marlin lives there."

"All by herself?"

"Yep," he answered, heaving a box of juice off the shelf and onto the dolly. I grabbed another and stacked it on top.

"Have I ever seen her in here?"

"No," he answered. "She doesn't leave her house."

"What?" I had visions of discovering a truly re-markable psychological case. I could study her, do a paper about her. I would become famous before graduating.

"I'd like to meet her," I said. "Does she see people?"

My uncle stopped bending and looked over at me. "Of course she sees people. I deliver her groceries once a week. She's just a lady who doesn't leave her house. Her parents were sort of eccentric, too."

"Actually, it isn't eccentricity. It's a condition called agoraphobia. It literally means an abnormal fear of open places. I didn't know it could run in families."

"She's not afraid of open places, Jason. She just doesn't leave her house. She used to, but she hasn't since her parents died."

"Why? How did they die?"

"They just died."

"Could I deliver the groceries next time she calls?" I asked.

He reluctantly agreed. "I'm only allowing this because you are a relative, not really an outsider. I'm trusting you not to bug her. We all like Kiri. She's part of this town and we don't want anything to happen to her."

"I'm not going to hurt her," I said. "I'm nice to old ladies."

Bob smiled. "Quit talking and get to work."

Two days later, Kiri Marlin called in her order. I helped get the requested items together and then I anxiously drove to her house. When I got out of the car, I noticed there wasn't any wind. I could hear it in the pine trees, a gentle whooshing sound I liked to listen to on nights just before a storm, but I could not feel it like I could in town—a damp wind that never seemed to stop. It was peaceful here, as if I had stepped into some kind of haven. I listened for a moment before reaching into the car for the groceries.

I rang the doorbell and a voice called for me to come in. I was mildly surprised that the door was not locked. I opened it and went inside. I expected cobwebs, darkness, perhaps a stale wedding cake or an old woman in a dingy wedding gown. Instead I was greeted by two cats, sunlight, bleached oak floors, vivid green ferns, and various hanging plants. The air was cool and fresh, as if a breeze were running through the house.

And then Kiri walked into the room, a totally different apparition from the one I had expected. She removed gardening gloves and held out her hand. I was struck dumb, but I managed to shake her hand.

"You must be Jason," she said, tucking the gloves into her jean pockets. "I'm Kiri Marlin." She smiled, and I guessed her age at around thirty. Light brown hair was pulled away from her face by two combs. Her pretty cheeks were flushed, as if she had been outside running.

She laughed. "Close your mouth, Jason. Emily Dickinson I'm not. Come on into the kitchen," she said, taking one of the bags from me.

I blushed and followed her into a large airy kitchen, where windows and plants outnumbered appliances and cupboards. One of her cats, a Siamese, leapt onto the counter and sniffed at the packages as I set them down.

"Are you enjoying your visit?" she asked as she began putting away the groceries.

"It's very different from where I come from," I answered.

"That doesn't answer my question," she said, "though I suppose it does in a way."

"Oh, I like it here, really, especially the ocean and the beaches."

"I like the ocean, too. Sunsets from here are spectacular," she said.

"You can see it from here?"

"Sure, I have quite a view," she said. "Come on, I'll show you."

She took me out of the kitchen and up a short flight of stairs into the living room. All of the west wall was made of glass. We were above the trees and had a panoramic view of the ocean. Today the water was dark green, flecked with white. A flock of birds flew over one of the shore rocks.

"It's nice, isn't it?" she said, smiling.

I nodded and turned from the window. I suddenly felt guilty for my earlier desire to examine her like some kind of specimen.

"Do you like games?" I asked, noticing several boxes on her bookshelves: a backgammon game, a go set, Scrabble.

"Yes, I guess I do."

"I've always wanted to learn go. Could you teach me?"

She turned and looked into my eyes for several seconds, as if she were trying to look deeper, to see into my soul.

"Sure, I'll teach you," she said. "You bring the pizza and be here at eight."

Kiri was a good and gentle teacher, but when I did something totally wrong, she reprimanded me, telling me I had not been listening. After nearly an hour in her company, I forgot she had this little quirk: she did not leave her house. We played and ate in the living room so we could watch the sun go down. As the evening passed, she asked me about school and my life, and I told her. She teased me when I told stories about parties I had attended in college.

"I don't want to hear about that," she said. "I want to know what you've learned. Not just at school, but in your lifetime."

"I'm not sure what I've learned," I said, "except how little I truly know." I was surprised at the things I could tell her—feelings and ideas I wasn't even aware of until I said them to her.

The cats each chose a lap and curled up to sleep.

"I've had Harlow, the Siamese, since my mother died," she said. She leaned against the couch and stroked the cat.

"When was that?" I asked.

"About eight years ago," she answered. "She's getting to be an old cat. I got Tori three years ago."

"How did your mother die?" I asked.

"Just like most people die," she answered. "She stopped living."

I remembered that my uncle hadn't told me how her parents had died, and I wondered what the big mystery was. I didn't pursue it, however, and the conversation moved away from her mother. We discussed books we had each read. I will remember that first evening always. Sometimes, now, I wish I could forget, or at least distort it so I don't remember how beautiful it was. That night, as always with Kiri, I was relaxed. There was no flirtation, no awkwardness between us. I just truly enjoyed the company of another person. The house creaked, the pines moved with the wind, and Kiri and I talked into the night.

Finally, when night was edging toward morning, I told Kiri I should leave. We cleaned the living room and then she walked me to the door. I hesitated, not wanting to go.

"May I come again?" I asked.

She looked into my eyes.

"You must know one thing, Jason," she said. "I do not leave this house. You must promise not to try to change that."

"I promise," I said, without thinking. She smiled. I would have promised anything that night just so I could see her again.

For the next week, I went over to Kiri's every night. Sometimes there were other people there, friends of hers. Some of them were people I had met in town or had seen roaming the beaches. They were nice, but I resented their presence. I wanted Kiri all to myself. She seemed to enjoy our time alone, too, showing me how she managed without leaving the house.

She was obviously proud of her greenhouse. It was filled with flowers and vegetables. I had never seen flowers so colorful or vegetables so lush, yet she used no fertilizers or other chemicals.

"Just my hands," she said.

I was not much of a gardener, but since Kiri enjoyed spending time in the greenhouse, I asked her to teach me how to be useful.

"I think teaching you to be useful would be a full-time job," she said, grinning.

I grabbed her. "I'll get you for that," I said. "I'll yell at your plants and give them neuroses."

She laughed, and I realized she was in my arms. My stomach seemed to twist inside itself. It still does when I think of that moment. I had never felt anything so wonderful—until I leaned over and kissed her. She put her arms around me, and we embraced.

She whispered my name and kissed me again.

"We're all dirty from the garden," she said. "I think we need a shower." She took my hand and we went upstairs.

I had never fallen so quickly and so much in love. We never ran out of things to say, yet often we just lay quietly in each other's arms, listening to the wind through the pines. One evening, we fell asleep on the couch together. I awakened to darkness; Kiri was gone. When my eyes adjusted to the dark, I could see Kiri by the window. I went and stood behind her. The moon was out, shining down on the beach and ocean. Two people walked along the tide mark. I put my arms around Kiri's waist.

"Do you wish you were down there?" I whispered.

"Good God, no," she answered, stiffening in my arms. "If all around you were flames and you were in the only safe spot, would you want to go into the flames?"

"Is that what it's like for you?" I asked. "Is it that frightening?"

"It is not so much frightening as . . ." She turned to me, searching for the right words. "As certain. I will die if I leave this house."

"But you will die inside this house someday, too," I said. "Think of all the things we could do together, places we could see before we die."

She covered my mouth with her hand. "Sssssh. You promised. You must accept me the way I am."

"Won't you even consider going for help?"

"Help? I don't need help, Jason." She pulled away from me.

I took her hand. "Can't you see it's not normal to be locked up in this house?"

She laughed, making it an almost unnatural sound. "Of course it's not normal. But it isn't just my psyche that's in danger, Jason. It's all of me." She sighed. "I've been out, and I'm nothing out there—insubstantial. Here, I'm something. I have control. Some people never find their niche in the world, I have. My parents tried to live outside this house. They failed. This is our spot. This is where I belong. I've accepted that. There is comfort in knowing where you belong, Jason."

"Kiri, I can help you if you let me," I said, as I took her face in my hands. "There is nothing outside this house that can't hurt you inside this house, too."

She stared at me, an unwavering look that made me think she was looking clear to my core. I dropped my hands.

"You can't understand," she said, "but you must accept that this is my place on earth. End of discussion."

The conversation ended, but I continued to think about it. I needed to finish college. I couldn't do that in Canyons, but I didn't want to leave Kiri. I had always imagined myself traveling one day. I couldn't do that with Kiri, and I didn't want to go without her. I was so blind; if only I had realized how many places we saw together in her own home.

I was determined to cure her. I went to the library and found out what I could about agoraphobia. There wasn't much. They described physical reactions: perspiration, accelerated heartbeat, severe anxiety attacks.

Therapists suggested gradually curing patients by taking them on small excursions outside the home.

One night I began looking through my uncle's library, hoping to find something to help me.

"Whatcha looking for, son?" Uncle Bob asked as he stood in the doorway.

"Psychology books."

He laughed. "Nothing but Zane Grey and Janet Dailey in this house," he said.

I smiled. I had never known anyone as well read as my uncle. The house was packed with books. Bob came into the room and sat down.

"Let it be, Jason. What does it matter?"

"I want to do things with her," I said. "It hurts me to see her holed up in that house all the time."

"Why? Is she unhappy?"

"She says she isn't. But how could she be happy? It must feel like a prison."

"Or a sanctuary," he said. He leaned back in his chair. "She knows what's best for her, Jason. Her folks have been in this town, in that house, for generations. Made their fortune in the stock market, I believe. Before they died, Kiri's parents were important people in town." He squinted. "You know, I can hardly remember them anymore. It hasn't been that long since they died."

"How did they die?"

"Mr. Marlin was in a car accident," he said. "There were rumors he died before the car actually crashed into the ocean. There wasn't much left of him when they pulled the car out. It was the first time in decades he'd left the house. No one knew why he left. Some said Kiri's mother talked him into it." He shrugged. "Maybe it was a nice day and he wanted to go for a ride. Soon after his death, Kiri's mother walked into the ocean and drowned."

"So you think Kiri's fear comes from what happened to her parents when they left the house?"

"You aren't listening," he said. "Maybe she's got reasons to fear."

I shook my head. "There must be a way to help her, to free her from this fear. There must be."

Bob stood and stretched. "She doesn't have a problem with it, Jason. You do." He started to say something else, but instead, he left the room. I sat on the floor, wondering what to do next.

For weeks I worried about the end of the summer and the rest of our lives. Then suddenly I had the answer and I was elated—and afraid. Kiri never suspected what I was going to do—at least I thought so at the time. I chose a day that was particularly cool and breezy. The air moved nicely through the house, filling it with the smells of the outdoors. Clouds covered the sun, taking the summer brightness away. Kiri and I worked in the greenhouse. I helped her take flowers and put them in the wheelbarrow. Later I was going to plant them outside, around the living room windows.

"I get enough sunlight from the windows, but sometimes I think my flowers need to be outside," she said. Harlow bounded into the room like a kitten and jumped onto my shoulders. Tori pawed at my leg and meowed.

"They're hussies, aren't they?"

"Just like you," I said. I reached over and kissed her nose.

"How did you get off work today?" she asked.

"I asked for it off."

"That was clever," she said, laughing. Then she scowled when I tugged too hard on a root and it broke. "Patience, Jas. In any case, I'm glad you're here. I love these kinds of days." She whirled around. "I can't believe how happy I am!"

I caught her in mid-turn. The cat jumped away from me. "Happy! Well, I've got something that will make you even happier. Close your eyes."

"What?" She closed her eyes. "A surprise?"

"Yes." I tied a kerchief around her eyes and across her ears. Then I twirled her around a few times. I led her around the house, going up and down stairs, trying to disorient her. We both laughed. My heart began pounding too hard. I broke out in a sweat. I hoped I was doing the right thing, but I was afraid she would be angry with me. I stopped her for a moment and kissed her. She lifted her head up, blind, and grinned.

"I love you very much," I told her, suddenly frightened of what I was doing.

"I love you, too," she said. "Now take me to my surprise."

I twirled her one more time, led her in and out of two more rooms, and then I took her through the open front door. I talked and laughed so she wouldn't notice the change. I had even put some old boards on the sidewalk, hoping they would feel like her living room floor. I stopped her just out of the shadow of the house, about ten steps from the door.

"Jason, where am I? Can I see now?"

I slowly untied the kerchief. "See, you're safe," I said.

I will never forget the look on her face as she turned to me. It still troubles me at night: I open my eyes from a nightmare and I will see her face, inches from my own. Her eyes were opened wide in terror—and disappointment. I had betrayed her.

"You promised," she whispered.

Suddenly, it seemed that the sky was black. Or was it? I couldn't breathe or move. Perspiration rolled down my back. I became overwhelmed with anxiety. I was dizzy. I covered my eyes, trying to still the twirling world. What was happening to me? I reached for Kiri, but my arms flayed air.

Seconds later, I opened my eyes. The dizziness subsided. I looked around. It was a gorgeous summer day. The cats stood in the doorway watching me. A breeze moved through the pine trees.

And Kiri was gone.

I ran toward the house, calling her name. Inside, I wandered about almost blindly, bumping into doors and walls: I knew when I found her she would not ever want to see me again.

But I didn't find her. She wasn't in the house. I looked around the yard, too, but there was nothing.

And then I went to the greenhouse and found something near the windows. I'm not certain what—it looked as if some living thing had suddenly become unglued and melted into the ground, leaving behind its shadow like a kind of marker. I closed my eyes and quickly backed away.

They never found Kiri. For a time I was suspected of murdering her. The more I went over the events in my mind, the more I believed that to be true, but when I confessed, they didn't believe me.

Soon after, Kiri's recently made will was read. She declared that her substantial fortune and the house be left to me if she was not seen in the house for thirty days. When my uncle told me, I cried out, calling for someone to take away the pain. I realized then she had known all along I would not keep my promise.

The house stood empty until my return yesterday. The cats had fled long ago. I stood at the door trembling. I turned the handle. It was unlocked, as it had always been. I wanted to be sick as I opened the door. It all came rushing back, every second of the happiness we had shared in this house. And then I stepped inside. This time I found the cobwebs and darkness I had expected that first day. The house smelled of decay. I breathed the damp air deeply. I had done this. I was the cause. I looked around. The house was empty, as if Kiri had never existed.

I started to back away, to run out of the house, but something made me hesitate. Perhaps I could fix it up, make it alive again. I had traveled for five years, running toward anything that could make the memories go away even for a little while. Now I was weary of it. This was my home, my place in the world. I looked outside once more, and then I closed the door and shut away the light.

THE UNCORKING OF UNCLE FINN

by Jane Yolen

According to legend churchmen and supernatural creatures have been engaged in conflicts for centuries. What is unusual about the following tale, which takes place in an Irish abbey, is the nature of the "war." The protagonists are its blasphemous Abbot and an extremely devout elf.

Uncle Finn had angered the Abbot. It had something to do with blasphemy—the Abbot's, not Uncle Finn's. Uncle had been converted several centuries before by the Irish saint Patrick and was deeply religious still, given to falling on his knees in the unlikeliest of places: rookeries, backstairs, tidal pools, butter churns. The Abbot, on the other hand, was a pagan and a drunk besides. It was inevitable that the two should clash over matters of faith.

Now I grant you that it is unnerving for the locals to have a fanatically Christianized elf forever exhorting them to eschew evil and seek the good, popping up unexpectedly in their most secret places of vice. He knew where every still was working, every mistress kept, every bit of falsified paper stored. He had a nose for venialness. But as he had been proselytizing for more than three centuries in his own curious way, one would have thought the humans would have grown used to it. And indeed, those who could stand it the least had long since left, moving to Killarney or Glocamorra or catching a ride with itinerant saints, sailing westward over the treacherous seas in coracles made of glass. There were some just that desperate to escape Uncle Finn's exhortations.

The Abbot, however, was newly appointed, being a sinner of great reknown on the Continent. It was thought by the bishop that a year or two in Kilkenny under the watchful eye of Uncle Finn would wear him down. It was the bishop's own version of a finishing school, and he was prepared to finish the Abbot or kill him in the process.

The war had begun as soon as the Abbot had set foot in the cellar, that being Uncle Finn's province. He was partial to dark places; his maternal great-grandmother had once lived with a troll, and Finn took after that side.

The Abbot's first trip to the cellar was without warning. He had disconnected the bell that rang over the cellarer's head, a precaution even his most fervid detractors had applauded. That way, of course, no one could count the number of times he visited belowstairs. Kilkenny Abbey was well known not only for its wines and a surprisingly good claret, but also for its hardier brews: kümmel made with an imported caraway seed, a plum drink concocted with the help of a recipe lent by the Slovakian saint Slivos, and a wild blackthorn gin that had been said to rock even the toughest of European soldiery.

To say that Uncle Finn was surprised by the Abbot is an understatement. He was astonished out of three Hail Marys. They bled from his lips and lost him the conversion of three recalcitrant mice and a reprobate rat.

One must also imagine the Abbot's astonishment, for no one had warned him about Uncle Finn. He had come tripping down the stairs, ready for further lubrication, and suddenly there was this wee attenuated creature garbed in green on knobby knees before a congregation of reluctant rodents. Is it any wonder the Abbot cried out and held his head? Or that Uncle Finn reciprocated with the bloody Hail Marys and an elvish curse that shattered three bottles of the best claret that the Abbot had hoped to save for after midnight Mass?

The Abbot fired the second shot of the war, a letter to the pope requesting excommunication for all faerie folk on the grounds that everyone knew they had no souls. But the pope refused the request, for he himself had once held similar views when he was but a seminarian. And then he had pronounced that his walking stick would sooner grow blossoms than a certain nixie of the local pond might enter heaven. He had not known she was a convert, one of the magdalens brought round by a recent crusade. No sooner had the words been out of his mouth, than his staff had sprouted a feathering of ferns and spatulate leaves and begun to bud. So the pope was not about to deny the possibility of souls to any of the Good Folk. In effect, he left the matter entirely in the bishop's hands.

This so displeased the Abbot, he turned his displeasure into a monumental drunk using the scaramental wine, a drunk that ended only when he awoke in his cell the Sunday before Lent to see Uncle Finn perched on his bedfoot, hands upraised, the spirit of the Lord and all the Irish saints moving in his mouth.

"Arise," cried Uncle Finn, "and go forth."

The Abbot arose, and his sandal went forth and smacked Uncle Finn right between the eyes while all the while the Abbot praised the Lord.

Now a sandal and Uncle Finn are about the same size, so there was more damage than either the Abbot or the Good Lord intended. So the Abbot was, indeed, forced to arise and scoop up Uncle Finn's body from the stone floor. He brought Uncle Finn, wrapped in a linen handkerchief, to the infirmarer, a certain Brother Elias.

"What can you do with this thing?" asked the Abbot. However, as he was holding Uncle Finn wrapped in the handkerchief in his left hand and his right was holding his own head (and it still ringing from the three days of steady drinking), it was no wonder Brother Elias' answer was confusing.

"If you'd stop bending your elbow, my lord Abbot," said the old monk, "your head would be marvelously improved. It's a wonder of anatomy, it is, that head and elbow are so connected." The infirmarer, being a reformed tippler himself, had plenty more salvos where that one came from. He had given up drink and taken up religion with the same fervor.

"Not my elbow and not my head, you Kilkenny clodpate! This!" The Abbot held out his left hand, where, in the linen, Uncle Finn was just coming to.

"Saints in heaven, but it's Finn," cried Elias, making the sign of the cross hastily and missing a fourth of it.

"That's not fine at all," said the Abbot, who had no tolerance for any accents save his own.

"Not fine. Finn," explained the infirmarer, but since he pronounced them the same, it led to a few more moments of misunderstanding until he reached over and gently removed Uncle Finn from his winding sheet. "You had better be asking his pardon, my lord. He's a Christian now for sure, which means he will turn the other cheek as often as not. But he's still quite a hand at elvish curses when he's riled. Better not to be on his bad side."

"He's already on *my* bad side," roared the Abbot, remembering with renewed fury the three bottles of claret. "Fix him up, tidy him up, and shut him up. Then report to me. The minute he can handle a good strong talking-to, I want to know."

But Finn was already beginning to sit up, and reaching his wee hands up to his wee head. What was not clear to the two monks was that Finn, while awake, was not aware. The sandal had quite addled him. His magic was turned around and about widdershins. He began to moan and speak in tongues.

"Oh, for Our Lord's sake," cried the Abbot with great feeling, his own head twanging like a tuning fork by the tone of those tongues.

The supplication to Our Lord brought Uncle Finn's eyes wide open, and he began to sing hosannas.

"I wish he'd put a cork in it!" cried the Abbot, his hands to his ears.

At the word *wish*, Finn's eyes got a strange glow in them, and everything not human in the room began to stir about as if caught up in a twisting wind. Faster and faster anything not pinned down began to move: glasses and retorts; bunches of drying patience, pepperwort, and clary; mortars and pestles; long lines of linen bandages; copies of *Popular Errors in Physick*, Mithradates' receipt for *Venice Treacle*, and Drayton's *Hermit*. All the while, Uncle Finn kept chanting:

> *Pickles and peas, knife and fork,*
> *Find a bottle, carve a cork,*
> *Wind it up and in the wine*
> *A sailor's life is mighty fine.*

Which, of course, is a terribly mixed-up version of the old bottle spell used mostly by drunken mages to call up spirits.

Sea winds began to blow, spouts of whales were sighted, dolphin clicks heard, and with one last incredible *whoooosh*, the whole of the whirling stuff was sucked in through the neck of a nearby bottle of Bordeaux '79 that Elias used for medicinal purposes only, it being too sour and full of sediment for a tippler of taste. The displaced wine splattered all over the infirmary, and the room smelled like a pothouse for a week.

Then, with a final *thwap*, the cork replaced itself. The stirring continued inside the bottle for fully a minute more, and when the wind and mist and moisture had resolved itself, there appeared inside the light green bottle a passable imitation of a sailing ship, with a pestle for a mainmast and linen bandages for sails. Clinging to the mortar steering wheel was Uncle Finn, looking both puzzled and pleased. He gave a weak smile in the direction of the cork, put his hand on his head, and slid down in a faint onto the papier-mâché deck on which the ingredients for *Venice Treacle* could still be discerned.

"Oh, my Lord," said the infirmarer, not really sure if he meant the salutation to have a capital *L* or a small one.

But the Abbot, taking it was himself addressed, said softly, "And *that* should do it."

For a week he was right, for the abbey was quiet and filled with plain-song laced only with the Abbot's own version of an old capstan chantey sung fully half note off-tune.

But the communications of the Fey, while sometimes slow, are sure. The rodent proselytes told their families, one of whose members was overheard by a wandering and early June bug. The June bug's connections included a will-o'-the-wisp who had married into Uncle Finn's family. It was scarcely a week later that word of Uncle Finn's incarceration came to my father's ears.

By the time he had sorted through his meager store of magicks and translated himself to the far side of the island, using a map in one of his books that was sadly too many years ahead of its time, twelve boggles, banshees, nuggles, and a ghost (all relatives) had been

to visit before him. The abbey had, in that short
week's time, gotten itself a reputation for being
haunted—as indeed it was, in a manner of speaking—
and the humans had summarily deserted the abbey
grounds until the proper exorcists might be found.

None of this, of course, helped poor Uncle Finn. No
one but a human could pull the cork from the Bordeaux bottle, for it had been placed there by a human
wish. And as long as the visits continued, no human
would venture near the place.

My father sighed and stared at his brother, whom he
remembered fondly as an elf of high promise and a
great sense of humor. Uncle Finn looked little like the
memory, being sadly faded and a bit green, a property
not only of the tinted glass but of his initial handling,
seasickness, and a week corked up in a bottle that still
reeked of wine.

Father shouted at him and Finn shouted back, but
their voices were strained through the layers of green
glass. Conversation was impossible. At last Father came
home, whey-faced and desperate-looking. In fact, all
the relatives had left, for there was nothing any of
them could do except sigh. As the last of them departed, the priestly exorcists arrived. Humans have
this marvelous ability to time their exits and entrances,
which is why they—and not the Fey—hold theatrical
events. They spoke their magic words and threw about
a great deal of incense and believed it was their own
efforts that rid the abbey of the Fey. But like a plumber
who gets paid after a sink has fixed itself, they were
praised for nothing. Visiting Fey never overstay their
welcome nor hang about when nothing can be done. It
is simply not in our nature.

The Abbot had, of course, sworn Elias to secrecy
concerning Uncle Finn and the bottle, and the two of
them had replaced the Bordeaux '79 on the wine
cellar racks without the cellarer's knowledge. But Elias,
after a week in a room smelling strongly of tipple,

returned to his old ways, and after that his vow of secrecy mattered little, for no one would have believed a word he had to say. As for the Abbot, after a year of the most flagrant misrule, he was sent by the pope on a crusade against the infidels from which he did not return, though there were frequent rumors that he had become a sheikh in a distant emirate and had banned all peris and jinn from his borders.

That left Uncle Finn corked up in his bottle on a back shelf in a cellar of a once-haunted Abbey, marked as a wine so degraded and unpopular that it would never be taken by any knowledgeable person from the shelf. And we were afraid he would remain so forever.

But one day, as I sat reading in my father's library, which is well stocked with books of the past, present, and future, I came upon a volume in section A. A for Archaeology, Astronomy, Ancestry, and Aphorisms. It was a splendid piece of serendipity, for the book told about the Americas, where, in some distant year, a man rich in coins but lacking in wisdom would take Kilkenny Abbey stone by stone over the great waters, a feat even a Merlin might envy. And—as one of the Aphorists wrote in another volume in that section, since Americans would have no wine before its time, surely the magical words "Bordeaux '79" will reek of such time. Uncle Finn, oh Uncle Finn, you will have before you an entire continent to convert, and proselytes beyond counting, for a land that saves its saviors in plaster and seeds the heavens with saucers should have no trouble at all accepting a bottle saint.

A PLACE TO STAY FOR A LITTLE WHILE

by Jim Aikin

It was a very unusual household among whose members were a man who patched holes in the world, a shapechanger, and even a talking radio. It was also a very peaceful domicile until a man who had the ability to control minds became a resident.

"I can't cope," Cynthia Lutz said to the radio. "I simply cannot cope."

"Oh, come on," the radio said. It was a wooden table model that dated from about 1933. "Things aren't that bad. Things have been this bad before."

"When?" Cynthia snapped.

"Well, they must have been, some time or other," the radio said evasively. "How would I know? My memory isn't worth a damn. What do you expect from vacuum tubes?"

"I've never been turned down for welfare before, that's for sure." Cynthia pushed long loose gray-streaked hair away from her bony face and paced up and down in the kitchen, sandals slapping on the worn linoleum. Her toes were calloused and her jeans were frayed. "They told me I make too much money. Too damn

188

much money selling candles, do you believe that? And I can't explain to them that I've got five dependents, or this place will be crawling with social workers, and you know what'll happen then. They'll lock Mrs. Simpston up and send Debby to a foster home and deport Mr. Alvarado, and probably put Toby in a hospital and arrest me for sanitary violations or something. So how am I supposed to feed this menagerie?"

"Fortunately, I require no sustenance," the radio said smugly.

Cynthia narrowed her eyes at the faded grille cloth. "Oh, yeah? What if I can't pay the electric bill?"

"I'm sure it won't come to that," the radio said uneasily. "You'll think of something."

"Your faith is touching." Above a teetering pile of dishes in the sink, an open window let in afternoon breeze through a green tangle of vines. The radio was sitting squarely on the big table against the opposite wall. Cynthia eyed the dishes with distaste, and transferred her attention to the refrigerator. She had left an apple in there. . . .

"There is one other thing," the radio reported.

"What?" She squinted at the naked white interior of the refrigerator. Peanut butter. Not quite half a jar.

"Somebody new. He'll be here soon."

"How soon? And what's his problem?"

"That's all the information I'm getting. Sorry."

"You're a big help. As usual."

"I do the best I can. I'm only a radio."

II

The street was quiet and shady. Here and there tree roots had buckled the sidewalk. He was walking aimlessly, content to let his feet lead the way, whistling soundlessly between his teeth and wondering what it would be like to live in one of these big old houses year after year instead of knocking around on the road. His name was Steven Raleigh, and it had been four months since he had last used his terrible power.

At the attic window of one house he saw a pale shape that moved and was gone, leaving a curtain swaying. He stopped and looked up at the window, shifting the duffel bag on his shoulder, but the shape failed to reappear. The house was a little more decrepit than its neighbors; the paint was badly peeled, and nobody had swept the dead leaves off the porch roof, and long spears of grass had grown up around the bone-dry birdbath. It looked like the kind of place where they could use some odd jobs done. On impulse, he stepped long-legged over the low picket fence and climbed the creaking steps to the porch.

He started slightly when he saw the old man sitting in deep shade on the porch swing. The old man stared straight ahead, not noticing Steven at all. He was a small, frail-looking old man wearing a threadbare but immaculate three-piece suit and a cream-colored hat that had been very fashionable forty years before.

"Excuse me," Steven said.

The leather face turned slowly toward him. "You wish to speak to Cynthia," the old man said in the meticulous accent of a Mexican whose English is very good. "She is inside." His hand twitched on his thigh, a gesture much too small to be called a jerk of the thumb, and his face rotated slowly away again.

Steven rapped on the glass pane in the door, and when nobody came he turned the knob and stepped inside. The hallway smelled of dust and cooking and scented candle wax. "Anybody home?" he called.

Cynthia Lutz set down her peanut butter sandwich and headed for the hall. She saw a slim, well-knit young man with a badly trimmed crop of fine blond hair, an expressionless mouth, and wary, haunted eyes. He was wearing boots, jeans, and a work shirt. He thumped the duffel bag to the floor and looked at her uncertainly. "Let me guess," she said, setting her hands on her hips. "You turn into a penguin."

"You shouldn't make jokes with me," he told her.

"Oh. I'm sorry. Why not?"

"Never mind. It's not important. I thought maybe you had some odd jobs you needed done."

She put back her head and laughed. "Is that what you thought? There's plenty of work to be done, all right, but I haven't got a cent to pay you. Not a cent. Would you like something to eat? Anything you like, as long as it's peanut butter. I could make you a peanut butter sandwich."

When he had washed down some sandwich with a swig of the strawberry Kool-Aid she found gathering dust on a top shelf, he said, "Why feed me? You don't know me."

"I take in strays." She was sitting across from him, admiring his healthy appetite. "What did you mean when you said I shouldn't make jokes?"

"Did I say that? I didn't mean anything." He ran his finger through a ring of the Kool-Aid, smearing it across the table.

"I think you meant something."

"Just that it might not be safe. When I get mad, I do things, sometimes. But don't worry," he added, holding up a palm, "you're safe. I won't do anything. I promise."

She chewed on her lip. "What kind of things do you do that aren't safe?"

"It's hard to explain. It doesn't matter."

"It does matter. You think I won't believe you, if you tell me. You think nobody could possibly believe you."

He gave her a smoldering look from under his eyebrows. "You'd believe me all right, if I showed you. But I don't dare." He took a big bite of sandwich and chewed purposefully.

"Why do you think you came here?" she asked conversationally.

"I told you. Looking for odd jobs."

"Stopping at all the houses? Or did you just come straight here and walk in the front door?" Outside the window a hummingbird was nuzzling among the vines. She watched until it darted away.

"I didn't stop at every house, no."

"Something about this house in particular attracted you. Shall I tell you what it was?"

He shrugged. "You're talking."

"It was me. I attract people. But not just anybody. People who have strange gifts. People to whom things happen, things that can't be explained. If you weren't one of those people, you wouldn't be here."

"I don't know what you're talking about."

She took a sip, without asking, of his Kool-Aid. "You saw that old man on your way in?"

"Sitting on the porch staring off into space."

"That's Mr. Alvarado. He's resting. Would you like to know why he's resting?"

"I guess so."

"Mr. Alvarado patches up the holes in the world. It's hard work. In between times, when there aren't any holes that need patching, he stays here. When a hole opens up, he senses it somehow, and he has to go off and patch it. He's never been able to explain very well *how* he patches holes, but he did tell me once that he's one of two or three hole-patchers left in the world. Maybe the only one left, by now. When they're gone, the world is going to come apart. He couldn't explain that very well either, but I have a feeling it may be serious. Anyhow, he takes it seriously. That's why he's resting. It's hard work patching holes, and he's eighty-three years old."

Steven made motions with his mouth, as though rolling the idea around on his tongue, or possibly cleaning peanut butter off his teeth. "You're kidding," he stated.

"I'm not kidding. I hope he's wrong about the end of the world, but I believe he does what he says he does. He's not the strangest person here."

"You're putting me on. That's crazy."

"Any crazier than the situation you're in?"

"I don't want to talk about that."

"Suit yourself." Cynthia shrugged. "You belong here. That much is obvious. We've got an empty room you're welcome to. All it's got is a mattress. Nobody will steal your stuff. The house rules are simple." She ticked them off on her fingers. "Don't pay any attention to anything Mrs. Simpston says; you won't be able to understand one word in three. Under no circumstances go into the attic—the person living in the attic does not like visitors."

He remembered the vague shape at the window.

"If you hear loud noises or see flashing lights, ignore them. Likewise for people walking through walls or floating around a foot off the floor. Don't annoy Mr. Alvarado. And as of this afternoon, if you want to get fed, go out and hustle yourself some grub. The hostess is flat broke."

After looking at her for a minute with his hands half-curled in front of him on the table like an exhausted boxer, he stood up. "I've gotta think about this. Can you show me where the room is?"

III

The mattress was thick and soft, and the blanket that went with it smelled of wood smoke. Steven Raleigh had walked a long ways. In a few seconds he was asleep.

An hour later he woke to a presence in the room—gentle breathing, the rustle of a garment. He lifted his head. The intruder's eyes met Steven's for a startled moment, then dropped to the floor. The longish untidy hair and pale hollow-cheeked face could have belonged to either a man or a woman. The contours of the body were concealed in a shapeless bathrobe.

"Oh, I'm sorry. I didn't mean to wake you." The voice was a husky contralto. "Cynthia said we had somebody new, and I wanted a look, that's all. I'd better go."

"No, don't." Steven raised himself on an elbow. "Stay a minute."

"I can't. Cynthia won't like it." But the figure lingered.

"Do you live here?"

"I live in the attic. But you won't see me. I don't come down much."

"What's your name?"

"I don't know. I kind of like 'Toby.' Mostly that's what they call me."

Toby's head cocked sideways, asking a silent question, and Steven remembered the posture. Her name had been Laurel, and she had looked at him just that way, standing in the darkened living room of her parents' house, that first night when she invited him into her bedroom. Laurel's voice echoed across the years: "Listen—do you want to make it, or what?" He hadn't thought of her for a long time, and the memory flooded in with an unexpected ache. There had been lots of other women since. It was easy; it didn't matter whether they wanted to or not. But with Laurel it had meant something, because that was before the power came to him.

"Are you all right?" Toby asked.

"Fine. I was thinking. You remind me of somebody I knew a long time ago."

Fear flashed in Toby's eyes. "Oh, no, it's starting already. I really do have to go. I can't afford to stay around you any longer."

"Why not? I won't hurt you."

"It's not you, it's me. Whenever I'm around some-body, I change. I can't help it. I'm sorry. I have to go. Good-bye." The figure slipped out the door.

Steven sat up and rubbed his neck. "I change," Toby had said. What the hell did that mean? Still, the woman was right—the inhabitants of this house were strange. He pulled on his boots and clomped down the stairs. There wasn't much furniture, and what there was had seen better days. The stained glass above the window seat had a forlorn look of lost elegance. On the sag-ging couch a large brown dog was asleep. As he went by, it lifted its head and blinked amiably at him.

Entering the dining room, he thought it was empty, but a voice halted him. An old woman said, "Twenty of them. My, my. How nice for you." She was sitting on a straight chair against the wall, a little round woman with wispy white hair and twinkling, if some-what rheumy, eyes, and she was smiling and nodding at a point up near where the chandelier would have been, if there had been a chandelier.

"Hello," Steven said.

"Oh. Oh, goodness, you frightened me. Orlanoi was just showing me the flaming chariots of the East-ern Kingdom. What a spectacular sight! I do declare!"

"You must be Mrs. Simpson."

"Simpston. With a 't.' And who might you be?"

"My name's Steven Raleigh. I just got here." He leaned forward and spoke loudly and distinctly to her, a courtesy to which she did not seem averse.

"Oh, that explains it." She smiled and nodded.

"Explains what?"

"The purple and silver robes, of course. You've been traveling."

He looked at his shoulders. Nobody had come up and draped purple and silver robes around him. "Have you seen Cynthia?" he asked.

"I believe she's at the palace."

Steven considered this. "Oh." He went on into the kitchen.

Cynthia was at the sink, her sleeves rolled up, steam roiling thinly around her. "I met Mrs. Simpston-with-a-tee," Steven said. "And Toby."

"Toby."

"Toby came to my room."

"Toby's not supposed to do that," she said, pressing her lips together.

He sat down at the table. "What was that you said before about us having to find our own food?"

Scrubbing a saucer savagely, Cynthia said, "And when she got there, the cupboard was bare. You heard right. We're going to have a meeting in a little while, as soon as I get things cleaned up, to talk about it. Want to come?"

"Yeah. I'd like to meet everybody."

"If they're here, you'll meet them. Sometimes I can't find Frank."

"Frank?"

"Frank Reeves. He has a tendency to fade."

"He's the one who walks through walls," Steven said, making the connection.

"Right. It's an effort for him to become visible. About three times a week I go up to his room and bang on a garbage can lid and yell at him until he condescends to condense, or whatever it is he does. I'm afraid if I don't do it, he'll evaporate completely."

"Must be tough." Steven sat and stared at a tattered poster on the wall. Under a green spray of marijuana was the legend, *Let A Thousand Parks Bloom*. "You don't expect me to believe any of this," he said.

"Believe what you like. Or better still, talk to the radio. That might do the trick."

"The radio." He saw it for the first time.

"I can't offer him any proof," the radio said. "Why should he listen to me?"

"Don't worry about that," Cynthia counseled. "Just talk to the nice man."

"What should I say?"

"Hey," Steven said. "This thing's *talking*."

"Mm-hmmm," Cynthia said agreeably, turning back to her dishes. "Are you beginning to feel less alone?"

Steven stared at the radio, breathing through his mouth. "You've got wires hooked up somewhere," he declared. He craned his neck to look under the table, stretched out an arm to pull the plug and examine it, and after replacing the plug straightened up and lifted the radio in both hands to look at the tabletop under it.

"Hey, don't do that!" the radio protested. "Put me down! Some of my components are *very* fragile."

He glared at the radio, then set it down gently. "That doesn't prove anything. You could have a transmitter hooked up inside of it, and a receiver in another room."

"Just to fool you?" Cynthia asked sarcastically. "Come on."

"Okay. Okay. You've got a radio that talks. You've got a guy that fixes holes, and a guy that walks through walls. What else have you got?"

Wiping her hands on her apron, she turned. "No. You first."

"Well, at least tell me what it is about *you*. You read minds, or you're a thousand years old, or something, right? What is it?"

"Nothing that exciting. As far as I can tell, I'm depressingly normal—except that I attract people who aren't. Nobody has walked into this house uninvited in a long time who wasn't some kind of a case. That's how I knew about you. So tell. What is it?"

He swallowed with an effort. "I control people."

A cold lump congealed at her stomach, and her scalp prickled. She looked at him silently, measuring him. This one could be dangerous.

"I don't do it very often. I try not to."

"Why try not to?"

"I start to like it. It feels good. Like a drug."

"So you try not to."

"It's been four months."

"When you say you control people, what do you mean?"

"I control them, that's all. I give them orders, in my head, in a certain way, and they do whatever I say. They don't have any choice."

"Show me," Cynthia said impulsively. "Make me do something."

He shook his head slowly and gravely. "I don't dare. Didn't you hear what I said? I might start to like it."

IV

There were seven of them around the table (eight counting the radio), Mrs. Simpston smiling and nodding in her black dress, Toby chewing slender fingers and darting dark looks this way and that, Mr. Alvarado sitting very still and erect with his hat in his lap, Cynthia Lutz, Steven Raleigh, and two people Steven hadn't encountered yet. Cynthia introduced Debby Weibel, a solemn, fidgety girl of nine or ten who looked like she was about to kick somebody, and Frank Reeves, an unremarkable middle-aged man who sauntered in through the door without bothering to open it. "Okay," Cynthia said without preamble, "here's the situation. We've got no money, and no food. Any hot ideas?"

They looked at one another uneasily. "We could help you make some more candles," Frank Reeves suggested. Reeves appeared to be sitting in a chair, and Steven found himself wondering whether this was an act put on to put the others at ease, or whether Reeves could solidify himself when necessary. Probably the latter, Steven decided. It would be too hard to maintain a sitting posture if you weren't sitting on anything.

"I'm counting on you to help with the candles," Cynthia said, "to pay next month's rent. But business is slow. Anyway, the street fair isn't until Saturday, and we're out of food *now*. Next?"

Debby Weibel started to cry. At the same moment the room was filled with large green sparks and a huge buzzing groaning noise that swooped up and down several octaves while pulsing painfully. "Debby, honey," Cynthia yelled, going over to the girl and squeezing her shoulders, "please try to control yourself. It's okay. Everything will be all right. Go ahead and cry if you want to, but please try not to make any of the big noises. Okay?" Snuffling, Debby nodded. The sparks faded and winked out, and the horrendous sound dwindled until it merged with the hum of the refrigerator. Steven realized he had been sitting on the edge of his chair. The sound affected him the way a dentist's drill did. He took a breath and relaxed.

The kitchen door swung open and the dog floated in, all four paws dangling limply a foot above the floor. The dog, Steven noticed now, was not only large but rather fat. "Come on in, General," Cynthia said. "Join the party. How would you like to hunt some rabbits?"

"Woof," said General helpfully. His tongue lolled out.

"I suppose I could apply to the county," Mrs. Simpston ventured. "Not that I like to beg, you understand, but I should like to do my part."

Cynthia shook her head. "We've been through that before. If Orlanoi happened to drop by while you were at the welfare office, they'd take you down to the county hospital and probably use electroshock on you. You wouldn't like the county hospital at all."

"I know, dear. It must be so hard on all of you, not being able to see the world as it really is. I don't blame you for getting confused."

"Why can't Mr. Alvarado apply?" Steven demanded. "He looks like he could cope."

"Among other things, he's an illegal alien," Cynthia explained. "Why don't you apply?" she countered.

"No identification. Also, I'm wanted for questioning."

There was some more silence.

"Pardon me for interrupting," the radio said, "but couldn't you work out a plan whereby Mrs. Simpston or Mr. Reeves could distract a grocery clerk while the rest of you take things off the shelves and put them in your pockets?"

"I hope we're not reduced to that," Cynthia said. "It's not a long-term solution. Sooner or later we'd get caught."

"You could plant a vegetable garden," the radio suggested.

"Gardens take months to grow, wirehead. We're talking about imminent starvation."

The little girl started to snuffle. Cynthia patted her absently.

"Isn't there some sort of charity dining room downtown?" Reeves asked.

"I'd thought of that already. It's ten miles, and we don't have bus fare. It would take so long to walk back and forth we'd end up down there living on the street. Anybody ready for that?"

"I have some money," Mr. Alvarado announced quietly. "A little money."

"No, Mr. Alvarado," Cynthia said gently. "What if you need it to get to the hole next time? What if you have to take a plane?"

"I do not like to see my friends in need. I will find a way to get to the hole. I will walk."

"No, Mr. Alvarado. What you're doing is too important."

"Nothing," he said with vehemence, "is more important than helping my friends."

Steven sat forward. "Wait a minute. If he's willing

to make a sacrifice like that, what am I doing sitting here on my butt?" An aside to Mrs. Simpston: "Excuse the language, ma'am." To the table at large, "I just got here, but I'd like to stay for a while, if it's all right with you folks. And if we've got to have some food, I'll get us some food. You," addressing Frank Reeves, "can you carry stuff without it slipping out of your hands?"

"It takes a little concentration, but I can manage."

"Okay, so you come—and you," nodding at Cynthia. "We're gonna get us some groceries."

V

I don't think we ought to be doing this, Cynthia told herself. It felt real bad. Not the stealing—she could live with that. She was worried about what it would do to Steven. She didn't like the spring in his knees, or the way he breathed through his teeth. But with all those mouths to feed, what choice did she have?

Steven was buzzing with reckless energy. Pushing the cart down the aisle while Cynthia selected boxes and cans, he felt his stomach twitching. Large, soft things that had been securely moored inside him had come loose and were drifting in the dark, bumping into the walls. But could he even do it after all this time? What a mess if they got up to the checkout counter and it didn't work! A fat woman was inspecting an apple, and he focused on her. She put the apple down, picked up an orange, tossed it high in the air, caught it, and set it down among the bananas. Oh, yes. Oh, yes. His whole body tingled. The woman was looking around in embarrassment and confusion. Steven winked at her.

"I think that's everything," Cynthia said a couple of minutes later. "Are you sure this is going to work?"

"I'm sure."

They had two heavily laden carts; Frank Reeves was

pushing the other one, frowning in concentration at his hands. "How do you shave?" Steven asked.

"It's tricky."

They stood waiting while a disinterested woman ran the groceries across the scanner. Cynthia noticed she was wringing her hands, and pulled them apart and wiped them nervously on her pants. "That comes to two hundred forty-two seventy-seven," the woman said at last.

We've already paid you. Give me the change. Those are the ones, in that slot.

Cynthia gasped. The woman was counting ten-dollar bills into Steven's hand, thinking they were ones. He tucked them into a pants pocket.

"Do you folks want help out to your car with this stuff?"

"We can manage," Steven said.

There were too many sacks to carry, so they loaded a cart and Cynthia pushed it while the men carried two sacks each. When they had walked half a block Cynthia said, "That's frightening. You can do that any time you want to?"

"Sure. It's easy. Pretty nifty, huh?" He grinned, pleased with himself.

"But what about the clerk? She'll come up three hundred short at the end of the day."

"Yeah. So what?"

"So she could lose her job, that's what."

Steven tried to meet her gaze and failed. "You're right," he admitted sourly. "See, that's the trouble with it. I always end up hurting people."

"Well, couldn't we have just loaded up the carts and wheeled them out the door without going past a cash register? I don't want to seem ungrateful, but . . ."

"That's too complicated. I'd have to control ten or fifteen people at once, to keep them from noticing. I'm not that good. The best I could manage would be to make them all fall down so they couldn't follow us.

They'd still call the police, and the police would get a description of us. So it wouldn't work. This way is a lot safer."

"Except that you may have cost that woman her job."

He looked at her coldly. "*We* may have cost that woman her job. You're gonna eat this stuff too, so don't get on your high horse. Anyway, would you rather have used Mr. Alvarado's plane fare?"

She sighed. "I guess not."

They walked along in silence for a while. The tingle had worn off, and Steven was beginning to feel depressed. After what had happened last time, he had promised himself he would never use the power again. It only led to trouble.

But hell, he wasn't responsible for the whole damn world, was he? If that woman didn't get fired today for losing three hundred dollars, she'd get fired tomorrow for showing up drunk, or something. What difference did it make?

The difference, his conscience pointed out, is that you wouldn't be the one making her get drunk. But it's not my fault! he protested. I didn't ask to have this power! To escape this oppressive line of thought, he said to Cynthia, "Tell me about the radio."

"Well, it's a nice old radio. I'm fond of it, even if it doesn't have much to say."

"It just wandered in, the way I did?"

"Not exactly. We've had maybe two dozen different people staying with us at one time or another. For a while there was this nice old guy—a farm hand from Missouri, he could barely read or write—who did things to machines. He never touched them; all he did was stare at them."

"You mean he could fix things that were broken?"

"It wasn't quite that simple. What things did after he got done with them was never exactly what they'd done before. The trouble was, he couldn't control it.

He never knew ahead of time what would happen. Anyway, somebody had given us an old radio that didn't work, and I asked him if he couldn't see about fixing it up somehow. He was tickled pink when it started to talk—said he'd never gotten anything to do something like that before."

"What happened to him?"

"We had an old car sitting in the driveway, and whenever he got tired of playing checkers with the radio he'd go out and stare at the car. One day he announced that he'd got it running and was going to take it out for a spin. We haven't seen him since. I figure the first time he tried to make a left turn, he took off into the fourth dimension."

VI

"You know, I'm starting to like it here," Steven said. He was sitting at the kitchen table snapping green beans the way she had shown him and throwing them in a pot.

"We like having you," Cynthia said. "You've been a big help."

"I could do a lot more. I could get you a car, and some good furniture, and some nice clothes. Maybe if Debby had a piano and some piano lessons, she'd stop making those damn noises."

"That's sweet of you, Steven. But we already have everything we really need. I thought you didn't want to use your power unless it was an emergency. You said it did something to you."

"I can handle it," he said in a surly tone. "I *want* to help. Why won't you let me help? You didn't mind when I got that money last week for Mr. Alvarado."

"Helping Mr. Alvarado is important. But I don't know. Maybe you shouldn't have done that either."

Mr. Alvarado had announced one morning that he must be off within the hour. Cynthia had packed some

sandwiches for him, and Steven had slipped out and
hit a couple of stores in a nearby shopping center.
When he pressed the bills into the old man's hand,
Mr. Alvarado said, "Gracias, amigo," and even though
the glorious buzz from using the power had already
worn off, leaving Steven bleak and gloomy as usual,
Mr. Alvarado's "gracias" made him feel good again.
But now Cynthia was saying he'd done something
wrong. He pushed back the chair and got to his feet.

"Where are you going?"

"Out."

"You aren't going to—do anything to anybody, are
you?"

"What if I am? Maybe I need to keep in practice.
You don't expect me to stay cooped up in here all
day."

"I thought you said you liked it here. I just don't
want you to get in any trouble."

"I can take care of myself."

But he didn't go out. He knew she was right—every
time he used the power he felt dirty afterward, and
defeated. Instead he went upstairs to his room and lay
down on the mattress with his fingers laced behind his
head and stared at the ceiling. Why did it have to be
so complicated? All he wanted was to have that feeling flowing through him like a soft fire, the thrill of
being absolutely in command. Things had been sim-
pler once. There had been other ways to feel good.
Playing touch football. Staying up late to watch a
meteor shower with his dad, sitting out in the back
yard in the dark with the fireflies buzzing around. And
those few times with Laurel. Laurel had liked him a
lot, and he had been crazy about her. No telling where
she was now. Married, probably, with kids. He remembered the silky contours of her body sliding over
him, the delicate fragrance of her sheets, the sound of
a moan catching in her throat. Tears stung his eyes.
He was alone. Even in a house full of people who

ought to understand, he was alone. Cynthia didn't understand, she just wanted to keep him penned up so he wouldn't get into trouble. Besides, she was ten years too old for him, and she didn't do anything to make herself sexy. Didn't even shave her legs. Now, Laurel . . . The closest he'd get to Laurel in this house was Toby. He hadn't seen Toby since that first day, but he remembered vividly how Toby had reminded him of Laurel. The more he thought about it, the clearer the resemblance became. At last he rolled to his feet. It couldn't do any harm to get another look, could it?

He climbed the narrow attic stairs and tapped on the door. "Who's there?" came the husky contralto.

"Steven."

"Go away."

"I wanted to talk to you."

"Talk to somebody else. Talk to the radio."

"You're not being very friendly," he chided.

"I can't afford to be friendly."

"It must get lonely, living up here."

There was no sound on the other side of the door.

"I got to thinking about that girl," Steven said, leaning his cheek on the wood. "The one you remind me of. You do look like her, just a little. She was real pretty."

"I don't look like her," said the voice. "I don't look anything like her. Now go away. Please."

"Do we have to talk like this? Can't you let me in for a minute? I won't hurt you."

Again there was silence. Bitterly, Steven slammed his fist into his palm. Shut out again. They were afraid of him. And he hadn't done anything to deserve it this time, not a thing! Why should he have to put up with this crap? *Come open the door.*

Soft footsteps, and the door swung open. The first glance shocked him—Toby looked nothing at all like Laurel. He brushed past the unmoving figure. "I wanted to see where you live," he said. The attic was warm and musty-smelling under the sloping roof. An unmade bed stood against one wall. There were two small curtained windows, one at the front of the house and one at the back.

"Did you make me open the door?" Toby asked.

"What if I did? Is that such a crime? I wanted to see you."

"You've seen me."

"I remembered you looking different."

"I always look different."

"Stand over there where the light's better," Steven directed. "Tilt your head a little. That's it. You *do* look like her." Even though he wasn't using the power, Toby seemed to have no will, and obeyed like a mannequin.

"I don't look like her. At least, I didn't. I'll start to before long. The longer you stay, the more I'll look like her. I change."

"Like a chameleon," he said. "So that's why you have to stay up here."

There was a tattered overstuffed chair by the front window. Toby sank into it. "Whenever I'm around somebody I start to turn into whoever they love. I can't help it. If I stay around them long enough, I become their ideal lover."

"You mean it's some kind of illusion? They look at you and think they're seeing somebody else?"

"No, it's a real physical change. My body molds itself according to whatever is in the other person's unconscious. Even my sex changes. Around you I'd become a girl. I can feel it happening already. Once it gets started, it happens very fast."

Steven squinted at Toby's face in the washed-out lighting from the window. Already it hinted at Laurel's. The cheeks and mouth were filling out, and the hair, black a moment before, had an auburn highlight.

"It must be frightening," he said, "to lose your identity like that."

Toby laughed humorlessly. "What identity? I thought I had an identity once, but it was only a cruel trick. Before I came here, I lived with a man named Tom Kittredge. He kept me locked up. He must have known what I was, but he never told me. I thought I was his wife. But then one day he didn't come home, and I started to get scared. After a while I ran out of food, and he still hadn't come, so I climbed out a window.

"When I got out on the street, I started changing. I was sure I was going crazy, because as far as I knew, I was Kitty Kittredge, but when I saw my face in a store window it was—it was *melting*." Toby put a hand to the cheek and jaw and stretched the skin. "That was a bad time. I don't remember everything that happened. I think I was in a hospital for a while, but then I wasn't, I was just wandering down the street, and Cynthia found me.

"Once I'd had a chance to sit here by myself for a while and think, I figured out how it is for me, how I have to live. Maybe understanding that counts as an identity, or anyway a piece of an identity. But I still don't know who I might have been before I was Kitty Kittredge. I'm not even sure I'm human."

The voice had grown higher and more animated as Toby talked. The nose had shortened and acquired a faint dusting of freckles. Steven felt a spasm of desire. "Don't do that," Toby said. "I can feel it. It goes through me like a wave. You'll have to go." But the protest had no force.

"How is it any better living like this—" Steven sat down on the bed and waved a hand at the attic. "—than living with a man thinking you're his wife? You're still a prisoner."

"At least this way I have my own thoughts. That's something very precious, that maybe you don't understand. If I become your friend, the one you're remembering, I'll lose whatever identity I have. I'll start to think I'm her. I'll want to be with you all the time, and make you happy. Making you happy will be the only thing that matters to me. And that's not right."

His groin was throbbing. As he stared, fascinated, the figure in the overstuffed chair flowed like a lump of wax under a sculptor's fingers, becoming less Toby and more Laurel. The arms were plumper now, and tanned. The hair was longer and lighter, the eyes set wider in a rounder face.

"Don't. Please don't. Please go away." But it was Laurel pleading with him, not Toby. The shapeless bathrobe fell away from a smooth thigh.

Come over here. Sit beside me. Toby/Laurel obeyed. Tears were streaming from the eyes, and they were Laurel's gray eyes. He touched Laurel's cheek with his fingers. "Don't be afraid," he said. Erotic excitement and the thrill of control surged in his blood. "I won't hurt you. It'll feel good, I promise. I know how to make it good for you."

"Oh, please . . ."

"Laurel. Laurel, honey." He kissed her neck. The perfume was Laurel's. He spread the robe open so it fell around her waist, and they were almost Laurel's breasts. He kissed her mouth, and her lips parted and her tongue darted out, seeking his. He lay back on the bed and drew her over him so the long auburn hair stroked his face, and her face was in shadow. *Unbutton my shirt,* he commanded.

VII

"How *could* you?" Cynthia stormed. "After I specifically told you not to go into the attic."

"I don't have to justify myself to you." He ran water in the sink and took a glassful, not to have to meet her eyes.

"Do you have any idea how much harm you've done? We've been working for months at strengthening its personality, so it can be around other people and not start changing. And now this! Anybody else, it knows to keep the door locked. There's only one way you could have gotten in."

"You don't know what you're talking about," he said belligerently. "She loved it. You should have seen how happy she was. So I'm happy, and she's happy, and what's *your* beef?"

Cynthia sighed in exasperation. "Of course Toby is happy. The trouble is, it won't stay happy. First it will want to move into your room, to be closer to you. Then it will start following you around. But every time you're with somebody else, it will get confused and start to change again. This has happened before, Steven. Last time it was Mrs. Simpston. Toby turned into an imitation Archangel Orlanoi—you know, the one that visits Mrs. Simpston? She was in heaven, having her Archangel around *all* the time, though she did get terribly confused whenever the real Orlanoi showed up. And I'll admit it was interesting for us to see what it is Mrs. Simpston has been having tea with, all these years. Toby became a Radiant Being.

"Until one afternoon when Mrs. Simpston wandered out into the garden and Toby spent a solid hour in the living room with the dog. When Mrs. Simpston discovered that her Radiant Being now had the muzzle and hindquarters of a Labrador retriever, she had hysterics. She tried to kill General with a fireplace poker. Poor General was so traumatized he hasn't walked a step since. So tell me—how are you going to feel when your 'Laurel' takes it into its head to help me out in the kitchen and winds up with a big black beard like my friend David used to have? Not to mention David's anatomical endowment. What you are going to do then?"

Steven scowled at her. "So what if Mrs. Simpston tried to kill the dog? That's not my fault. I'm just trying to live my life, and I've got as much right as anybody. I don't know why everybody's always blaming me for things."

"Because you're creating problems, dear heart. That's why."

"I don't see any problem. She can stay in the attic, just like always. If we have to, we can padlock the door from the outside."

"Oh, really. How cosy. All right," Cynthia said, spreading her hands, "I'm not going to ask you how fair you think it is that with a being in the house who could give any one of us the complete fulfillment of our erotic fantasies, *you're* the one that gets that being all to yourself. I'm not going to ask you that. And I'm not going to ask you why, when you could have your way with anybody in the world, you pick somebody helpless and vulnerable like Toby, instead of somebody who's strong enough to deal with it. I just want you to think this one over." She leaned forward and spoke with quiet intensity. "You said before that you felt bad about controlling people. But this is worse than controlling. You're completely wiping out another person's life." Her voice rose. "That's not Laurel up there, it's just a projection that originated in your mind. You're destroying everything that makes Toby an individual, and replacing it with some kind of phantom out of your own unconscious. Whatever Toby really is, you're killing it. How do you feel about that? How does it feel to be a murderer?"

Go away. Leave me alone.

Cynthia turned on her heel and left the kitchen. Steven slammed his fist into the wall.

"You're certainly causing an uproar around here," the radio commented.

He willed it to burst into flames, but nothing happened. "That won't work on me," the radio said. "I'm an inanimate object."

He was still sitting at the table an hour later, leaning his head on his hand, when Mrs. Simpston toddled in.

"Oh, there you are, dear boy. Cynthia asked me if I wouldn't find you. Would it be too much trouble to come out on the front porch and undo whatever it was you did to her? She says she can't come back into the house—and it's nearly dinnertime."

Reaching out with his mind, he found Cynthia Lutz nearby and released her. A minute later, having poured herself a cup of coffee with shaky hands, she sat down across from him and looked at him sorrowfully. "We've got a new house rule," she said. "As of right now. You don't do that to anybody who lives here. Not in any way, shape, or form, and not for any reason. If you ever do that again, you'll have to leave."

"You can't make me leave if I don't want to," he mumbled.

She put out a hand to touch his wrist. "You've been in situations like this before, haven't you, Steven? Wherever you go, sooner or later this kind of trouble starts."

His throat filled with tears. He nodded, mute.

"I'm sorry. I'm so sorry." She wiped her eyes with a finger.

"I only wanted to help with the groceries," he said, choking, "and then I got lonely. You can't blame me for that."

"But once you start, it's hard to stop. Isn't that what you said?"

He nodded, biting his upper lip.

"Steven, listen to me. We want you to live here with us, for as long as you want to. We want to help you learn to control this power, so you can make friends with people. We want to be your friends. Do you understand?"

"Yeah. I guess so."

"But you mustn't use your power on your friends. That's what's hurting you."

"Using it at all is what's hurting me. What difference does it make if it's a friend or a total stranger?"

"Well, there's a difference between using it for good

and using it to hurt people." Her eyes glowed. "What if you were a lifeguard at a swimming pool? Nobody could ever drown. You could just sit up in your tower and if anybody got in trouble you could take over and swim for them and guide them back to the side. Wouldn't that be wonderful? Wouldn't it?"

"I don't know. What if I decided to drown them instead?"

"You wouldn't do that, would you?"

"I might. Why shouldn't I?" Half to himself, he added, "What's scary is knowing that I *could* drown them if I wanted to. Nobody in the world could stop me."

"That would be very sad. But Steven, I think you're missing something. The reason you need to learn to use your power wisely isn't to keep from hurting other people, though you *can* hurt us very badly. The reason is to keep from hurting yourself. You're the one I'm worried about. I'd like to see you lead a healthy, happy life. And you can *do* it. I believe that. But unless you learn to control the power, it will destroy you."

"I can take care of myself," he said sullenly. But after glaring at the table for a minute his eyes softened, grew troubled. "I don't know, maybe you're right. I gotta think." He struggled to his feet and left the kitchen, his shoulders slumped.

VIII

For the next two days, wanting to prove how cooperative he was, Steven threw himself into yardwork, sweeping the roof and gutters, shoring up a sagging railing, hacking at weeds with a rusty hoe. Three dozen times he glanced up at the attic window, but always it was empty. He knew Cynthia was right, but at the same time he resented her for confronting him. "What does she know?" he muttered. "Hell." At night he lay on his back and stared at the ceiling and envisioned scenarios in which he and Laurel ran away from this place to start a new life together. But in every scenario, he had to use the power again and again, to get them money and a place to stay, to keep other minds with other erotic images away from his Laurel. And he knew that wouldn't work, because he knew what using the power did to him. The only way to keep Laurel isolated without using the power was to stay here— and as long as he stayed here, he couldn't see her at all. There she was, a few feet overhead, untouchable. He shuddered and wept in frustration.

The third morning he was dragging the sprinkler around to the front to water the brown patches of grass when Mr. Alvarado came back. The old man shuffled slowly up the sidewalk, like a paper cutout inching forward frame by frame, and turned in at the gate without even looking up at the house. Steven paused, holding the hose. "How did it go?"

Mr. Alvarado ceased his forward progress and considered the question remotely. "The hole—I got it closed. It was much bigger than usual. Hard to bring the edges together."

"Cynthia was putting some bread in the oven."

"Ah." An imaginary whiff of baking bread stirred the old man's impassive features. He slid one foot forward, then the other, and resumed his motion in the direction of the house. At the front steps he paused with one hand on the railing, gathering his strength.

"Here, let me help you," Steven offered.

"No. Gracias. If I cannot do this myself, it is finished. We are all finished." After deliberating for another moment he hoisted a foot onto the first step.

"Cynthia said what you're doing is important."

"Yes. I close the holes in the world."

"Closing holes—how do you do it?"

The old man's eyes went soft as he looked into inner distances. "It is like wires. Like lightning. The world unravels, and I must knit it up. I seize the strands in my hands, so—" He clutched both hands into fists, suddenly and with surprising strength. "—and weave them back together." His torso weaved from side to side like a snake. "Sometimes they whip this way and that, very fast. I have to grab them and hold them. It is very tiring."

They had reached the porch. "This power," Steven prodded. "It just came to you, right?"

"No. Many years ago, I had a teacher. My teacher found me by the lightning he saw in my hands. I had not yet learned to see it. He taught me. When I was his apprentice there were two others like him in Mexico alone, and others around the world. And it seems to me that the holes were smaller then, but perhaps that is only my memory." He paused in the hallway to hang his hat on the rack. "Now the others are gone. Soon there will be nobody left to patch the holes."

"Couldn't you teach somebody else?"

"Always, as I travel, I search for one who has the—" He spread his fingers, palms facing one another from opposite sides of his chest as though he were holding a large cat's cradle. "— the lightning in his fingers. But there is nobody."

"Does it have to be somebody like that? Couldn't you teach somebody else?"

"No. Impossible."

"Mr. Alvarado, I don't know what you're saying, exactly, about lightning in your fingers, but I've got a kind of power, and maybe it's a little like yours. Maybe we could team up. You could teach me about this lightning stuff, and maybe I could learn it. I might surprise you. But even if it took me a while to learn, I'd be glad to go along with you when you go somewhere, and make sure nobody gives you any trouble, or anything."

"I am sorry. I must go to my room now, and lie down."

"But Mr. Alvarado," Steven said, "you don't un-

derstand. I want to help. I've never done anything in
my life but cause trouble, and I want to make a fresh
start. I want to do something good for once. If you'll
just let me . . ."

Cynthia appeared in the door to the kitchen, wearing an apron and holding a big bowl under her breast
like a baby. "Steven," she said, waving a long wooden
spoon at him, "don't annoy Mr. Alvarado."

He glared at her, and put his head down. "I'm
sorry, Mr. Alvarado. I only wanted to help."

But the thought ate at him. The old guy needed
somebody, that was for sure. Cynthia wouldn't let him
near Laurel, and now this. What was he supposed to
do around here, with Cynthia giving the orders? Just
go for groceries whenever she snapped her fingers,
and slave away in the yard, and talk to Mrs. Simpston,
who never made any sense, or to the radio, which
made sense but had nothing to say. He stomped back
out the front door and scowled at the sprinkler, which
hadn't been turned on yet, and instead of turning it on
went back inside and upstairs to his room.

He had been lying there only seconds when the
concert started. At first the low rumble pulsed soothingly like a passing train, but suddenly he was assailed
by the screech of metal parts grinding against one
another, a prolonged shriek with an uncomfortably human voice. He sat up and grimaced at the wall beyond
which was Debby Weibel's room and shouted, "Shut
up!"

Far from abating, the noise erupted. After an ava-
lanche of thumps and crashes his own voice was thrown
back at him distorted and echoing shut-up-shut-up-
shut-up. Simultaneously the wall began to waver and
shimmer in a moist organic rhythm that made him
nauseous. He staggered out into the hall. Here a waterfall of pink globules was oozing sinuously down,
accompanied by a dizzying antiphonal cacophony of
invisible mourning doves. He leaned against the wall

outside the girl's room to gather his strength. *Stop that.* The waterfall evaporated and the doves fell silent.

He listened at the top of the stairs, expecting to hear Cynthia coming to point an accusing finger, but the stairwell remained empty. I wasn't supposed to do that, he told himself. Well, what if I did? A man's entitled to a little peace and quiet, isn't he? Am I gonna let that bitch control *me?* Why should I let her run my life?

He went up the attic steps two at a time and pounded on the door. "Laurel! Laurel, open the door!"

There was no response. He knocked again, more gently. "Laurel, it's me. I just want to see you for a minute. That won't hurt anything, will it?"

"Go away," said the muffled voice.

"Laurel—"

"I'm not Laurel. Can't you understand that?"

"But you could be," he said in his most seductive tone. "Remember how good it was? It could be that good again. Better. Wouldn't you like that?"

Below him the noise surged up again. This time it was a grinding of huge gears that rolled and swelled until the walls were rattling. Holding his ears, Steven staggered down the narrow steps, intending to make the girl eat her fingers, when suddenly Cynthia was below him, eyes flashing, wiping flour on her apron. "What's going on here?" she demanded. "What are you doing?"

"Nothing. I was going to ask her to stop, that's all."

"What were you doing in the attic?" Cynthia yelled over the din.

"Nothing! I wasn't up in the attic. Can't you get her to stop that?"

"What were you doing in the attic?"

"I can't stand this any longer." He strode to the girl's door and rattled the knob, which was locked, then stood back and kicked. The latch splintered. Debby Weibel was standing in the middle of the room, head back, eyes closed, swaying, hugging herself with thin bare arms.

Stop that. She faltered. *Stop that noise.* She crumpled in a heap and lay on the floor, twitching. Silence descended.

Behind him when he turned Cynthia stood, arms folded, eyes leveled at him. "You go," she said. "Right now. Leave this house."

Go back to the kitchen. Bake your bread.

She turned and marched down the stairs. Oh, yes. Exulting, he mounted again to the attic. "Laurel, honey. Come on, open up. Don't you know I've missed you?"

Silence.

"Lau-rel."

Silence.

"I can make you open the door. I'd rather not do that, sugar. I'd rather you do it because you want to. Don't you want to?"

"No! Go away!"

He worked his jaw stiffly. *Open the door.*

The door opened. She was more disheveled than before, and some of the gauntness had returned, a hunted look. He stepped in and closed the door. "Hey, baby. Aren't you glad to see me? Not going to give me a kiss?" He tilted her chin with a forefinger.

"I hate you. You're a monster."

"Oooh, strong language. Well, if I'm a monster, what do you think that makes you?"

"I don't know what I am," Toby/Laurel said, troubled.

"Tell me you don't like being with me. Go on."

"I *do* like being with you, Steven. I can't help liking it. That's the trouble. Don't you see? Your strength and my weakness fit together perfectly. That's why you've got to stop. It feeds on itself. I get more and more dependent, and you get more and more cruel."

Shut up.

Laurel/Toby stared at him in mute appeal with the

terrified eyes of a fawn caught in a bear trap. He stroked the hair away from the cheeks and held the head immobile, bringing the mouth very slowly closer and closer to his own. Laurel's lips were trembling, and wet. "Now, see," he said. "This isn't so bad, is it? You might even start to like it. Mmm?"

IX

"We've got to do something," Cynthia Lutz said to the radio.

"Agreed. What do you have in mind?"

"I was hoping maybe you'd have a suggestion. For once." She was leafing nervously through the recipe book. The problem was, she had been ordered to bake bread. And she was running out of ingredients. The flour and eggs and yeast were lined up in neat loaves to the right of the oven, waiting for their turn, with a misshapen oblong of Bisquick with onion and dill bringing up the rear. Somewhere in here, she remembered vaguely, there was something about corn starch, sunflower seeds, and zucchini . . .

"You've already tried asking him to leave," the radio said.

"Right."

"Why not ask him to stay. Flatter him."

"Make him king of the mountain." She considered the idea.

"Only until you have a chance to dispose of him," the radio added.

"And what if I don't want to be disposed of?" Steven asked, leaning in at the kitchen door with an expansive grin. "You know, that's quite a little piece of action you've got up there. I might be starting to like it here." He took in a noseful of air. "Mmm, smells good. Did we get any strawberry jam, or are you gonna have to go get some?" He fished in the refrigerator. "He-e-ere we go." Setting the jar on the table, he grabbed an uncut loaf from the already-baked-and-still-warm row on the other counter and pawed through the drawer under the drainboard looking for a big sharp knife. Brandishing it with a slightly ironic flourish, he said, "An implement of destruction." He threw himself into a chair and stabbed the loaf of bread. When he had carved loose a thick slice, he dug jam from the jar with the blade and smeared it on the bread. Staring into her eyes wickedly, he took a big bite and chewed.

Inside she was squirming with fear, but she met his eyes. "Steven," she said slowly, "we've got to talk." He munched bread. "Steven, honey—"

"Don't you honey me. You only want me to back off so you can take charge of this place again. You're scared of me."

"That's right, Steven. We're scared of you, Steven—"

"You want to run everything. You want to tell me what to do. Don't you? Isn't that what you want? You want to tell me to go to my room. You try to tell me I'm nasty because I take over a lousy grocery clerk in a lousy supermarket. I'm nasty, huh? I'm not fit to associate with nice people like you. That's what you're thinking, isn't it? Well, I'll show you nasty. *I'll* show you nasty." He looked at the jellied butcher knife in his hand. "Here. Catch."

He tossed it to her, and she caught it deftly, by the hilt.

"That's good. Now. Dance."

The knife rotated inward toward her belly, and her shoulder and arm vibrated with the double effort of bringing the point closer and pushing it away. She bit her lip, and tasted iron blood. Very slowly she backed away from her own hand, and the hand followed, bringing the gleaming blade in to press an indentation into the apron. She heard a spastic moan and realized dimly that it was coming from her own throat.

"Let her alone!" cried the radio. "Let her alone! Stop it, do you hear? Stop it!"

Turning, he picked up the radio in both hands and hurled it across the kitchen, where it crashed into the wall. But in the moment when he was distracted, Cynthia flung the knife away and plunged toward the door.

He dashed after her. She lurched across the hall and out the front door and across the porch and hit the first step crooked and twisted her ankle and went down hard, banging an elbow and a hip and her head. She grabbed her head and pressed against the agony, until it started to subside.

He leaned over the railing and grinned down at her. *Die, bitch, die. Don't breathe. Forget how to breathe.*

She goggled up at him. Gradually her face turned rosy. Her torso heaved.

Oh, yes. It was hot wine in his veins. Oh, yes. But suddenly, he saw how it would be. This was what he loved, not Laurel. In another moment the image of Laurel would be burned forever out of his brain, and this purpling monstrosity would take its place. He would go back to the attic, and the attic-dweller would have the same staring hideous face, the tongue dripping bloody foam, the eyes popping, and wherever he went in the world the creature that had this face would pursue him and call endearments to him and reach out bony hands to clasp him to its cold, cold bosom.

He let go. He let go of her throat and ribs and diaphragm and turned and stumbled back into the house. Behind him came the rasp of air into tortured lungs. From the kitchen he grabbed an unsliced loaf of bread and tucked it in his shirt as he scampered upstairs for the duffel bag. Got to get out of here, got to get out of here. He looked around the bare room. He had left nothing. Back down the stairs, he staggered into the blazing afternoon. Cynthia was lying on the lawn, up on one elbow, gagging. He took the steps three at a time and sprinted past the dry birdbath and leaped the short fence. She saw legs flash past, but she was busy sucking in air to ease the burning. When her brain swam into focus so she could look, he was already out of sight. Away down the crooked sidewalk diminished the thud of running boots.

X

The next day they held a funeral for the radio. Cynthia had to call about twenty places to find the right tubes, but when they plugged them in the radio only hummed and got Fresno through a lot of static, no matter how much they begged and pleaded with it. So Cynthia dug a hole in the back yard and they buried it. She couldn't think of anything to say at the funeral of a radio, which made her so damn mad she cried. Mrs. Simpston had picked a bouquet of wild mushrooms, for no reason that anybody could fathom, to put on the grave. Mr. Alvarado clutched his hat before him in both hands, and Frank Reeves put in a wavering appearance. Little Debby Weibel held Mrs. Simpston's other hand and snuffled. And from the attic window a face looked out.

When Cynthia had tamped down the dirt and put the shovel back in the garage, she went back into the kitchen and looked in all the cabinets to figure out how much food they had left. They were going to eat a lot of bread for the next few days, that was for sure. She made a list, and planned some meals. It came to about two weeks, depending on how many meals Frank Reeves did or didn't show up for. After that, they would be back where they started.

She looked over at the empty spot on the table where there wasn't any radio. "Got any hot ideas?" she asked. The empty spot didn't say anything. After a while she said softly, "Thanks for saving my life."

The empty spot didn't say anything to that either.

THE BOY WHO PLAITED MANES

by Nancy Springer

He was a very strange boy who seemed content to practice his only apparent talent without ever uttering a sound. Then one day a situation developed that did cause him to speak, and things were never the same in Lord Robley's realm.

The boy who plaited the manes of horses arrived, fittingly enough, on the day of the Midsummer Hunt: when he was needed worst, thought Wald the head groom did not yet know it. The stable seethed in a muted frenzy of work, as it had done since long before dawn, every groom and apprentice vehemently polishing. The lord's behest was that all the horses in his stable should be brushed for two hours every morning to keep the fine shine and bloom on their flanks, and this morning could be no different. Then there was also all the gear to be tended to. Though old Lord Robley of Auberon was a petty manor lord, with only some hundred of horses and less than half the number of grooms to show for a lifetime's striving, his lowly status made him all the more keen to present himself and his retinue grandly before the more powerful lords

223

who would assemble for the Hunt. Himself and his retinue and his lovely young wife.

Therefore it was an eerie thing when the boy walked up the long stable aisle past men possessed with work, men so frantic they did not look up to glance at the stranger, up the aisle brick-paved in chevron style until he came to the stall where the lady's milk-white palfrey stood covered withers to croup with a fitted sheet tied on to keep the beast clean, and the boy swung open the heavy stall door and walked in without fear, as if he belonged there, and went up to the palfrey to plait its mane.

He was an eerie boy, so thin that he seemed deformed, and of an age difficult to guess because of his thinness. He might have been ten, or he might have been seventeen with something wrong about him that made him beardless and narrow-shouldered and thin. His eyes seemed too gathered for a ten-year-old, gray-green and calm yet feral, like woodland. His hair, dark and shaggy, seemed to bulk large above his thin, thin face.

The palfrey's hair was far better cared for than his. Its silky mane, coddled for length, hung down below its curved neck, and its tail was bundled into a wrapping, to be let down at the last moment before the lady rode, when it would trail on the ground and float like a white bridal train. The boy did not yet touch the tail, but his thin fingers flew to work on the palfrey's mane.

Wald the head groom, passing nearly at a run to see to the saddling of the lord's hotblooded hunter, stopped in his tracks and stared. And to be sure it was not that he had never seen plaiting before. He himself had probably braided a thousand horses' manes, and he knew what a time it took to put even a row of small looped braids along a horse's crest, and how hard it was to get them even, and how horsehair seems like a demon with a mind of its own. He frankly gawked, and other grooms stood beside him and did likewise, until more onlookers stood gathered outside the palfrey's stall than could rightly see, and those in the back demanded to know what was happening, and those in the front seemed not to hear them, but stood as if in a trance, watching the boy's thin, swift hands.

For the boy's fingers moved more quickly and deftly than seemed human, than seemed possible, each hand by itself combing and plaiting a long, slender braid in one smooth movement, as if he no more than stroked the braid out of the mane. That itself would have been wonder enough, as when a groom is so apt that he can curry with one hand and follow after with the brush in the other, and have a horse done in half the time. A shining braid forming out of each hand every minute, wonder enough—but that was the least of it. The boy interwove them as he worked, so that they flowed into each other in a network, making of the mane a delicate shawl, a veil, that draped the palfrey's fine neck. The ends of the braids formed a silky hem curving down to a point at the shoulder, and at the point the boy spiraled the remaining mane into an uncanny horsehair flower. And all the time, though it was not tied and was by no means a cold-blooded beast, the palfrey had not moved, standing still as a stone.

Then Wald the head groom felt fear prickling at the back of his astonishment. The boy had carried each plait down to the last three hairs. Yet he had fastened nothing with thread or ribbon, but merely pressed the ends between two fingers, and the braids stayed as he had placed them. Nor did the braids ever seem to fall loose as he was working, or hairs fly out at random, but all lay smooth as white silk, shimmering. The boy, or whatever he was, stood still with his hands at his sides, admiring his work.

Uncanny. Still, the lord and lady would be well pleased. . . . Wald jerked himself out of amazement and moved quickly. "Get back to your work, you fellows!" he roared at the grooms, and then he strode into the stall.

"Who are you?" he demanded. "What do you mean coming in here like this?" It was best, in a lord's household, never to let anyone know you were obliged to them.

The boy looked at him silently, turning his head in the alert yet indifferent way of a cat.

"I have asked you a question! What is your name?"

The boy did not speak, or even move his lips. Then or thereafter, as long as he worked in that stable, he never made any sound.

His stolid manner annoyed Wald. But though the master groom could not yet know that the boy was a mute, he saw something odd in his face. A halfwit, perhaps. He wanted to strike the boy, but even worse he wanted the praise of the lord and lady, so he turned abruptly and snatched the wrapping off the palfrey's tail, letting the cloud of white hair float down to the clean straw of the stall. "Do something with that," he snapped.

A sweet, intense glow came into the boy's eyes as he regarded his task. With his fingers he combed the hair smooth, and then he started a row of small braids above the bone.

Most of the tail he left loose and flowing, with just a cluster of braids at the top, a few of them swinging halfway to the ground. And young Lady Aelynn gasped with pleasure when she saw them, and with wonder at the mane, even though she was a lord's daughter born and not unaccustomed to finery.

It did not matter, that day, that Lord Robley's saddle had not been polished to a sufficient shine. He was well pleased with his grooms. Nor did it matter that his hawks flew poorly, his hounds were unruly and his clumsy hunter stumbled and cut its knees. Lords and ladies looked again and again at his young wife on her white palfrey, its tail trailing and shimmering like her blue silk gown, the delicate openwork of its mane as dainty as the lace kerchief tucked between her breasts or her slender gloved hand which held the caparisoned reins. Every hair of her mount was as artfully placed as her own honey-gold hair looped in gold-beaded curls atop her fair young head. Lord Robley knew himself to be the envy of everyone who saw him for the sake of his lovely wife and the showing she made on her white mount with the plaited mane.

And when the boy who plaited manes took his place among the lord's other servants in the kitchen line for the evening meal, no one gainsaid him.

Lord Robley was a hard old man, his old body hard and hale, his spirit hard. It took him less than a day to pass from being well pleased to being greedy for more: no longer was it enough that the lady's palfrey should go forth in unadorned braids. He sent a servant to Wald with silk ribbons in the Auberon colors, dark blue and crimson, and commanded that they should be plaited into the palfrey's mane and tail. This is the strange boy did with ease when Wald gave him the order, and he used the ribbon ends to tie tiny bows and love knots and leave a few shimmering tendrils bobbing in the forelock. Lady Aelynn was enchanted.

Within a few days Lord Robley had sent to the stable thread of silver and of gold, strings of small pearls, tassels, pendant jewels, and fresh-cut flowers of every sort. All of these things the boy who plaited manes used with ease to dress the lady's palfrey when he was bid. Lady Aelynn went forth to the next hunt with tiny bells of silver and gold chiming at the tip of each of her mount's dainty ribbon-decked braids, and eyes turned her way wherever she rode. Nor did the boy ever seem to arrange the mane and tail and forelock twice in the same way, but whatever way he chose to plait and weave and dress it seemed the most perfect and poignant and heartachingly beautiful way

a horse had ever been arrayed. Once he did the palfrey's entire mane in one great, thick braid along the
crest, gathering in the hairs as he went, so that the
neck seemed to arch as mightily as a destrier's, and he
made the braid drip thick with flowers, roses and great
lilies and spires of larkspur trailing down, so that the
horse seemed to go with a mane of flowers. But another time he would leave the mane loose and floating, with just a few braids shimmering down behind
the ears or in the forelock, perhaps, and this also
seemed perfect and poignant and the only way a horse
should be adorned.

Nor was it sufficient, any longer, that merely the
lady's milk-white palfrey should go forth in braids.
Lord Robley commanded that his hotblooded hunter
also should have his mane done up in stubby ribboned
braids and rosettes in the Auberon colors, and the
horses of his retinue likewise, though with lesser rosettes. And should his wife choose to go out riding
with her noble guests, all their mounts were to be
prepared like hers, though in lesser degree.

All these orders Wald passed on to the boy who
plaited manes, and the youngster readily did as he
was bid, working sometimes from before dawn until
long after dark, and never seeming to want more than
what food he could eat while standing in the kitchen.
He slept in the hay and straw of the loft and did not
use even a horseblanket for covering until one of the
grooms threw one on him. Nor did he ask for clothing,
but Wald, ashamed of the boy's shabbiness, provided
him with the clothing due to a servant. The master
groom said nothing to him of a servant's pay. The boy
seemed content without it. Probably he would have
been content without the clothing as well. Though in
fact it was hard to tell what he was thinking or feeling,
for he never spoke and his thin face seldom moved.

No one knew his name, the boy who plaited manes.
Though many of the grooms were curious and made

inquiries, no one could tell who he was or where he had come from. Or even what he was, Wald thought sourly. No way to tell if the young snip was a halfwit or a bastard or what, if he would not talk. No way to tell what sort of a young warlock he might be, that the horses never moved under his hands, even the hot-blooded hunter standing like a stump for him. Scrawny brat. He could hear well enough; why would he not talk?

It did not make Wald like the strange boy, that he did at once whatever he was told and worked so hard and so silently. In particular he did not like the boy for doing the work for which Wald reaped the lord's praise; Wald disliked anyone to whom he was obliged. Nor did he like the way the boy had arrived, as if blown in on a gust of wind, and so thin that it nearly seemed possible. Nor did he like the thought that any day the boy might leave in like wise. And even disliking that thought, Wald could not bring himself to give the boy the few coppers a week which were his due, for he disliked the boy more. Wald believed there was something wrongheaded, nearly evil, about the boy. His face seemed wrong, so very thin, with the set mouth and the eyes both wild and quiet, burning like a steady candle flame.

Summer turned into autumn, and many gusts of wind blew, but the boy who plaited manes seemed content to stay, and if he knew of Wald's dislike he did not show it. In fact he showed nothing. He braided the palfrey's mane with autumn starflowers and smiled ever so slightly as he worked. Autumn turned to the first dripping and dismal, chill days of winter. The boy used bunches of bright feathers instead of flowers when he dressed the palfrey's mane, and he did not ask for a winter jerkin, so Wald did not give him any. It was seldom enough, anyway, that the horses were used for pleasure at this season. The thin boy could spend his days huddled under a horseblanket in the loft.

Hard winter came, and the smallpox season.

Lady Aelynn was bored in the wintertime, even more so than during the rest of the year. At least in the fine weather there were walks outside, there were riding and hunting and people to impress. It would not be reasonable for a lord's wife, nobly born (though a younger child, and female), to wish for more than that. Lady Aelynn knew full well that her brief days of friendships and courtships were over. She had wed tolerably well, and Lord Robley counted her among his possessions, a beautiful thing to be prized like his gold and his best horses. He was a manor lord, and she was his belonging, his lady, and not for others to touch even with their regard. She was entirely his. So there were walks for her in walled gardens, and pleasure riding and hunting by her lord's side, and people to impress.

But in the wintertime there were not even the walks. There was nothing for the Lady Aelynn to do but tend to her needlework and her own beauty, endlessly concerned with her clothes, her hair, her skin, even though she was so young, no more than seventeen—for she knew in her heart that it was for her beauty that Lord Robley smiled on her, and for no other reason. And though she did not think of it, she knew that her life lay in his grasping hands.

Therefore she was ardently uneasy, and distressed only for herself, when the woman who arranged her hair each morning was laid abed with smallpox. Though as befits a lady of rank, Aelynn hid her dismay in vexation. And it did not take her long to discover that none of her other tiring-women could serve her nearly as well.

"Mother of God!" she raged, surveying her hair in the mirror for perhaps the tenth time. "The groom who plaits the horses' manes in the stable could do better!" Then the truth of her own words struck her, and desperation made her willing to be daring. She smiled. "Bring him hither!"

Her women stammered and curtseyed and fled to consult among themselves and exclaim with the help in the kitchen. After some few minutes of this, a bold kitchen maid was dispatched to the stable and returned with a shivering waif: the boy who plaited manes.

It was not to be considered that such a beggar should go in to the lady. Her tiring-women squeaked in horror and made him bathe first, in a washbasin before the kitchen hearth, for there was a strong smell of horse and stable about him. They ordered him to scrub his own hair with strong soap and scent himself with lavender, and while some of them giggled and fled, others giggled and stayed, to pour water for him and see that he made a proper job of his ablutions. All that was demanded of him the boy who plaited manes did without any change in his thin face, any movement of his closed mouth, any flash of his feral eyes. At last they brought him clean clothing, jerkin and woolen hose only a little too large, and pulled the things as straight as they could on him, and took him to the tower where the lady waited.

He did not bow to the Lady Aelynn or look into her eyes for his instructions, but his still mouth softened a little and his glance, calm and alert, like that of a woodland thing, darted to her hair. And at once, as if he could scarcely wait, he took his place behind her and lifted her tresses in his hands. Such a soft, fine, honey-colored mane of hair as he had never seen, and combs of gold and ivory lying at hand on a rosewood table, and ribbons of silk and gold, everything he could have wanted, his for the sake of his skill.

He started at the forehead, and the lady sat as if in a trance beneath the deft touch of his hands.

Gentle, he was so gentle, she had never felt such a soft and gentle touch from any man, least of all from her lord. When Lord Robley wanted to use one of his possessions he seized it. But this boy touched her as gently as a woman, no, a mother, for no tiring-woman or maid had ever gentled her so. . . . Yet unmistakably his was the touch of a man, though she could scarcely have told how she knew. Part of it was power, she could feel the gentle power in his touch, she could feel—uncanny, altogether eerie and uncanny, what she was feeling. It was as if his quick fingers called to her hair in soft command and her hair obeyed just for the sake of the one quick touch, all the while longing to embrace. . . . She stayed breathlessly still for him, like the horses.

He plaited her hair in braids thin as bluebell stems, only a wisp of hairs to each braid, one after another with both his deft hands as if each was as easy as a caress, making them stay with merely a touch of two fingers at the end, until all her hair lay in a silky cascade of them, catching the light and glimmering and swaying like a rich drapery when he made her move her head. Some of them he gathered and looped and tied up with the ribbons which matched her dress, blue edged with gold. But most of them he left hanging to her bare back and shoulders. He surveyed his work with just a whisper of a smile when he was done, then turned and left without waiting for the lady's nod, and she sat as if under a spell and watched his thin back as he walked away. Then she tossed her head at his lack of deference. But the swinging of her hair pleased her.

She had him back to dress her hair the next day, and the next, and many days thereafter. And so that they would not have to be always bathing him, her tiring-women found him a room within the manorhouse doors, and a pallet and clean blankets, and a change of clothing, plain coarse clothing, such as servants wore. They trimmed the heavy hair that shadowed his eyes, also, but he looked no less the oddling with his thin, thin face and his calm, burning glance and his mouth that seemed scarcely ever to move. He did as he was bid, whether by Wald or the lady or some kitchen maid, and every day he plaited Lady Aelynn's hair differently. One day he shaped it all into a bright crown of braids atop her head. On other days he would plait it close to her head so that the tendrils caressed her neck, or in a haughty crest studded with jewels, or in a single soft feathered braid at one side. He always left her tower chamber at once, never looking at the lady to see if he had pleased her, as if he knew that she would always be pleased.

Always, she was.

Things happened. The tiring-woman who had taken smallpox died of it, and Lady Aelynn did not care, not for the sake of her cherished hair and most certainly not for the sake of the woman herself. Lord Robley went away on a journey to discipline a debtor vassal, and Lady Aelynn did not care except to be glad, for there was a sure sense growing in her of what she would do.

When even her very tresses were enthralled by the touch of this oddling boy, longing to embrace him, could she be otherwise?

When next he had plaited her mane of honey-colored hair and turned to leave her without a glance, she caught him by one thin arm. His eyes met hers with a steady, gathered look. She stood—she was taller than he, and larger, though she was as slender as any maiden. It did not matter. She took him by one thin hand and led him to her bed, and there he did as he was bid.

Nor did he disappoint her. His touch—she had never been touched so softly, so gently, so deftly, with such power. Nor was he lacking in manhood, for all that he was as thin and hairless as a boy. And his lips, after all, knew how to move, and his tongue. But it was the touch of his thin hands that she hungered for, the gentle, tender, potent touch that thrilled her almost as if—she were loved. . . .

He smiled at her afterward, slightly, softly, a whisper of a smile in the muted half-light of her curtained bed, and his lips moved.

"You are swine," he said, "all of you nobles."

And he got up, put on his plain, coarse clothing and left her without a backward glance.

It terrified Lady Aelynn, that he was not truly a mute. Terrified her even more than what he had said, though she burned with mortified wrath whenever she thought of the latter. He, of all people, a mute, to speak such words to her and leave her helpless to avenge herself. . . . Perhaps for that reason he would not betray her. She had thought it would be safe to take a mute as her lover. . . . Perhaps he would not betray her.

In fact, it was not he who betrayed her to her lord, but Wald.

Her tiring-women suspected, perhaps because she had sent them on such a long errand. She had not thought they would suspect, for who would think that such a wisp of a beardless boy could be a bedfellow? But perhaps they also had seen the wild glow deep in his gray-green eyes. They whispered among themselves and with the kitchen maids, and the bold kitchen maid giggled with the grooms, and Wald heard.

Even though the boy who plaited manes did all the work, Wald considered the constant plaiting and adorning of manes and tails a great bother. The whole fussy business offended him, he had decided, and he had long since forgotten the few words of praise it had garnered from the lord at first. Moreover, he disliked the boy so vehemently that he was not thinking clearly. It seemed to him that he could be rid of the boy and the wretched onus of braids and rosettes all in one stroke. The day the lord returned from his journey,

Wald hurried to him, begged private audience, bowed low and made his humble report.

Lord Robley heard him in icy silence, for he knew pettiness when he saw it; it had served him often in the past, and he would punish it if it misled him. He summoned his wife to question her. But the Lady Aelynn's hair hung lank, and her guilt and shame could be seen plainly in her face from the moment she came before him.

Lord Robley's roar could be heard even to the stables.

He strode over to her where she lay crumpled and weeping on his chamber floor, lifted her head by its honey-gold hair and slashed her across the face with his sword. Then he left her screaming and stinging her wound with fresh tears, and he strode to the stable with his bloody sword still drawn, Wald fleeing before him all the way; when the lord burst in all the grooms were scattering but one. The boy Wald had accused stood plaiting the white palfrey's mane.

Lord Robley hacked the palfrey's head from its braid-bedecked neck with his sword, and the boy who plaited manes stood by with something smoldering deep in his unblinking gray-green eyes, stood calmly waiting. If he had screamed and turned to flee, Lord Robley would with great satisfaction have given him a coward's death from the back. But it unnerved the lord that the boy awaited his pleasure with such mute— what? Defiance? There was no servant's bow in this one, no falling to the soiled straw, no groveling. If he had groveled he could have been kicked, stabbed, killed out of hand. . . . But this silent, watchful waiting, like the alertness of a wild thing—on the hunt or being hunted? It gave Lord Robley pause, like the pause of the wolf before the standing stag or the pause of the huntsman before the thicketed boar. He held the boy at the point of his sword—though no such holding was necessary, for the prisoner had not moved even to tremble—and roared for his men-at-arms to come take the boy to the dungeon.

There the nameless stranger stayed without water or food, and aside from starving him Lord Robley could not decide what to do with him.

At first the boy who plaited manes paced in his prison restlessly—he had that freedom, for he was so thin and small that the shackles were too large to hold him. Later he lay in a scant bed of short straw and stared narrow-eyed at the darkness. And yet later, seeing the thin cascades of moonlight flow down through the high, iron-barred window and puddle in moonglades on the stone floor, he got up and began to plait the moonbeams.

They were far finer than any horsehair, moonbeams, finer even than the lady's honey-colored locks, and his eyes grew wide with wonder and pleasure as he felt them. He made them into braids as fine as silk threads, flowing together into a lacework as close as woven cloth, and when he had reached as high as he could, plaiting, he stroked as if combing a long mane with his fingers and pulled more moonlight down out of sky— for this stuff was not like any other stuff he had ever worked with, it slipped and slid worse than any hair, there seemed to be no beginning or end to it except the barriers that men put in its way. He stood plaiting the fine, thin plaits until he had raised a shimmering heap on the floor, and then he stepped back and allowed the moon to move on. His handiwork he laid carefully aside in a corner.

The boy who plaited moonbeams did not sleep, but sat waiting for the dawn, his eyes glowing greenly in the darkened cell. He saw the sky lighten beyond the high window and waited stolidly, as the wolf waits for the gathering of the pack, as a wildcat waits for the game to pass along the trail below the rock where it lies. Not until the day had neared its mid did the sun's rays, thrust through the narrow spaces between the high bars, wheel their shafts down to where he could reach them. Then he got up and began to plait the sunlight.

Guards were about, or more alert, in the daytime, and they gathered at the heavy door of his prison, peering in between the iron bars of its small window, gawking and quarreling with each other for turns. They watched his unwavering eyes, saw the slight smile come on his face as he worked, though his thin hands glowed red as if seen through fire. They saw the shining mound he raised on the floor, and whispered among themselves and did not know what to do, for none of them dared to touch it or him. One of them requested a captain to come look. And the captain summoned the steward, and the steward went to report to the lord. And from outside, cries began to sound that the sun was standing still.

After the boy had finished, he stood back and let the sun move on, then tended to his handiwork, then sat resting on his filthy straw. Within minutes the dungeon door burst open and Lord Robley himself strode in.

Lord Robley had grown weary of mutilating his wife, and he had not yet decided what to do with his other prisoner. Annoyed by the reports from the prison, he expected that an idea would come to him when he saw the boy. He entered with drawn sword. But all thoughts of the thin young body before him were sent whirling away from his mind by what he saw laid out on the stone floor at his feet.

A mantle, a kingly cloak—but no king had ever owned such a cloak. All shining, the outside of it silver and the inside gold—but no, to call it silver and gold was to insult it. More like water and fire, flow and flame, shimmering as if it moved, as if it were alive, and yet it had been made by hands, he could see the workmanship, so fine that every thread was worth a gasp of pleasure, the outside of it somehow braided

and plaited to the lining, and all around the edge a
fringe of threads like bright fur so fine that it wavered
in the air like flame. Lord Robley had no thought but
to settle the fiery gleaming thing on his shoulders, to
wear that glory and be finer than any king. He seized
it and flung it on—

And screamed as he had not yet made his wife
scream, with the shriek of mortal agony. His whole
hard body glowed as if in a furnace. His face contorted, and he fell dead.

The boy who plaited sunbeams got up in a quiet,
alert way and walked forward, as noiseless on his feet
as a lynx. He reached down and took the cloak off the
body of the lord, twirled it and placed it on his own
shoulders, and it did not harm him. But in that cloak
he seemed insubstantial, like something moving in
moonlight and shadow, something nameless roaming
in the night. He walked out of the open dungeon
door, between the guards clustered there, past the
lord's retinue and the steward, and they all shrank
back from him, flattened themselves against the stone
walls of the corridor so as not to come near him. No
one dared take hold of him or try to stop him. He
walked out through the courtyard, past the stable, and
out the manor gates with the settled air of one whose
business is done. The men-at-arms gathered atop the
wall and watched him go.

Wald the master groom lived to old age sweating
every night with terror, and died of a weakened heart
in the midst of a nightmare. Nothing else but his own
fear harmed him. The boy who plaited—mane of sun,
mane of moon—was never seen again in that place,
except that children sometimes told the tale of having
glimpsed him in the wild heart of a storm, plaiting the
long lashes of wind and rain.

DAW

Don't Miss These Exciting DAW Anthologies

ANNUAL WORLD'S BEST SF
Donald A. Wollheim, editor
- ☐ 1986 Annual   UE2136—$3.50
- ☐ 1987 Annual   UE2203—$3.95

ISAAC ASIMOV PRESENTS THE GREAT SF STORIES
Isaac Asimov & Martin H. Greenberg, editors
- ☐ Series 13 (1951)   UE2058—$3.50
- ☐ Series 14 (1952)   UE2106—$3.50
- ☐ Series 15 (1953)   UE2171—$3.50
- ☐ Series 16 (1954)   UE2200—$3.50

SWORD AND SORCERESS
Marion Zimmer Bradley, editor
- ☐ Book I   UE1928—$2.95
- ☐ Book II   UE2041—$2.95
- ☐ Book III   UE2141—$3.50
- ☐ Book IV   UE2210—$3.50

THE YEAR'S BEST FANTASY STORIES
Arthur W. Saha, editor
- ☐ Series 10   UE1963—$2.75
- ☐ Series 11   UE2097—$2.95
- ☐ Series 12   UE2163—$2.95

Attention:

DAW COLLECTORS

Many readers of DAW Books have written requesting information on early titles and book numbers to assist in the collection of DAW editions since the first of our titles appeared in April 1972.

We have prepared a several-pages-long list of all DAW titles, giving their sequence numbers, original and current order numbers, and ISBN numbers. And of course the authors and book titles, as well as reissues.

If you think that this list will be of help, you may have a copy by writing to the address below and enclosing one dollar in stamps or currency to cover the handling and postage costs.

DAW BOOKS, INC.
DEPT. C
1633 Broadway
New York, N.Y. 10019